NO RETREAT

BOOK 4: THE EUPHEMIA SAGE CHRONICLES

ROSY FENWICKE

WONDERFUL WORLD

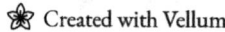

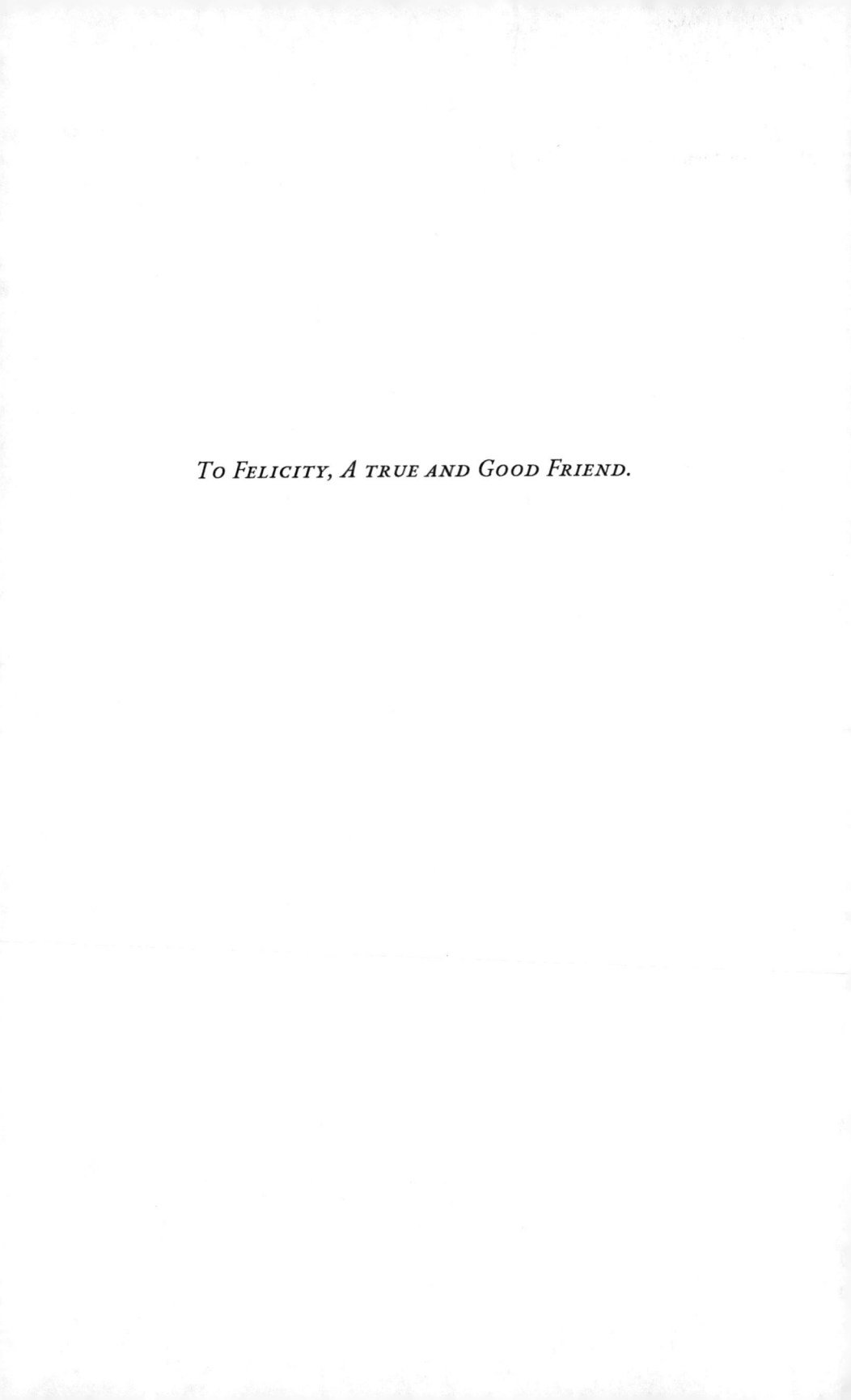

To Felicity, A true and Good Friend.

PROLOGUE

THE BELL TINKLED MERRILY AS JANE PUSHED OPEN THE DOOR
to the jeweller's shop on Cuba Street. It was a small space, economically
decorated. Loose sisal matting covered the black painted floor. A fake
tree, a ficus, its leaves dulled by dust, leaned drunkenly from a chipped
terracotta pot in one corner. Badly painted white walls backed two
wooden glass cases on legs which were set at right angles to each other
leaving the window to the street unobstructed.

Normally, Jane avoided shops like this. She deplored tattiness in all
its forms. In her opinion, which she was willing to share with anyone
who asked, relabelling second-hand and calling it vintage was a concept
invented by millennials to compensate for their propensity to make do.
Besides, tattiness in a jeweller's shop was not just lazy, it was suspicious.
She sidled over and inspected the pieces on display. Gold bangles, new
and used, recreated the Olympic symbol on a black velvet tray occupying the centre of one case. Untidy lines of pearl necklaces, used
judging by the colour of the knots between the beads, littered one side
and racks of plain gold wedding bands occupied the other. It was sad
looking at old treasures waiting for their new owners.

'Can I help you?'

Startled, Jane looked up guiltily. 'I think so,' she said.

It was too late to back out now. She had come to do what had to be done, and now she had to go through with it. Even though she didn't want to. Even though she could see her mother's eyebrows frowning in displeasure over her winged blue glasses. She could almost feel the breeze from her mother's finger, wagging at her from the family vault in the Karori cemetery. Her dead mother's voice informing her that the women in their family received jewellery, expensive jewellery, from men, sounded in her head. They never sold their jewellery. Ever! No matter the reason. The pieces were only to be accumulated, cared for, worn regularly, and passed down to the next generation. These had been the Watson family rules, since they had first arrived in New Zealand in the mid-nineteenth century.

'I heard you buy jewellery,' Jane blurted.

Now that she had said the words, she wanted to run, to get out of this horrible little shop. But she needed the money or the two week stay she had booked at the Retreat on Waiheke Island would go to someone else. It was only at the Retreat Nell assured her, that she would find the meaning of life. A meaning Jane had been seeking since Justin died, since Kevin whisked her off for a wild weekend in Palmerston North, since Dan insisted she go hiking with him to places with no flushing toilets and no running water. And since dear, kind, sweet Alastair had attached himself to her and declared his undying devotion something she wasn't sure she wanted.

'What have you got?' asked the young woman.

Jane reached behind her head, undid the fine gold chain, and lifted the diamond pendant out from where it had been resting between her breasts. She held it dangling in the air and looked pointedly at the young woman. Who, in return, looked mystified? A light bulb moment followed, and she jerked into action, digging around in a drawer before pulling out a black velvet mat which she spread on the top of the glass case. Reverently, Jane placed the diamond and chain on the mat and stepped back.

The young woman bent over the diamond, screwed up one eye and studied the jewell. She moved her head, screwed up her other eye, and looked at it again.

'This is quite good,' she said, straightening up.

'I know that,' said Jane. She wiped her palms on her sides as she tried to speak without yelling. The uneasiness she felt when she first walked into the shop had morphed into full-blown anxiety. This girl knew nothing about diamonds, but this was the place Nell had insisted she come. Nell, she trusted. Nell had helped her so much already. No one had truly understood her before she met Nell. The last month had been a revelation and Nell said it would get even better, but only if she came to the Retreat. Only there could she do the work she needed to do to understand what life had in store for her. Jane absolutely and unequivocally had to get to the Retreat.

'How much will you give me?'

'She won't give you anything,' said a short, dark-haired, big-bosomed woman who emerged from the back of the shop. 'But I might. Tracy, make us both a coffee, will you?'

The younger woman sniffed and made way for the older woman. 'Black or white?' she asked.

'Nothing for me, thank you,' said Jane.

'Black,' said the older woman. She positioned herself in front of the necklace, her hands leaning on the counter. 'Sorry about my niece, she's doing work experience from school.' She pulled a loupe out of her pocket, spat on the end and rubbed it dry with the point of her elbow, then she wedged it into her left eye and bent over the diamond. 'Hmm, interesting,' she said eventually. She picked up the pendant, tossing it in her hand to assess the weight and then holding the diamond between two fingers, held it up to the light and peered at it again.

'I need to weigh it,' she said.

'Look, it's very simple, said Jane. Her palms were sweating and her heart thumped against her ribs. 'This is a 2 carat, G colour, SI 1, round diamond with an excellent cut, weighing 245 milligrams. The registered valuation of the diamond in 2005 was $5,895 dollars. The chain, which is 14 carat gold, is worth $3799 dollars.'

'Hmmm,' said the woman.

'There's nothing hmm about it,' replied Jane.

'$4500 for both.'

'That's daylight robbery. Certainly not.'

'I thought you might say that. How about $5000?'

'Are you mad?' asked Jane. 'I need at least $6000.' Damn, she thought as soon as she uttered the words. She had revealed too much.

The eyes of the other woman lit up. 'Done! Six thousand.'

'No, I meant at least six thousand. Not that exact amount. Over six thousand.'

'I'm afraid,' said the woman. 'It isn't worth any more than that. Look,' she said, standing back. 'I'm not in this business for fun. You're more than welcome to take your piece to another jeweller and get a comparison quote. In fact,' she said. 'Do that. I have a reputation for honest dealing. Why do you think Nell recommended me? She trusts me and I don't want you to think I'm trying to put one over on you.'

Jane looked again at the pendant. She had never liked it. It reminded her of Justin. Too small to sit well with the rest of the collection, it was meant to be a placeholder until Justin's business ventures took off and he could afford to buy her the significant piece she deserved. The pendant was a broken promise, not a diamond.

'Six thousand,' Jane said and felt instantly lighter.

'What's your bank account number?' asked the woman.

Jane gave it to her and waited while the money was transferred into her account. Then she walked out of the mean little hole in the wall shop and left Justin behind. She was going to have a bigger and a better life. The life she deserved, the life Nell told her would be hers. But only if she went to the Retreat.

CHAPTER 1

Euphemia couldn't bear to look at the shiny black cars parked outside the house. This morning's rain had stopped and although the clouds hadn't parted to reveal the sun, the polished paint-work of the hearse and its attendant cars gleamed against the grey of the street even on this dullest of days. It was better to focus on the van parked in the driveway and to watch the steady procession of food and drink which the caterers were ferrying into the kitchen.

She walked across to the bed and put her hand on Sarah's shoulder. 'Are you ready?' she asked.

Sarah didn't look up. 'No.'

'Me neither,' replied Euphemia, sitting down beside her.

Sarah took her hand and squeezed it. 'I don't think I will ever be ready. We're too young. It's so unfair. This wasn't supposed to happen until we were old and finished living our lives. He'll never see Kezia's baby. Have you thought of that?' She dropped Euphemia's hand, searched the pockets of her coat for a tissue and, when she found it, wiped the tears from her cheeks and blew her nose. She threw the soggy tissue into the rubbish bin with the others. 'Has my mascara run?' She turned her face so Euphemia could inspect her make-up for damage.

'You look fine.' Euphemia meant it. They were the same age, but

Sarah looked several years younger. Her porcelain complexion was unlined and flawless, unlike Euphemia's, which showed the effects of years of outdoor running. Sarah's make-up cleverly disguised the slight puffy redness around her eyes so that only those closest to her would know she had been crying. With a flick of her shoulder-length, thick brown hair, she stood up, smoothed down her coat and picked up her handbag.

'I don't know how you do it,' she said. 'You are always so calm and reasonable. About everything. You have not only organised the funeral but also comforted those who should have been comforting you. It's true what everyone says.'

'What does everyone say?' Euphemia held up her hand. 'No. Don't tell me. I don't want to know. Not today. Today is about him. Not me. I keep telling myself that and it works. It's how I stay so calm and reasonable. It helps me cope.'

A soft knock on the door interrupted their conversation. 'Mrs Baillie, the cars are ready.'

'We'll be right down, Gordon,' said Sarah. She raised her eyebrows and smoothed her coat again. Euphemia stood up and collected her handbag.

Their children were waiting in the living room when they walked in. Nicky and Kezia, Euphemia's daughters, were standing in the middle of the room, their faces strained by grief and exhaustion. Beside them stood Sophie and John, Sarah's and Roger's children. The four of them had grown up together, sleeping over at each other's homes, going on holidays with each other, taking it in turns to give their fathers hell for playing golf instead of spending time with them. When they saw Euphemia and Sarah, they opened their arms and the six came together for a group hug. The caterers stopped setting up the dining room, waiting respectfully while the families murmured their comforts to each other.

Behind them, Gordon Campbell, the funeral director, coughed. 'I don't mean to hurry you,' he said, 'but the deacon is waiting. As expected, Old St Paul's is full and the hall we set up to take the overflow is almost full. We need to make a start.'

Sarah squeezed Euphemia's hand one last time and, supported by

Sophie and John, led the way. Kezia and Nicky linked arms with their mother and followed. Ben, Kezia's husband, attached Petal's lead to her collar, picked her up, and carried her out to one of the waiting cars.

Old St Paul's, a charming wooden church in the inner suburb of Thorndon, had absorbed the grief of the citizens of Wellington at funerals since it was built by the early settlers in 1866. It had been constructed of fine native timbers, its arches reminiscent of the cathedrals of the middle ages, but on a much smaller scale. Parklike gardens had once surrounded it. Now hemmed in by a one-way thoroughfare into the city on one side and hill on the other, all that remained of the garden was an ancient Pohutukawa tree shading the entrance. By the time the hearse and the cars drew up under its branches, the church and the hall across the road were full to overflowing.

Hushed conversations stopped when the families walked down the central aisle towards the closed casket at the front of the church. One by one, each paused to caress the polished wood before taking a seat in the front pew. Cameras had been set up around the church to relay the service to the mourners in the hall and via the internet to those unable to make the trip to Wellington. Barbara Scarsdale had called earlier that morning to tell Euphemia she would watch from her home in Sydney and that her thoughts would be with them.

Euphemia, Nicky, Kezia and Ben faced forwards, their eyes on the casket, bracing themselves for what was to come. Sarah let out a sob, and the congregation responded with a gasp of sympathy. Sophie and John, linking their arms through their mother's, shuffled closer.

The minister took up her place next to the casket and, with arms half-raised, asked the congregation to stand. She had a wonderful voice, resonant, warm and strong, and her prayer inspired everyone present, even the doubters who would not normally set foot in a church. When she finished, she lowered her hands and, amidst coughs and the scuffing of feet, everyone took their seats. Kenneth slipped in beside Euphemia, passing her and the others copies of the Order of Service which he had been distributing in the hall across the road.

'We have come together today,' said the minister, 'to celebrate the life of Roger Baillie. Sarah's loving husband of thirty-three years, Sophie and John's devoted father, and Kenneth and Euphemia Sage's best friend and business partner. A friend to all of us here today, we remember Roger not only as an excellent and respected solicitor but as a warm-hearted, loving, enthusiastic, intelligent, giving, fun-filled human being. His death, along with so many others in the tragic aircraft accident last week, was both premature and tragic.'

Euphemia took Kenneth's hand and squeezed it tightly.

CHAPTER 2

EUPHEMIA, THEN KENNETH, HUGGED SARAH BEFORE THEY walked her out to her car. 'Anything you need, let me know,' said Kenneth, shutting the door.

'We're here for you any time, night or day,' said Euphemia. She kissed Sophie and John, telling them the same thing.

Kenneth hugged his godchildren one last time before John got into the driving seat, and Sarah climbed in behind her mother. Standing together, their arms around each other's waists, they waved as the car drove away slowly.

'They did well to stay this long,' said Euphemia as they walked back inside. Ted, Kenneth's and Roger's business partner in their firm, 'Desserts are Us', had catered to the gathering . He and his crew had packed up and left two hours earlier. The furniture was still pushed back against the walls, and the carpet needed vacuuming, but otherwise the house was back to normal. Euphemia looking at Kenneth tried not to feel guilty he was still alive. She couldn't imagine what Sarah must be going through returning to her empty home and, worse, an empty bed.

The last seven days had been exhausting. People were in shock as they tried to absorb the news of Roger's death. Sarah and the children were inconsolable. Kenneth, losing his best friend, was not much better.

It fell to Euphemia to organise the funeral, the official paperwork, the catering and general logistics as well as be there as a friend and comforter at all times of the night and day. She was used to looking after others and was good at not only attending to details but also ensuring everything went according to plan. She was the lynchpin of her family and business. Everyone depended on her. This left her no time to attend to her own need to grieve. But, she told herself she didn't mind. She would do it later, when everyone else was okay. As for exercising her body to maintain her super powers, that could wait until life got back to some semblance of normal.

She had organised an afternoon tea at the hall for the hundreds of mourners who attended the service. Tea, coffee and sandwiches for those who knew Roger from his legal practice, the golf club, the Chamber of Commerce, his school and university days. The second gathering at the Sage family home in Thorndon was for those who were closest to him. Alcohol helped the mourners relax and as the evening wore on, stories of Roger's exploits grew more honest and thus more outrageous. There had been the time he had fallen off the yacht into Sydney Harbour when he and Kenneth were negotiating the deal with RS Holdings to set up their business 'Desserts are Us'. Then the time when he and Kenneth had gone trout fishing on Lake Taupo. Gin was the cause of Roger falling into the water when he tried to get back on the jetty. He plunged feet-first into the watery depths, rod and reel still in hand. Sarah reported he was no better on their honeymoon in Fiji. Too keen to try para-gliding behind a jet boat, he hadn't done up his harness correctly, despite the instructor going over everything twice. It was fortunate he was only twenty feet in the air when he slipped free, plummeting into the ocean metres from a shallow reef. Roger, in true Roger fashion, had been unfazed by this and insisted he go up again immediately after he clambered back into the boat. Toasts followed, each one more revealing about Roger than the last. Invitations to Sarah and the children to stay at holiday houses and to come to social functions were extended and, with hugs, backslapping and tears, his friends called it a night. They left satisfied their friend had had the send-off he would have wanted, but saddened he was not there to enjoy it with them.

In bed that night, Kenneth pulled Euphemia into his arms. 'Roger did everything in that family. What will Sarah do without him?'

'Too soon to tell,' said Euphemia, cuddling into his side. 'She'll be okay financially?'

'More than okay. Roger might have acted the fool, but he was a savvy investor. She is a very rich widow. Richard, the other partner at Baillie Law, sent me an updated copy of his will yesterday as a courtesy. With Sarah's permission in case you were wondering.'

'I assumed it was because you were Roger's trustees,' she said, twisting one of Kenneth's wiry chest hairs around her finger.

'I was. When we started 'Desserts are Us', he asked if I would mind his giving the trustee role to Richard. He wanted to keep things tidy. I didn't mind. Being in a strictly advisory role for future Baillie finances suits me better. His death means I'm going to be much busier.' He kissed the top of her head. 'So much for me stepping back so we can have more time together.'

'Does that mean you'll be going overseas again?'

'Until I hire more staff. I will have to if I'm to get the company up and running properly.' He trapped her hand on his chest and absent-mindedly caressed it with his thumb. 'You can hold the fort at Sage. Besides, the girls and Sarah need you here. I can't imagine Kezia will want you gallivanting off with me now that she's pregnant.'

'But...' she said.

'What?' he asked.

Euphemia shook her head and interlaced her fingers tightly through his. She had been about to say, what about what I want to do, but stopped herself. Kenneth had commitments he couldn't avoid or delegate. Not if the business was to succeed. Both Ted and Sarah depended on him to look after their financial interests in the fledgling enterprise.

'Nothing,' she murmured. 'I'm just grateful you're alive.'

'Me too,' he said, lifting his head to plant another kiss on the top of her head. He rolled on to his side and wriggled down the bed, so their faces were level. 'It could easily have been two of us in boxes at Old St Paul's today. If Barbara hadn't insisted I take her call, I would have been sitting in the seat next to Roger when the plane crashed off the runway into Evan's Bay. I feel guilty I wasn't with him. That I lived and he didn't. I can't look at Sarah without thinking, what if?'

Euphemia knew what he meant. She had been at Wellington Airport waiting for Kenneth's plane to land when they heard the news. Kezia and Ben had arrived on an earlier flight and just told her they were pregnant. It was one of the worst autumn storms ever experienced in Wellington, the capital city of New Zealand. With next to no visibility, and the wind gusting to over one hundred and twenty miles an hour, the pilot had done his best under the circumstances. No one could have anticipated the one freak gust which came out of nowhere. The one and hundred and thirty miles an hour blast of southerly air hit the plane just as it was touching down. It tipped the aircraft sideways, ripping out two wing flaps and a rudder aileron at the same time. With no ability to alter direction or speed, the plane propelled by the tailwind skidded through the fence at the end of the runaway, soared over the road below and pitched headfirst into the sea. The pilot and co-pilot died instantly, along with those in business class. Those in economy class made it out because of the bravery of the cabin crew, who did everything right to prepare the emergency exits before releasing the inflatable escape chutes into the water.

Of course, Euphemia knew none of this when she heard about the crash. She kissed Kezia and Ben and ran straight out the door into the storm. She ran past the parking building, down the ramp and on down Calabar Road to Evan's Bay. Traffic travelling in both directions along the waterfront had stopped before she arrived at the crash scene, which only delayed the emergency airport vehicles getting to the stricken plane. Without hesitating, Euphemia leapt down the boulders forming the seawall. Desperate to get to Kenneth, she didn't care who saw her. She was about to dive into the churning water when her phone vibrated in her pocket. She nearly didn't answer it. Peeling salt-wet hair away from her eyes and face, she saw it was a text from Kenneth apologising for missing his flight, telling her he would see her tomorrow.

'What I don't understand,' she said, gliding one finger lightly down the side of his face and stopping at his lips, 'is why you waited so long before you texted me you weren't on the flight?'

'I thought I had,' he said. 'It was only when I checked my phone later that I saw I hadn't pressed send. The text was sitting there unsent. I guess the phone call from Barbara asking for an update on my meeting distracted me.'

'Why do you think Barbara asked only you to go to the meeting and not Roger? He would be alive today if both of you had gone.'

'Don't think I haven't asked myself that question over and over in the last week,' said Kenneth.

'And?'

'You can ask her on one of your many Zoom calls with her. I don't know. What I know is,' he said stopping to kiss her properly. 'I am very proud of my wife. For saving so many lives.'

'I did what anyone would do.'

'That's what impresses me the most. You didn't lift the plane out of the sea using your super powers. You stuck to the rules.'

'I considered it,' said Euphemia. 'I couldn't take the chance of it not working. Still not knowing the extent of my powers is so frustrating. It's been over a year since I got them and I don't know what I can reliably do. Or what I can't do or shouldn't do.'

'Does it matter? What you did was amazing enough. You organised the human chain into the sea to get the passengers to shore quickly. They have you to thank for saving their lives and you did it without using your super powers.'

'I used them a little. But not so anyone would notice. The emergency crew got their boat launched quickly, so I didn't have to stay in the water for long. They are very professional.'

'Yes, they are.' He nuzzled her neck and whispered in her ear. 'But everyone is talking about the brave heroine, Euphemia Sage, the business consultant who put her life at risk to save a planeload of people. You will never hear the end of it. You're famous. You might even get an award from the Queen.'

'That's the problem,' whispered Euphemia, enjoying the feel of his lips on her neck. 'The last thing a super woman, two words lower case, ever wants to be, is famous. According to Barbara, it's the worst thing ever for the powers. I won't be able to operate in secret. Someone will always point me out. She is furious.'

'She's furious with you for saving lives? I don't believe it.'

'She has this thing about the no one finding out about the switch until we know the genetic code for it. I've told you before. She is fanatical about secrecy. Sometimes I wonder if she wants to keep the powers all to herself and was disappointed when she found out about me. That I might put her precious foundation at risk. What do you think?'

A soft, puttering snore was her answer. She reached up and smoothed the hair from his forehead. 'You are my rock Kenneth Sage,' she whispered. 'Thank you for not dying.'

CHAPTER 3

A MONTH LATER, AFTER ROGER'S WILL HAD BEEN MADE probate, Sarah called to make an appointment to discuss her financial situation with Kenneth and Euphemia. Jane, the receptionist at Sage Consulting, was ready to greet her when Sarah walked out of the elevator on the tenth floor. Unable to leave the reception desk on the day of Roger's funeral, Jane expressed her sympathy on the day of Sarah's appointment by wearing the same black dress she had worn to Justin, her dead husband's, funeral. She also wore the same triple strand pearl necklace and drop diamond and pearl earrings because pearls signify mourning. That she hadn't worn them for a while was also a factor. Wearing different pieces from the jewellery collection she had inherited reminded her of her mother and the rank her family once occupied in Wellington society. The Sages had made it clear she wasn't to wear the more expensive pieces to the office anymore, but they could say nothing about her wearing pearls when it was appropriate. Her mother had told her the Queen had a similar necklace which she wore every day. What was good enough for the Queen was good enough for her.

Jane had opened three boxes of tissues, placing one each in Euphemia and Kenneth's offices and one in the boardroom. It was typical that no one had thought to tell her where the meeting would take place. Cups and saucers, a plate of biscuits, milk, sugar and the coffee plunger were ready on a tray.

Jane hadn't been friends with either Roger or Sarah, but she had met them in passing at the golf club where Justin had been the president at the time of his death. Justin's routine quoting of Shakespeare, 'First kill all the lawyers,' every time they met, went down like a lead balloon, but he did it anyway. Why her husband was so uncomfortable in the presence of lawyers was revealed after he died and the unsavoury tangle of his business affairs became apparent. Left to tidy up, Jane had coped only because of Euphemia's cool, calm assistance. With her help, the insurance company quickly paid up and Jane repaid every creditor except one.

Sinclair Finance did not receive a cent. Alison and Malcolm could rot in prison for the rest of their lives if she had her way. Loan sharks, they had put her and darling Petal through hell over one unforgettable twenty-four-hour period. All because she owed them a measly one hundred thousand dollars. Alison, the receptionist at Sage Consulting before Jane, was the mastermind. Not only had the evil bitch waylaid clients in financial difficulties, but she had dragged Justin into her murky world and into Jane's marital bed. Jealous, Alison plotted to get her hands on Jane's inheritance, the jewellery. It was beyond forgiveness. Thankfully, the hearing in her left ear had almost recovered and the plastic surgery had not only restored but enhanced her poor broken nose. Jane derived immense satisfaction from knowing Alison Sinclair would stay locked up in the psychiatric wing at the local women's prison for eight years.

While she might not grieve for the lying, deceitful, smug, adulterous, thieving, arrogant mansplainer her husband had turned out to be, Jane knew what it was like to suddenly and unexpectedly become a widow. Justin was a terrible husband, but he was a husband. In a world where couples reign supreme, it had been a shock to have to suddenly fend for herself, socially and financially.

Jane planned to offer Sarah all the support and sympathy she would need to get through this time in her life. She had received no such support from her old friends when the truth came out about the fire.

Euphemia and Kenneth had been there for her and Jane would remain eternally grateful, but before the disaster they hadn't mixed in the same social circle as the Frenches, and their kindness took a bit of getting used to. Her daughter, Justine, brought up by her parents to expect the best from life as was her birth right, was less than impressed when Euphemia locked away what remained of the insurance pay-out in a superannuation scheme for her mother. She had flounced off to New York where, Jane reported, she was doing spectacularly well.

Roger Baillie, the exact opposite of Justin French, had been a good man. His peers genuinely liked, trusted, and respected him. He had provided financially for Sarah and her children. He would be a tremendous loss to poor Sarah, and Jane was determined to help in any way she could. She imagined how devastated Sarah must be. In fact, she had felt the other woman's grief so intensely that last night she had woken up crying into her pillow.

It was thus a surprise when Sarah emerged from the elevator wearing a bright red velvet trouser suit, and black Louboutin high heels, the black patent leather So Kate 120s, which Jane immediately recognised as the ones Victoria Beckham wears. Shoes that any other midlife woman could barely wear sitting down, much less actually walk in.

Sarah blitzed Jane with a smile, her fire-engine red lipstick highlighting a row of perfect white teeth. She peered over the rim of her huge black sunglasses and said, 'I'm Sarah Baillie. I have a two-forty-five appointment with Ken and Euphemia.'

'Yes,' said Jane. 'I know. I wanted to say how sorry I was to hear of your loss.' Confused by the glamorous appearance of the grieving widow, she didn't know whether to carry on with the rest of her prepared condolences. Her mother had brought her up to behave courteously and appropriately in every social situation, so she continued. 'Roger was a lovely man and you will miss him terribly. If there is anything I can do, this is my number. I would be very happy to help you any time, day or night. As a recent widow myself, I know...'

Jane stopped talking when Sarah held up her hand, then reached inside her Chanel handbag, pulled out a tissue and dabbed at her eyes under her glasses. The intertwined back-to-back Cs figured on the arms of the sunglasses, too.

'Thank you,' said Sarah. 'So kind. Roger told me what happened to you. We widows understand the pain we feel in a way no one else can.'

'You're right,' breathed Jane, Sarah's words resonating inside her.

'A month ago,' said Sarah, 'I was a mess. At the funeral, I almost collapsed. I don't know what I would have done without Kenneth there to hold me up. I didn't sleep for three days, I hadn't eaten for a week. All I could think about was Roger and how much I was going to miss him and the life we had planned. I could barely breathe. I was so afraid.'

'I know that feeling,' said Jane. 'What did you do, because you look fabulous?'

'A friend from the golf club told me to call Nell, and she came straight away. Sophie and John, my children, were sceptical, but as soon as I met her, I knew she would help me. She performed a widow's ancient healing ceremony. It was like a miracle because I felt instantly lighter. She said I was one of the worst cases she had ever seen, so she dropped everything to come and work with me. She came every day without fail and Voila! You see before you a woman who is reborn. Of course I miss Roger, but life is a journey and we pack our grief in our suitcase and bring it with us. I have her contact details if you would like to call her. You won't regret it.'

'She sounds fabulous,' said Jane. She was being polite. Doubtful she could afford Nell's services, she nevertheless was desperate to keep up appearances.

Sarah dug around in her bag again and pulled out a card with an embossed yellow sun on a blue background on one side and an embossed silver moon on a black background on the other. Printed in the middle of the sun was a phone number. Nothing else.

'I can feel your pain,' said Sarah. 'You must call her.'

CHAPTER 4

'I WAS SHOCKED WHEN RICHARD TOLD ME HOW MUCH Roger left,' said Sarah. 'I knew we were comfortable, but I didn't know we were rich.' The report listing her assets lay in front of her on Kenneth's desk.

'He was a very smart investor,' said Kenneth. 'You own a well-diversified portfolio of commercial and residential properties, shares, bonds, cash in fixed term deposits, gold and crypto-assets. As well as one third of the shares in 'Desserts are Us'. I will arrange an up-to-date valuation of the company, and tell you how much that's worth.'

'Why didn't he say anything?' asked Sarah.

'Would it have made a difference?' asked Euphemia.

'Probably not.' Sarah paused. 'Maybe. I don't know. Sophie slummed it on her trip to Europe. She and her friends dumpster-dived for food outside French supermarkets to save money. Roger laughed when she posted the photos on Insta, but he didn't offer to bail her out. He said it was good for her to learn how the other half lives.'

'He would have helped her if she really needed it,' said Euphemia.

'I guess so.' Sarah folded the report in half and attempted to squash it into her handbag, but the bulge meant the clasp refused to stay shut. 'I should have bought the larger size.' She took out the report and smoothed it flat. 'Nell told me to buy this. And the trouser suit. And the sunglasses. She said a decent splurge is healing. Presbyterian-Roger would not have approved. Party-Roger would have loved it.' She ran her hand over the quilted leather, her eyes closed, a dreamy look on her face. 'When I touch it and feel the softness, I think of him. It's a technique Nell taught me. It grounds my grief in mundane objects.'

Euphemia had never heard a Chanel bag called mundane before, but now was not the time to point this out. If it helped Sarah get over Roger, who was she to nit-pick?

'Who is Nell?' asked Euphemia, exchanging a look with Kenneth. 'I haven't heard you talk about her before.'

Sarah opened her eyes. 'What did you say? Oh. Nell. She has literally saved my life. When I wasn't getting out of bed, Tina from the golf club put me onto her. She is an intuitive healer, except she's more than that. She's an empath. All the girls have been to see her. She understands exactly what you are thinking and everything you are going through because she feels what you feel, but deep inside of her. Within five minutes of meeting me, she was sobbing like a baby. Since then, she has given up most of her other clients and is devoting her time to healing my profound grief and improving my holistic well-being.'

Kenneth's eyes had grown wide at the word 'empath'. By the time Sarah finished, he was shifting in his chair and coughing into his hand. Euphemia stared at him, willing him not to say something which would embarrass them both. He was well-known in their family for his intolerance of all things spiritual and religious. He accepted Euphemia's super powers only because he had seen them in action and because he was satisfied a genetic basis for them was scientifically feasible.

'Is she charging you for feeling your pain or is she helping you out of the goodness of her heart?' he asked.

'I donate to the Acceptance Institute, where she works. It's completely voluntary. I couldn't expect her to do what she does for nothing.'

'Who decides the quantity of your donations?' Kenneth asked, his voice tight.

Sarah squared her shoulders, and eyeballed him. 'I do,' she said. 'The

Acceptance Institute doesn't send invoices. You pay whatever you can afford.'

'Does this institute take on poor clients?'

Euphemia prayed Sarah hadn't seen the smirk on his face, but her prayers went unanswered.

'I'm not some deluded rich woman being robbed blind by the first person who offers me a shoulder to cry on.' She stood up. 'Nell said you'd be like this. Roger was down-to-earth, like you. That's why you got on so well together. He admired your ability to deal with facts by putting aside your emotions. But there was another side to my husband which you didn't know, a side which Nell has revealed to me in her communications with him. Roger had a softer side, an accepting questioning side which he was too afraid to show you, but which I always knew in my heart was there. He supports me seeing Nell, because he's told me. No, Kenneth,' she stopped, her hand raised. 'Don't look like that. You have no right to judge me. Nell is worth every cent. Not that it is any of your business what I do or how I choose to spend MY money.'

Euphemia groaned inwardly. She knew what was coming next. First Kenneth would react.

'Tell me Sarah, what do you mean exactly by saying he had 'an accepting questioning side'?'

The quote marks he made in the air would be enough to rile any woman. Even Euphemia felt the skin crawl up her spine in response. The non-questioning, non-accepting side of Kenneth was something few people ever saw, because it was rarely on display. Normally urbane and courteous, Sarah had found the one chink in his otherwise perfect composure. That chink was his total lack of tolerance for what he called 'woo-woo'. Sarah's next reaction was as predictable as Kenneth's had been.

'You haven't got the emotional intelligence to understand,' she said. 'I am sorry, Euphemia. You have been our friends all our lives, but it would horrify Roger to hear you speaking to me like that, Kenneth.'

Please don't let him shrug, thought Euphemia.

He shrugged.

Sarah picked up the report and tucked it under her arm. She put on her sunglasses, slung her bag over her shoulder and walked to the door, where she stopped and turned to face them. 'Nell advised me to remove all negativity from my life. Euphemia, this is nothing to do with you. I hope you and I can remain friends. Kenneth, consider yourself removed from my life.'

'Why don't we get a coffee and talk this over,' said Euphemia, getting up from her chair. 'This wouldn't be happening if Roger were here.'

'He's not here,' said Sarah. 'I am, and I have to do what's best for me and the children. I won't be ridiculed for my beliefs or what I choose to spend my money on,' said Sarah. 'By the way, Richard was just like you, condescending and patronising. I have a new solicitor, as well as a new financial advisor. My new solicitor will send you the relevant transfer documents in the next twenty-four hours.'

CHAPTER 5

EUPHEMIA PLUNKED DOWN IN THE CHAIR OPPOSITE KENNETH after seeing Sarah into the elevator.

'That went well,' she said.

'Do you think she means it?' he asked.

'Oh, she means it,' said Euphemia. 'Didn't you see me staring at you willing you to be quiet?'

'What can I say? I failed Staring 101. I flunked the translation module. You heard her. It's not just me. She has a new solicitor too.'

'I wish Richard had called ahead to warn us she was having a clean-out,' said Euphemia. 'But then he's probably embarrassed to be sacked,' she added. 'I am. I feel like we have let Roger down.'

'He would be the first person to understand. If he was here, he would have put Nell on the first bus out of town quick-smart,' said Kenneth. He ran his fingers through his hair and stood up. 'As long as she goes to a reputable law firm, it will be okay. In a way, it's good for us. We were going to be too busy over the next six months sorting out the company to advise the Baillie portfolio. I haven't told you yet, but I have to go to Oz again at the end of the week.'

'No, you haven't told me. I'll have your clients and mine to look after?'

'Afraid so. I know you don't mind. Not really. You love the work and it's not like you have anything else to do now the girls are gone.'

This was a statement, not a question, and it rankled. Kenneth, her loved husband, assumed he could do whatever he wanted when he wanted. To accommodate him, her life would once again go into its familiar holding pattern of propping everything and everyone else up. He got to fulfil his dream of building a company from scratch while she held the fort at home and at Sage.

Logically, she knew neither of them could have foreseen these circumstances. She also knew if she complained it would sound like a petty stamping of feet. She settled for a sigh and said, 'So much for us winding down and spending more time together.'

He got up, went to her, and held out his hand. She gave it to him and he pulled her up and into his arms. She stood with her head on his shoulder listening to his breathing, letting the familiar sound ease her mood as it had done throughout their married life. He was her refuge, his body her bulwark against the world. It wasn't his fault Roger had died and their plans had changed. Someone had to run Sage and so it fell to her to step up just as she always had. If only she could shake off the feeling of shackles tightening around her.

Kenneth pulled back. He looked at her, keeping his arms around her waist. 'You're a good woman, Euphemia. You're solid, reliable and damn good in bed, to boot. Where I would be without you?'

'And me without you?' she replied. They kissed gently and he let her go.

'Any idea who this Nell is?' he asked. 'Sarah taking her business elsewhere doesn't matter. Roger would still expect me, us, to look out for her just the same. He'd do the same for you.'

'He wouldn't need to. I can look after myself and you know it.' She straightened her shoulders. 'I've never heard of Nell, but I know someone we can ask.'

Jane was down on her hands and knees, playing hide and seek with Petal when Euphemia went to reception. It was puzzling because her pug wasn't the sort of dog who enjoyed playing games. Petal was more a 'feed me, cuddle me and let me sleep' kind of dog. When she saw Jane was holding treats, she understood. This wasn't hide and seek. It was the old 'I'll bribe you to run after me' game. It was Petal's favourite, but only if the treats were the ones she liked.

Sage Consulting's receptionist crawling along on her hands and knees playing with Euphemia's dog, who was panting and gobbling strips of duck jerky, was hardly the image she wanted their clients to get when they walked out of the elevator. But as there were no clients and none expected and as Jane and Petal both had huge smiles on their faces, she let it go.

'I'm hoping you can use your social networks to help us,' said Euphemia, peering under the desk.

'What do you think, Petal my little, poochy, moochy pooch?' asked Jane in that high-pitched, sing-songy voice people use for cute animals and all babies. 'Should I help your mummy and daddy? Should I? Should I?' Jane rolled the pug onto her back and scratched her bulging tummy. The little dog squirmed closer to the remaining treats until she was within snatching distance. With a flick of her long pink tongue, she licked them from Jane's hand, rolled upright, and in one swallow, the treats were gone. Game over, she licked her lips and trotted off to her bed in Euphemia's office for a well-earned rest. Jane stood up, dusted carpet fluff from the front of her dress, and sat down.

'Are you still in touch with the ladies at the golf club?' asked Kenneth, who had joined them. He leaned on the desk.

'Hardly,' said Jane. She swivelled around to look at him. 'I can't afford the subs and since the business with Justin and the fire, they've avoided me.'

'But they were your friends,' said Kenneth.

Jane twisted the pearls in her necklace. 'People are not always who they say they are.' She smoothed her dress over her knees. 'Why do you ask?'

'A woman at the golf club put one of our clients in touch with Nell and we want to find out more about her,' said Euphemia.

'Sarah Baillie is the only client you've seen this afternoon and your next appointment isn't until 3.30 PM. It's Dr Hegel and he wants to discuss expanding his business and where to put the profits from his appearance medicine clinic.'

'How do you know that?' asked Euphemia.

'He told me. His clinic here is making money hand over fist. Botox, fillers, skin scrapes, he says there aren't enough hours in the day to meet demand. He's very good. You should think about paying him a visit, Effie. He could take years off your face.'

The hairs on the back of Euphemia's neck stood to irritable attention whenever she was called Effie. Jane was the only person who called her that and the hairs still reacted. She had asked her so many times to stop with no result and so had given up. Now the woman was telling her she needed work on her face; the cheek of her. It was a mystery how they had become friends. Jane had delighted in bullying Euphemia at school, snubbed her when Justin was alive, then nearly had her killed when she begged for help after her jewellery got stolen. And yet, despite all the above, and despite Jane calling her Effie, their friendship had grown.

Euphemia shook herself and brought her thoughts back into the room.

'He could put filler in your puppet lines, the ones running down from your nose along the sides of your lips. They are deep, aren't they?' said Jane leaning back in her chair and focusing on Euphemia's face. 'He could inject Botox to get rid of those frown lines, put more filler along the line of your jaw...,'

Euphemia held up her hand. 'Enough. About my face. I am quite happy with it as it is, thank you.'

'Just saying,' Jane said. 'You could look years younger and quite attractive if you tried.'

'Enough.'

'Anyway,' said Jane. 'Dr Hegel wants to start clinics in the Wairarapa, the Kapiti Coast, and Auckland. There are plenty of women and men who understand the benefits of looking as good as they can nowadays.'

'Forget Dr Hegel,' said Euphemia. Heat rose from the waistband of her trousers up her chest to the base of her neck, pursued by a film of sticky sweat and a weird feeling of almost but not quite shivering. She shrugged off her jacket and plucked her shirt away from her body. The sooner this conversation ended, the better. Jane might be her friend, but talking to her was like being sucked into a whirlpool of information which, while related, was not always relevant. You had to struggle to get back to the original question. Experience had taught her it was better to take the direct approach. 'Do you know any of Sarah Baillie's friends? If so, who would have put her in touch with a healer-type person called Nell?' she asked. The hot flush was subsiding, but the stickiness stayed. If only she could take HRT like a normal woman. But she had been told her powers would disappear if she did, so that option was unavailable.

'Sarah gave me this,' said Jane. She handed the card to Euphemia. 'She suggested I see her. I haven't had time to call, but I'm thinking about it. I mean, what harm could it do?'

Euphemia picked up the card, turning it over in her hands. 'A phone number, no name, no address, no website. That's odd, don't you think?'

Kenneth shrugged.

'I suppose, but a word-of-mouth referral and a phone number is all anyone really needs,' Jane said.

'What if we both go to see her? You and me,' said Euphemia. 'I would go as your support person.'

Jane cocked her head to one side. 'So you'll pay?'

She nodded. 'I guess so.'

'You can write it off as a business expense, so it wouldn't be like it would cost you anything,' said Jane.

'One day I'm going to sit down with you and explain how business expenses really work and how the Inland Revenue Department takes a dim view of many of the things you assume to be deductible,' said Euphemia.

They heard the elevator door open, and looked up to see a short, balding man with an all-over tan and teeth too big for his mouth walking towards them.

'Dr Hegel. What are you doing here?' asked Jane. 'Your appointment isn't until 3.45 PM.'

'It says 2.45 in my diary.'

Euphemia remembered she still hadn't organised the timetable training course for Jane and made a mental note to get onto it. 'Dr Hegel,' she said, smiling. 'How lovely to see you again! Come down to my office.'

CHAPTER 6

WHEN KEZIA AND EUPHEMIA ARRIVED, IT WAS TO A TINY, overcrowded waiting room. The worn grey carpet, white scuffed walls and stained chairs inspired little confidence in Euphemia, but Kezia assured her the clinic's ultrasound department had an excellent reputation. Her google search had been the usual Kezia-deep-dive. She knew the backgrounds of each of the radiologists, their subspecialties, and had read most of their scientific publications. The machines purchased in the last five years were at the forefront of technology and the radiographers had undergone the appropriate training in both their maintenance and use. Privately, Euphemia wondered if such in-depth knowledge was strictly necessary, especially as child-bearing was such a natural and straightforward process, but she said nothing. It was not her place to dent the pregnancy experience of her eldest daughter. Her only concern was that if she and Ben were this intense at twelve weeks, what were the next twenty-eight weeks going to be like? They would go mad if they researched every last detail. She dreaded to think about how they would cope with the uncertainties of actual parenthood.

Ben was supposed to have been at this appointment, not Euphemia. After all, it would be the first time they would see their baby. But there had been a report of a suspicious death in Khandallah, one of the pricier suburbs in Wellington, and his being a detective meant he had to go when called. It wasn't possible to reschedule the appointment, so Kezia had asked Euphemia to come with her instead.

They checked in and by the time Kezia had filled out the necessary forms, two seats had freed up and they sat down. Euphemia picked up a tatty *House and Garden* magazine, turning to the garden section at the back. The article about growing hydrangeas from cuttings was very good with lots of useful tips she hadn't known before. She had been wondering what to put in the gap next to the oak tree in the corner, and the white hydrangea featured would be perfect. She was debating the ethics of quietly ripping out the relevant page or slipping the magazine into her handbag when Kezia groaned and clamped her hand on her arm.

'I can't hold on any longer,' she said, crossing her legs and wrapping one foot behind the opposite calf at the same time jiggling in her seat. 'Ask how long before I'm seen?' Euphemia had just stood up when Kezia's name was called. They followed a pleasant woman in a white uniform to an open door at the end of a corridor.

The sonographer Jill, according to her name badge, directed Euphemia to the chair on other side of the bed while Kezia climbed onto the bed itself. Jill explained what she was going to do. The full bladder issue now partially relieved by Kezia's anticipation at seeing her baby and partially because she was lying flat on the bed. Euphemia watched as Jill expertly ran the probe over her daughter's flat belly.

'See that,' she said. They looked at the snowy black-and-white image on the large screen next to the bed. A head and arm appeared, then disappeared. Jill twiddled the knobs and the sound of a baby's heart beating fast and insistent broke the silence. Kezia's face lit up, and she squeezed Euphemia's hand. Euphemia squeezed hers back. They had tears in their eyes as the image slipped into focus. Now they could see arms and legs moving, and it looked like the baby was hiccupping.

'One, two, three, four, five limbs,' said Jill.

'Five?' chorused Kezia and Euphemia.

'You're having twins,' said Jill. She turned a dial and two heartbeats filled the little room, one after the other, joggling each other along. 'Wait. I'll make sure there aren't any more in there.'

'Mum!' breathed Kezia.

'Kezia,' said Euphemia.

'No,' said Jill. 'Only two.'

'Twins,' they said together. Now they were both crying.

Jill moved the probe again, turning it around and sliding it over Kezia's belly and suddenly, there they were. Two babies lying head to tail, arms and legs kicking each other, little mouths opening and closing.

'Can you see what they are?' asked Kezia.

Jill squirted another dollop of jelly onto her tummy and pushed the probe deeper, sweeping it backwards and forwards over the babies who moved in and out of view. 'Not yet, maybe at the next scan when you are eighteen weeks,' she said.

'Are they all right? Is everything normal?' asked Kezia.

'Everything looks fine,' said Jill. 'But the radiologist will look at the scan and send a report to your midwife. Prue Thomson is looking after you, isn't she? You're lucky. She's one of the best.'

'I know. How long before she gets the report?'

'Should be the end of tomorrow,' she said. She looked at the screen again, checking through the contact details which Kezia had provided earlier. 'I've got your email address, so I'll send you a video of the scan to show their father. If he doesn't believe you, this will convince him.'

Neither Euphemia nor Kezia said a word on the walk back to Sage Consulting. Pedestrians split around them, some making rude comments about speeding up and moving to the right side of the footpath, but neither Euphemia nor Kezia noticed. Each was so absorbed by the news. When they reached a café, Euphemia pulled Kezia's elbow to sit down at one of the empty tables outside, where they waited for the server to come and take their orders.

'No wonder I felt so pregnant, so early,' said Kezia. She wrinkled her nose when the coffee arrived and asked the server to bring her a glass of water instead. 'I've gone off it. The smell makes me want to be sick,' she said. 'You have it.' She pushed the offending object towards her mother.

'Gladly. How do you feel otherwise?'

'About the fact I am going to get as big as a house with stretch marks to match and have two babies, not one to look after? How do you think I feel, Mum?' She burst into tears. The sole other patron picked up her handbag and left. Euphemia leaned over and put an arm around her daughter.

'It's a shock,' she said. 'Plenty of women have had twins. We'll all help. You won't be alone.' If they hadn't been in a public place, Euphemia was certain that Kezia would have put her head back and howled.

'Who else do you know with twins? How will we manage? We don't have a house. We're renting a tiny flat. It's barely big enough for us, let alone two babies and all the stuff they will need.'

'There's plenty of time to sort out the details.'

'Is there? I've only researched one-baby pregnancies. I have to go back to the beginning and start all over again.'

'That can wait.'

The server arrived with a glass of water and Kezia gulped it down. 'Do you know what I was really worried about today, Mum?'

'No, tell me.' Euphemia had finished one cup of coffee and started on the second.

'I was terrified she would say it was a girl.'

A scooter rider went past too closely, clipping Euphemia's chair with his handle-bars just as she was about to take a sip of her coffee. The milky liquid spilled onto the legs of her trousers, burning her skin.

'Hey', she yelled. 'Slow down.'

The rider didn't slow down or look back, instead he hoisted a one finger salute above his head. Few people with grey hair make the choice to have a ponytail, and for very good reason she thought. She studied his departing outline, committing it to memory as she mopped the coffee from her trousers.

'Mum?'

'Sorry. Did you see what he did? Some days, I don't understand how people have become so rude. As Aunt Maree used to say, common courtesy costs nothing, and it makes the world a better place. What were you saying?'

'Never mind,' said Kezia. 'We should get back to the office. Don't tell Dad. Not yet. Ben and I need to get our heads around the twin thing and work out what we are going to do.'

'What you are scared about? I don't understand. Girls are great.

You're a girl. Your sister and I are both girls. I like girls. I enjoy being a girl. Always have and I loved having daughters.'

'I like girls too – ordinary girls,' she paused. 'You know what I'm talking about. The stuff in Great-Aunt Maree's letters. Just because I haven't talked about it, doesn't mean I haven't been thinking about the Switch. I am the eldest daughter of an eldest daughter. My eldest daughter will develop super powers at menopause just like you and me, although I find that very hard to imagine. Not to mention preparing for. You were lucky. You didn't know what was coming or what was going to happen to you until long after you became a mother.'

'Only because Freddie, abandoned me when I was three. If she'd been there when I was growing up, like she was supposed to be, it wouldn't have been such a shock.'

'Was it a shock knowing you were going to develop the powers or actually getting them?'

'Both. If it wasn't for B...' Euphemia stopped.

'If it wasn't for who?' asked Kezia. 'Oh. Barbara.' She rubbed a finger up and down the side of her perfect nose while she considered what to say next.

'Concentrate on your good news,' said Euphemia. 'And the fact you are going to have two delicious babies. Don't think about something which won't happen to you for another thirty years,' said Euphemia.

'I'm twenty-eight, Mum. The average age of menopause is fifty-two, so I have twenty-four years of freedom left. That's all. Also, I have you to worry about. You've been involved in some dangerous stuff. I don't want anything bad to happen to one of my two babysitters. Nicky will be useless. She hates babies and told me not to rely on her. Ben's mother died years ago and his father lives in Auckland. That leaves you and Dad, and he's busy with the company. My friends are so jealous I have a mother living in the same town. Free babysitters are like gold.'

'Who said anything about free?' said Euphemia, standing up. 'I'm a professional woman and I will charge accordingly. But because you're family, I'll make an exception and give you a two for one discount.'

CHAPTER 7

KENNETH SUGGESTED LUNCH AT TED'S RESTAURANT IN CUBA Street and Euphemia agreed immediately. Anything to get away from the megalomaniac Dr Hegel and his torrent of texts and phone calls. Almost overnight, the previously mild-mannered doctor had morphed into a voracious property developer keen to extract every last cent of profit from the expansion of his clinics.

'Appearance medicine is an excellent and recession-proof business,' he said, sitting forward in the chair opposite Euphemia. If he had been smoking a pipe, he would have poked it at her to emphasise each statement. 'It's a pity I didn't expand sooner. I should have done this in my forties instead of my fifties.'

Euphemia, pretending to cough, turned away to restore her neutral face. Tony Hegel was easily in his early sixties, if not older. No amount of Botox, filler or flashy white veneers could make him look younger. The turkey neck, the wrinkled backs of his hands and his stiffness when he rose out of a chair betrayed him as surely as if his birth certificate had been tattooed on his forehead.

'We all wish we'd done things when we had the chance,' she replied turning back to him. 'It's true what they say about life passing by quickly.'

'It is indeed. Which is why I need the cost-benefit analyses for the different clinics ASAP. And by ASAP, I mean exactly that,' he said. He winced as he attempted to stand, his left leg giving way as he awkwardly pushed himself up from his chair.

Euphemia sprang forward to see if he was all right, but he waved her away. 'My foot went to sleep,' he said. 'It'll be all right in a minute.' He hobbled across the room, and stopping to lean on the door handle, he said, 'This afternoon is ASAP?' She nodded. Gathering his strength, he straightened his back and left.

She called the ninth floor and spoke to one of the tech modellers to convey their client's wishes, only to be assured the CBAs were almost done and would be in Dr Hegel's inbox by 3 PM.

'Like a well-oiled machine,' she said, finishing her story. Kenneth, concentrating on his meal, was uncharacteristically silent.

'What do you think about his expansion?' she prompted.

'He's right,' said Kenneth. 'There are a lot of things I wish I'd done in my forties and didn't. I keep wondering if it's too late to start something new now. At this time of our lives, I mean.'

Euphemia took a deep breath. Having dealt with the ego of one menopausal male already this morning was bad enough, but having to massage another over her mushroom risotto was too much. 'Regrets are a waste of time,' she said, laying down her fork and picking up Kenneth's hand. 'You forget how much you did in your forties. You achieved more than most so remember the positives, the good times. Hasn't Roger's death taught you anything?'

Kenneth's eyes flicked up from the table to look at her. 'You're right. If I hadn't done what I did then, I wouldn't be the person I am. I wouldn't be able to take advantage of the opportunities I have now.'

Euphemia picked up her fork and took a large mouthful of risotto.

'Speaking of Roger,' said Kenneth. 'That's why we're here. Ted wants to discuss plans for 'Desserts are Us'. The Asia trip was successful in terms of orders and opening up a distribution centre, but his death has left an enormous gap in management. We've decided Ted will step back from the restaurant to concentrate solely on production. Which will free me up to look after marketing, distribution, et cetera. We will employ new people as we develop. We're suddenly very busy but that can't be helped. I'm not complaining but I haven't had time to play golf for over a month.'

Euphemia raised her eyebrows in commiseration. Now was not the time to point out she hadn't been for a long run for over a week. Her short runs were great for speed and reaction training, but her long runs in the hills behind Wellington not only built up her stamina, they gave her time to think. 'Maybe you could play on Saturday,' she said.

'Maybe. It's not the same without Roger,' Kenneth replied. 'He kept me on my toes. Never had a chance of beating me, but he came close a few times.'

'Does Ted play?' she asked.

Kenneth brightened. 'I don't know. If he doesn't, I could teach him. What a good idea! He's no Roger in the banter stakes, but it's worth asking.' He looked around the restaurant, his face breaking into a broad grin. 'That's Charlie Watson. I need to have a chat with him about packaging,' he said, getting up. 'Back in a minute.'

They were sitting at a table for two in the window of Ted's restaurant, looking onto historic Cuba Street. The older shops offering vintage clothing and quirky ornaments were gradually being replaced with high end fashion boutiques, cafés and whole foods shops. The residents of the newly constructed apartment buildings had changed the area from being seedy, down-at-heel, to cosmopolitan inner city chic. It was still Wellington but with more of an international flavour. The influx of wealthy work-from-homers brought back a vibrancy last experienced in the 1950s when New Zealand was a much wealthier country and Wellington was both its commercial centre and the capital.

The designer shops with their young customers gave Euphemia hope for her poor old city. Poor management and tired infrastructure meant there had been an exodus of corporate headquarters from Wellington to the much larger Auckland with the resulting economic hit. Ten years ago, many of the heavily graffitied and abandoned buildings had been marked for demolition. Thanks to a mobilised public, smart developers and heritage organisations, their facades had been strengthened against the ever present threat of earthquakes, and their insides gutted to make way for modern high-rise buildings giving the inner city the best of both worlds – the old supporting the new.

Across the street in a small jeweller's shop, Euphemia recognised Jane standing at the counter talking to an assistant. A moment later, another woman approached and continued the conversation. Jane reached up behind her neck, unclasped the diamond pendant she was wearing, and set it on the counter. The woman put one of those lenses in her eye, picked up the diamond and examined it. They exchanged more words. Euphemia concentrated on reading Jane's lips as she provided her contact details for the woman, who was now writing everything down.

'Ted's new desserts,' said Kenneth, touching her hand to get her attention. Euphemia looked down at three desserts which had appeared on their table without her noticing; she had been so engrossed in watching Jane. The aromas tickled the back of her nose and her taste buds responded straight away, saliva flooding her mouth in anticipation. Ted joined them, pulling up a chair to sit and watch their reactions as they sampled his creations. Euphemia glanced quickly across the road. The shop was empty, Jane had gone. She took another spoonful of the dessert nearest to her.

'I vote the coconut lime tart with the roasted peach and macadamia nut ice-cream,' said Kenneth. He dived in with his spoon for a second helping.

'Hey, that's not fair. I haven't tried it yet,' said Euphemia.

For five minutes, they tasted the desserts while Ted organised a server to bring coffee.

'I vote the Baked Alaska with kiwifruit and cherry ice-cream,' said Euphemia finally.

'That's my favourite,' said Ted. 'And it will photograph well so it should be easy to sell to our distributors.'

'Decision made,' said Kenneth. 'The coconut lime tart it is.'

Ted and Euphemia howled in protest, but they could not sway Kenneth. The lunch crowd having departed, he enlisted the support of the servers who agreed with him. It crossed Euphemia's suspicious mind, he had bribed them to agree with him when he was supposed to have been talking to Charlie Watson.

'Baked Alaska next time,' said Ted. He sipped his espresso. 'There's something else,' he said. 'It's awkward, so I'll come straight to the point. Sarah Baillie came to see me last week. She wants to sell Roger's shares and she wants to do it quickly. Her lawyer told her how much they are worth and she has offered them to me. I asked about you taking half, but she specifically said she did not want you to have them.'

Kenneth stiffened, then reached for his glass of water. 'How has it come to this?' he breathed. He took a sip and shakily replaced his glass on the table.

'I can't believe it,' said Euphemia. 'We've been friends for thirty years.'

'I thought she would see sense,' said Kenneth. 'We're the people she should trust, not some lawyer she has only just met.' He looked at Ted. 'How much?'

'Two hundred and fifty thousand dollars.'

'That's ridiculous,' said Euphemia. 'Her share is worth three times that. In a year, it will be worth even more. It makes no sense selling now. Roger would want her to keep her share for the children. It's part of their inheritance, and she's giving it away for nothing.'

'I know,' said Ted.

'So what did you say?' asked Kenneth.

'I have to look after my children, too. So I did what anyone would do. I said Yes. I've spoken to my bank and the final settlement is in six weeks.'

Kenneth put down his cup. 'You really should have re-read the partnership agreement first,' he said. 'I understand your motives and I don't blame you for seizing an opportunity when it presents. In fact, I admire you for it. It just won't work the way you hope it will. Not according to the agreement you signed.'

'I'm sorry you feel that way,' said Ted. 'I guess my lawyer will be in touch then. With an opinion about our agreement.'

'It's business, Ted, not personal and I hope we're good because we need to run the company in the meantime. Your lawyer can talk to my lawyer and it will get sorted one way or another.' He wiped the corner of his mouth with his napkin and stood up, motioning for Euphemia to do the same. 'The new desserts are excellent by the way. You're very talented.' He stepped back so Euphemia could pass in front of him before patting Ted on the shoulder.

'I guess you won't be playing golf with him on Saturday,' said Euphemia when they went to pay the bill.

'You guessed right,' he replied.

CHAPTER 8

THE SUN HAD COME OUT WHILE THEY WERE IN THE restaurant, so they walked back to the office taking the long route around the waterfront. It was after one. Office workers leaving their air-conditioned cubicles behind in favour of fresh sea air strolled around the bay to inspect the council's latest gimmick for the city. Near the yacht harbour, at the back of Te Papa, the national museum, the council had erected a sign spelling Wellington in giant multi-coloured letters. There was a gap where the letter 'I' was supposed to be. The implication being that tourists would stand in the gap to have their photos taken, thus putting the 'I' in Wellington.

'Children might like it,' said Euphemia when she saw it.

'I'm not so sure,' said Kenneth. 'Children are quite sophisticated nowadays.' He took her arm and looped it through his for their walk past the yacht basin. 'What do you make of Sarah's fire sale?'

'Roger would be horrified,' said Euphemia.

'Do Sophie and John know?'

'I doubt it. Should we tell them, or is that poking our noses in?'

'The latter,' said Kenneth with a sigh. 'I need to face the facts. Sarah likes you, but she has taken against me and there's nothing I can do about it except wait to see if she comes around.'

'Sad but true,' said Euphemia. She looked up at him and smiled. How anyone could take against this man was bewildering. He was the kindest person in the world. Underneath his occasional intolerance. 'Did you see Jane? She was in the shop across the street when we were at lunch.'

'I wondered what you were looking at. By the way, the coconut and lime pudding is the right one to choose. No matter what Ted says, the Baked Alaska wouldn't arrive at our restaurants intact.'

'Desserts are Us', a great idea brought down by crumbling meringue,' said Euphemia, laughing.

Kenneth pulled her around into his arms and kissed her lightly on the mouth. 'Not on my watch,' he said. He let her go and they strolled on. A group of seagulls crowded around a man eating fish and chips, their loud caws demanding that he share.

'I think Jane was selling her diamond pendant. The little one Justin gave her when they got married.'

'She said she wouldn't sell,' said Kenneth.

'I know. Does she need the money?'

They stopped beside a low wall to watch a small yacht motor through the gap in the breakwaters shielding the yacht harbour. It slowed down to putter along the line of boats to find a berth, the deep green water stirred up by its exhaust contrasting with the clear blue sea it had just left. Two old men were in charge, their faces those of seasoned sailors. One stood at the helm steering, the other at the front with his back to him was making signs with his hand about when to slow down. He lowered his flat palm and the man at the helm turned off the engine. The yacht coasted neatly into their berth and the man in front leapt ashore to tie up. Except he leapt too soon and fell straight into the water between the wooden pontoon and the boat. Euphemia waited for him to bob up, but he didn't. The water had closed over him. Worse, the man at the back hadn't seen what happened and had gone below.

'Hold this,' she said thrusting her bag at Kenneth, before hurdling the fence. She raced along the front of the boat sheds, stripping off her coat as she ran. There were two ways to get to the pontoon and the man in the water. The long way running around the waterfront and the short way swimming across to where he had gone. Euphemia took the short way. She waded into the sea and struck out for the boat. When she reached the spot, there was still no sign of him so, taking a huge breath, she dived. Deep. The murkiness of the water prevented her from seeing anything. Keeping one hand on the hull of the yacht, she swam around, feeling blind with her other hand. Luckily, the rope trailing in the water brushed against her arm. She grabbed it and pulled it towards her. A foot struck her leg, then another foot. She fumbled up the man's body until she could grip him under the arms. With an almighty heave, she threw him up, out of the water and onto the pontoon, where he lay like a beached fish; lifeless and draining foul-smelling water from his mouth and nose.

Euphemia hauled herself onto the pontoon to find that Kenneth had taken the long way and was already there, kneeling beside the unconscious yachtie. He whacked the old man on the back, laid him flat, cleared out his mouth and started CPR. The first sailor emerged from the cabin to see Kenneth, in his business suit, bent over his mate singing 'Staying Alive' by the Bee Gees and performing cardiac compressions in time to the music. A dripping wet woman standing alongside was phoning 911. Once she had finished the call, she yelled at the old guy to go up to the wharf and wait for the paramedics to show them where to come. Thankfully, he didn't need to be told twice.

They took turns giving chest compressions and mouth to mouth resuscitation for the next ten minutes, by which time several people had arrived with offers of help. One had brought the AED machine from the yacht club and said he knew how to use it. Another said she was a paramedic and offered to take over. A look passed between Kenneth and Euphemia. Happily, they handed over the resuscitation efforts to the experts and once they were sure the arrivals knew what they were doing; they slipped out of the back of the crowd and quietly left.

Everyone was so focused on the ambulance staff arriving, they didn't notice Euphemia and Kenneth. If they had looked for them, they would have seen a trail of wet footprints and the drips from Euphemia's clothes leading to Sage Consulting. It was a nice day. The sun was out and her trail soon dried away to nothing. It was as if they had never been there.

CHAPTER 9

EUPHEMIA SQUEEZED HER LITTLE HATCHBACK INTO THE GAP next to a lamppost outside the old wooden villa on the slopes of Mount Victoria. She was pleased she didn't own an enormous car or they would have had to park miles away. One-storey wooden villas on small sections lined both sides of the narrow street. The suburb was being gentrified, judging by the number of tradespeople's vans and rubbish skips occupying most of the parking spaces. Cars driving up and down the hill had to pull over and wait for each other to pass, as there was only room for one vehicle at a time to proceed in either direction.

'Are you sure this is the right place?' she asked.

Jane checked the address on the post-it note stuck to the back of her phone. 'Yes, this is it. Number twenty-three. Nell said there was no signage. It's only two-thirty. My appointment is at three. I told you we were too early.'

'We could wander down to a café on Majoribanks Street and grab a coffee,' said Euphemia.

'Nell said no stimulants before the appointment.'

'I could have coffee and you could have water.'

Jane undid her seatbelt and opened the door keeping a hold of it so it didn't get caught by the wind, blow back and slam into the lamppost.

'I suppose I'll never hear the end of it if I get between you and your caffeine fix.'

They had waited a week for an appointment with Nell. They would have had to wait longer if Jane hadn't mentioned Sarah Baillie's name several times. The confirmation had come as a text, along with a detailed email containing a list of instructions for detoxification prior to the consultation.

'No coffee has been easy,' said Jane as they sat down at a table in the café's window. 'The no alcohol for five days was impossible. Alastair took me to dinner at Ombre to celebrate his new bike arriving from the States – the replacement for the one you wrecked.'

'It wasn't me who wrecked it,' muttered Euphemia. She sipped her flat white and waited for the caffeine to revitalise her flagging energy. 'I was merely holding it when someone else attacked it.'

'You shouldn't have been holding it.' Jane made a face as she sipped her water. 'As I was saying, we went out to dinner to celebrate and before I knew it, I drank a glass of champagne. That was two days ago. I stopped as soon as I realised. Poor Alastair had to finish the bottle alone.'

'I can't see that a glass of champagne would make a difference. Besides, how would she know?' said Euphemia. 'And don't confess, whatever you do.'

'That's what I thought,' said Jane. 'I won't be telling her about the chocolate cake, either.' She pushed the glass of water away from her. 'Why did Roger and Kenneth call the business 'Desserts are Us' and not 'Puddings are Us'? Pudding sounds much better.'

'Apparently not in the Australian, Asian or American markets.'

'People would come around. Pudding is a smarter word than dessert.'

'Apparently only for the English, and the company isn't planning to go to England,' said Euphemia. 'I didn't realise desserts would be this stressful. Kenneth is working too hard. Ted can't help, he's busy overseeing the manufacturing. Roger's death has left an enormous gap. It's getting to the stage where either Kenneth employs someone or they might have to shut it down. Good people are so hard to find.'

'I'll keep my ear to the ground,' said Jane. She sipped her water.

'Justin was involved with some smart business people over the years and one of them might be looking for a new challenge.'

Euphemia shifted in her chair. Anyone who worked with Justin was instantly off the list of possibilities. Jane's husband had been a con man living off his wife's family's reputation and what remained of their money until he had committed suicide in the most horrific manner. Jane had been lucky to escape alive. She was far better off with Alastair, who worked in HR at Sage Consulting. He might not be the dynamic go-getter Justin pretended to be, but he was kind and, more importantly, he loved Jane.

'Are you listening?' asked Jane, waving her hand in front of Euphemia's face.

She jumped. 'You said that pudding is the snobby word for dessert?'

'Actually, I was explaining the instructions Nell sent me,' said Jane. She held up her hand and used her fingers to count them off. 'No sugar, no cigarettes or other substances, no alcohol, no stimulants of any kind. She surely demands a lot from people she hasn't met yet. I'm surprised she's so busy.'

'So am I,' said Euphemia. 'I'm very surprised Sarah has given up drinking. She enjoyed her evening gin and tonic and she's never turned down a glass of champagne as long as I've known her.'

'I don't smoke, so that part was easy,' said Jane. She twisted her mother's engagement ring around her finger. The large white diamond sparkled in the weak sunshine streaming through the window.

'Should I hold that for you?' asked Euphemia, pointing at the ring.

'Why? People like Nell are spiritual beings. She won't be interested in jewellery.'

'If you say so.' Euphemia checked her cup to see if there was any coffee left. There wasn't. 'It's just that sometimes if you give the impression of being wealthy when you're not, then people take advantage of you.'

'I can assure you no one takes advantage of me,' said Jane dusting an imaginary speck off her sleeve. 'I see those sorts of people a mile away.'

Euphemia looked at her watch. 'Time to go,' she said. She waved to the barista at the door. 'Great coffee, thanks.' She meant it. Wellington is renowned for its café culture and the quality of the coffee. So much so that Aucklanders make jokes about it. This barista was better than most, and Euphemia made a mental note to come back.

'Any time,' he called, looking up from behind his monstrous machine.

It took a few minutes to walk up the hill to the villa. An intercom had been built into the architrave beside a black-lacquered wooden door. Jane pressed the button and waited while Euphemia tried not to look directly at the tiny lens tucked into a corner above them. Jane identified herself. The door clicked open, and they went inside.

A receptionist met them in the hall. 'I am Gaia. Welcome to the Acceptance Institute,' she said. She looked at them before settling her gaze calmly on Jane. 'You must be Jane French, here for your consultation. And you,' she said, 'must be Euphemia Sage, here to support your friend. Welcome. Follow me. Nell will be with you shortly.'

Gaia was a tall young woman with perfect hair, perfect teeth, a perfect figure and a beatific smile. Serenity radiated from her in the way she held herself, the way she walked in front of them, and in the tone of her voice. She held out her arm as if to display the waiting room which had been simply but elegantly furnished. Two chairs faced each other in the middle of the space. The walls were empty; the floor polished boards covered by a thick blue rug. There were no windows. The door had been removed, and the gaps where the hinges used to be were painted over. Gaia led Jane to one of the chairs, indicated that Euphemia should sit in the other, then left. They were so close Euphemia could see Jane's pupils dilating as the music, the incense, the soft lighting and muted colour contributed to an unavoidable rush of relaxation and a sense of well-being. Stress had no relevance here. Pain had a solution. Happiness was possible. Joy imminent. Suffering banished and fulfilment waited on the horizon.

Euphemia folded her hands in her lap, and pinched herself hard on the fleshy part of her thumb. It was the only way she could focus on resisting the seduction of her senses and allow her to reclaim her thoughts. At the back of the house, a door opened. Footsteps came towards them.

'You must be Jane. I'm Nell,' said the woman standing where the door had been.

Nell was older than Euphemia expected. She guessed the dark-haired woman with her hands now placed securely on Jane's shoulders was in her mid to late forties. She had dark eyes, curated eyebrows, a thin nose, and thinner lips. Nell looked over Jane's head and focused her eyes on Euphemia.

'You must be Euphemia. I've heard such a lot about you from Sarah,' she said.

Euphemia stood up. Nell moved around Jane and pressed her palms on either side of Euphemia's outstretched hand. Both felt the tingling, the surge of energy radiating up their arms, and they stepped back, registering the shock of the other. Nell smiled, gave a slight bow, and murmured about having to check something in the consulting room before she could see Jane.

'I don't know what I was expecting, but she's lovely,' whispered Jane. She got up from her chair. 'I understand what Sarah means about this place now. I feel relaxed, don't you?'

'Yes, of course. It is a very professional set-up,' said Euphemia. The tingling had settled to a low hum in the bones of her forearm.

'Is that all you can say? Professional? It's amazing, not professional. I haven't felt like this in ages and I haven't had my consultation yet.'

Euphemia was about to reply when Nell returned. She spoke only to Jane. 'Come with me, Mrs French,' she said.

'I'm here to support Jane,' said Euphemia.

'As we all are,' replied Nell smoothly. 'Unfortunately, I can't work with clients if there are observers present. Gaia will see you out, Mrs Sage.' She put her arm around Jane and guided her out of the waiting area and down the hall.

'Jane,' said Euphemia. 'Don't you want me to come with you?'

'I'll be fine,' called Jane, not looking back, their previous arrangement completely forgotten.

The door at the end of the hall shut, leaving Euphemia standing in the waiting room. Gaia opened the front door.

'We request our support people to wait outside,' she said. 'Nell can't work if there is the slightest aura of negative energy anywhere near her.'

Euphemia had no choice but to leave. No sooner had she crossed the threshold than the door closed behind her. She looked up. The lens in the corner winked. Just as the lenses in the waiting area had done.

CHAPTER 10

'BACK SO SOON?' ASKED THE BARISTA.

'You looked quiet, so I thought I'd come in and give you something to do,' said Euphemia. After leaving the clinic, she had strolled to the top of Majoribanks Street and on up to the pine forest that ringed the higher slopes of Mount Victoria. The council maintained the paths, and as it was a working day there were no mountain bikers descending without warning and at speed. It was pleasant enough wandering through the trees. If she had had her trainers in the car, she would have gone for a run. Instead she walked a short distance in her work shoes then turned back. Another coffee was a better way to fill in time.

'Is your friend at the Institute?' asked Joel. Euphemia liked the fact that people wore name badges nowadays. What would have been a stilted conversation became a friendly exchange when you knew who you were talking to. She thought about asking the staff at Sage if they would like name badges, but then remembered the twenty employees knew each other already. The clients worked with dedicated personal teams and introductions were routine, so her idea of name badges was redundant before it began.

'Another flat white please. How did you know she would be there?'

Joel set about grinding the beans and then tamping the coffee into the bowl, which he clicked into the machine. He pressed the button and the dark liquid ran into a cup. 'I get a lot of business from them. Support people.' He half-filled a stainless steel jug, dipped the nozzle into the milk, and turned on the steam with a hiss and a roaring gurgle. He poured the thick mixture into the coffee, adding a flourish at the end to create a fern pattern in the froth.

'How many people do they see in a day?' asked Euphemia. She tapped her card on the terminal and it beeped to show she had paid.

'It depends if Nell is working alone or if Selina is there too.' He wiped the steam nozzle with a cloth and thumped the used grounds into the bin.

'Is it just the two? Selina and Nell?' she asked. She saw no point in taking her coffee to a table, preferring to stand at the counter so she could chat to Joel. It was one of the best cups of coffee in Wellington. Hot, strong and not overpowered by the milk. She normally went into town for café coffee. This place was in the opposite direction but the same distance as her usual haunt, and it had a loyalty card for regular customers. Euphemia liked that. It was a commitment on both their parts. Joel would see a lot of her from now on.

'I can see the Institute from here, so I see everyone coming and going. Nell is there most days, or she takes an Uber to visit her clients in their homes. Selina spends more time at the retreat on Waiheke Island, but she comes down once or twice a month to monitor things.'

'Gosh,' said Euphemia. 'We're a long way from Waiheke.'

'The clients like the distance. They like the anonymity of being away from home. You'd be surprised at the famous faces I see going into the Institute.'

Euphemia finished her coffee and pushed the empty cup and saucer across the counter. He put them in the dishwasher. She guessed he was around thirty. Bearded, his eyes were clear and intelligent and he had a warm smile, which he gave often during their conversation. No wonder he knew so much about the goings on at the clinic. People would happily speak openly in front of him.

'I've met Nell. What's Selina like?'

'She's more intense than Nell,' he said. 'Dark eyes, long black hair. She looks part Indian because she wears that eye-liner stuff.'

'Kohl?'

'That's it. Huge almond-shaped eyes which draw you in. Selina runs the residential programme.'

'You could be their marketing department, you know so much.'

'Mum says I have to stop eaves-dropping on people's private conversations but I say that if people speak loudly enough for me to hear, their privacy can't be important.'

'I agree with you,' she said. 'And I've got time for another coffee. Single shot this time. There's no one else here so tell me everything you've heard about them.'

Ten minutes later, Euphemia was much better informed. The electrical sensation she felt when Nell clasped her hand was still a mystery, but there would be a rational explanation. There always was. Despite her experiences with Rachel and the old chest in the attic, Euphemia was on Kenneth's side in regard to spooky happenings. Most were contrived and a healthy scepticism was important, especially when a fee was required in return for the unexplainable.

The door opened, and Jane stepped into the café.

'I thought you'd be here,' she said. She nodded at Joel, who smiled freely in return. 'Do you mind taking me home? Nell said I should sleep after a session.'

'It's only three-thirty. Aren't you coming back to work?'

'I can't,' said Jane. 'Nell said I did well to release so much negativity after only one session and now I have to process it. It was wonderful, by the way. She even had time to devise a programme, especially for me. If I am to heal, I have to see her every second day for a fortnight.'

'Oh,' said Euphemia. 'Can I assume that your next appointment will be later in the day so you can sleep in your own time and not Sage Consulting's time?'

'Nell said my body's meridians are most receptive at two-thirty, so it's the same time.'

Euphemia rolled her eyes. Joel laughed and threw a tea-towel over his shoulder. 'I'll have the coffee ready and waiting.'

'Discovering your café is the one good thing to come out of the Acceptance Institute,' she said.

CHAPTER 11

Kezia popped her head around the living room door to tell the men that dinner was ready. Her father was the most relaxed she had seen him in months. He was in bloke heaven. Ben, her lovely husband, was lolling sideways in the big leather armchair. Alastair and Dave were sitting at either end of the sofa with Petal perched between them, scoffing up any dropped crisps which fell within reach. In front of them, empty bottles and cans covered the coffee table while beneath it empty tubes of Pringles lay discarded on their sides. A once respectable cheese board was now a mess of crumbled crackers, and a single dill pickle stuck drunkenly out of the middle of a remnant of melted brie. The men suddenly perked up and leaned towards the television screen, yelling at their team to keep it together for the last five minutes of the game. Correctly judging now was not the time to interrupt, Kezia returned to the kitchen and advised her mother to delay serving until after the game was over.

Nicky, who wished she was in the sitting room with the men, poured another glass of wine for herself and her mother.

Kezia made a show of taking a bottle of apple juice from the refrigerator. 'I don't care if I never drink alcohol again,' she said, looking down her nose at her sister's wine. 'It's over-rated.'

'That's your opinion. There is nothing better than a cold beer on a hot day or a chardonnay with a good meal,' said Nicky.

'I'm with Kezia,' said Jane. 'Alcohol is legalised poison which props up the right wing consumerist patriarchy. Nell told me and she's right. Look how much money the industry takes out of the pockets of everyday people.'

'But you love champagne,' said Euphemia. 'Pol Roger is your favourite. You've always said if it was good enough to help Winston Churchill lead Britain through the war, it was good enough for you.'

'That was before I understood who actually profits when I poison my system with alcohol,' said Jane. She poured another glass of water from the gigantic jug she had brought with her rather than take the risk of drinking water from Euphemia's tap. 'Tap water has additives in it like chlorine and fluoride. Both are poisons.'

'Only if you inject them in massive doses,' said Euphemia. 'Chlorine in minute quantities stops us from dying of diarrhoea and fluoride protects the teeth of young children and adults. I think my body can cope with a little scientifically flavoured water.'

'Nell and Selina developed this system,' she explained. 'The filters built into this jug adds the micro-nutrients I need every time I fill my glass. I have been using it for ten days and I can feel the difference already.'

'You look different too,' said Euphemia.

'Do I? That's incredible,' she said. 'I knew it was working.'

Euphemia had to bend down, and check on the roast despite having only checked it a few seconds ago. Nicky picked up Petal and buried her face in the pug's fur so Jane wouldn't see her face. Kezia suddenly found something interesting to look at in the garden.

'I get it,' said Jane, looking around. 'Mock me all you like. Nell is a brilliant woman. She knows what she's talking about. I'm not the only one who feels better. Sarah is healthier than she has ever been and Kate doesn't have back pain anymore.'

Euphemia couldn't believe how quickly Jane had adopted everything on the programme Nell had set out for her at their first consultation. She didn't begrudge anyone the benefits of eating a sensible diet, exercising more and sleeping longer. What she begrudged was Nell charging Jane a hefty 'donation' for this advice, as though it was a secret new discovery. What was also concerning was that Jane was now a health-zealot of the worst kind. And not just at home, but at work, too. She had thrown Olivia's chocolate biscuits in the rubbish, telling the poor girl that someone so young should look after their teeth and their waistline. Eat raw carrots instead, she ordered. Strangely, after the initial shock, Olivia had complied and so far had lost two kilos.

Poor Alastair, Jane's ever hopeful suitor, could no longer have coffee with his mates after his Saturday morning cycle club ride. Jane, on Nell's advice, insisted he have a kale smoothie instead. She had immediately phoned the café, where they stopped and dictated the recipe to the staff. Then she followed up by randomly popping in to check they were following her instructions. The club was seriously considering banning Alistair from the Saturday outings. Euphemia thought Jane had gone too far and taken pity on him. She arranged to meet him at Joel's café for double shot lattes while Jane was having her sessions with Nell – the only time she knew Jane wouldn't catch them.

A low rumble emanated from the living room, followed quickly by victory whoops and triumphant yells. Kenneth pushed open the door, his hands full of rubbish, and announced. 'We are the champions! The Hurricanes are in the quarter-finals.'

'I wish I could have seen it,' said Nicky. She took another sip of wine.

Kenneth, hearing the peevish tone in Nicky's voice, deposited the cans and bottles in the bin and went over to give her a hug. 'Next week,' he said. 'You and me, okay? There's a home game and I've got two tickets.'

Nicky accepted the bone he had given her with a shrug.

'Hey,' said Kenneth. He squeezed her shoulders, forcing her to look up at him. 'I appreciate you giving me time with the boys. I used to watch the games with Roger, but now he's not here... well, you understand?'

She sighed and met her father's eyes. 'I know. Guy-time. But next Saturday is a date. You can't back out.'

'I won't.' He tapped her on the nose with his finger. Nicky, now a detective constable and a grown woman, would have objected if the gesture hadn't reminded her of when she was a little girl. It made her feel loved, something which is hard to object to.

'Something smells good,' said Kenneth. He turned his attention to Euphemia. 'When's dinner?'

'Ten minutes ago,' she replied and opened the oven door to reveal an enormous platter stacked high with vegetables surrounding a slab of rump steak. 'Carry that through to the dining room, please,' she said. 'Nicky, Kezia, can you bring the potatoes and gravy? Ben, would you organise the seating? Jane, if it doesn't go against your conscience, would you please bring the wine?'

CHAPTER 12

IT WAS TEN O'CLOCK, AND THE DINNER HAD BEEN A SUCCESS.
No one wanted to leave the table. The conversation had been interesting
but relaxed and everyone was in a good mood after such a delicious
meal. Most evenings, if they were at home together, she and Kenneth ate
dinner on trays, while watching the news on TV. If she was home alone,
Euphemia snacked. The days of regular sit down family meals had
stopped when the girls left home. It was heart-warming to see the large
dining room table surrounded by guests again, all having a good time.
She looked across the empty pudding dishes and glassware and smiled at
Kenneth. He raised his glass in a silent toast and beamed back at her
before turning to talk to Dave about the game. How men could
remember plays long after the match was over was bewildering. It had to
be something in their DNA because she had never known a woman
with the same memory for tries, touchdowns and who tackled who
three years ago.

She looked at Ben, Kezia's husband. The father of her grandchil-
dren. He wasn't like most men. He was a detective like Nicky. In fact,
they had gone to police college together. At one time, she had thought
Ben was interested in her. Smart, personable and with a good sense of
humour, Ben was a lot like Kenneth. He was comfortable knowing his

wife was smarter than he was. He neither competed with her, nor tried to bring her down to his level. Being strong in himself meant he could be strong for Kezia when she needed him to be. They had told no one about the twins, preferring to wait until after the scan at eighteen weeks when they would find out if everything was all right with their babies. But Ben knew Euphemia knew, and she knew he knew, and so they shared their excitement. It made her feel special to be part of their secret. A secret which might be hard to keep for much longer. Although Kezia's tummy was still as flat as a board, she kept smoothing her clothes over the imaginary bump. So much so that Nicky had told her to stop it because it was annoying.

Nicky's relationship with Dave Richards was progressing. That's all she was allowed to know and Euphemia didn't dare ask for details in case she jinxed it. Nicky had told her as much. 'Don't ask. Don't put any pressure on me. Just let us work it out,' she said as soon as Euphemia mentioned his name. 'I was only going to ask you to ask him for dinner,' she replied. Nicky had sniffed. 'That's all right then. But don't say anything else.'

Dave was a detective sergeant in the police force. He understood how important Nicky's career was to her. From what Euphemia could gather from the few crumbs Nicky gave her, he hadn't pushed her to commit to their relationship. He knew that if he did, Nicky would run a mile, fearful that her independence was being compromised. Dave, like Ben, was a top bloke, and would be an excellent addition to the family, according to Kenneth. If only Nicky was less prickly, thought Euphemia, looking at her daughter sitting at the end of the table. She was arguing about the make-up of the Hurricanes team with Dave. Neither was giving an inch. Perhaps they were suited after all.

Alastair and Jane had been an item for three months. Again Euphemia didn't want to pry in case too much light on a budding romance killed it before it had really taken root. Alastair might not be a star in life or at work, but he was competent, obliging, reliable, and unlike Jane's previous men, he was decent. Euphemia knew nothing about him other than that he enjoyed cycling, owned several expensive bikes, lived alone, and he loved Jane. Jane wasn't used to being loved. The men in her life, primarily her husband of thirty years, had treated her appallingly. Thankfully, Justin was dead and, for the first time in her life, Jane could take responsibility for her own destiny. Her budding renaissance as a woman was a joy to see. The devotion to all-things-Nell was only a minor glitch. Jane would grow past the psychologically slick dogma offered by the Acceptance Institute. Euphemia knew that underneath her need for approval Jane was a sensible woman with a good dollop of common sense.

The only people missing from the table were Roger and Sarah. Roger's gauche jollity had enlivened dinners throughout their married lives. Roger would drink as much as he liked and Sarah, more restrained than her husband, was the sober driver. His opinions were often outrageous, but he always had good reasons for them and Euphemia had enjoyed their debates. She had called Sarah and invited her to dinner, leaving a message on her phone when there was no answer. She even followed up with a couple of texts. That had been two days ago. She called again and left another message and still had heard nothing, so she could only assume Sarah wasn't ready for a full-on Sage dinner yet.

'Ahem, everyone.' Kenneth stood up at the end of the table, his glass raised to propose a toast. 'Thank you to my wife, the cook, for such a fabulous meal.' He stopped and waited while everyone filled their glasses. There was a tussle between Jane and Alastair when she tried to fill his glass with water from her jug, and he whisked his glass away and filled it with the remains of the Dry River Pinot Noir.

'Roger, my best friend, would have been your ally in that, Alastair,' said Kenneth. 'I don't know how many times I heard him quote WC Fields. "I don't drink water. Fish make love in it." Anyway,' he said, when the groans died down. 'My toast is to absent friends.'

'To absent friends.' There was silence as they drank to Roger, but it was short-lived. The doorbell rang. Not once, not twice, but continuously. Petal leapt up from under the table, barking and running around in circles until Nicky caught her up and cuddled her into silence. Kenneth got up and when he came back, Sophie Baillie was with him. Clearly distressed, she shrank back when she saw how many people were there. Kenneth put his arm around her. Euphemia got up and suggested they all go into the kitchen.

Sophie shook her head. 'I'll be fine,' she said, sweeping her hair back over her head. 'It's Mum. She's gone. And she left without telling us. She put everything on the market, the house, our furniture, the cars and she's gone to the Acceptance Institute Retreat on Waiheke Island.'

Jane perked up. 'Don't worry,' she said. 'I'm going too. I'll tell her you're upset and to call you.'

This was the first Euphemia had heard of Jane's plan and she was wondering who was going to staff reception when she saw Sophie start to cry.

'You don't understand,' said Sophie, gulping back tears. 'She's going to live there. Permanently. Her new lawyer told her to sell everything and donate the proceeds to the Institute, in return for living there for the rest of her life. She said we could come and visit her but only if we accept her decision and stop arguing with her. John is furious. He told her he hated her. He yelled at her that Dad hadn't worked hard all his life so she could get conned. She didn't like hearing that, but she still left. I'm sorry to barge in, but I came because I don't know what else to do.'

CHAPTER 13

EUPHEMIA WALKED INTO THE KITCHEN AND KENNETH looked up. 'How is she?' he asked. The dishes were done, and he was putting the large platters away on the top shelf in the pantry.

'Asleep,' replied Euphemia. She automatically picked up a cloth to wipe down the bench. 'She's exhausted. They have been staying with Sarah for the past week to talk her out of ruining all their lives. She's terrified the Acceptance Institute will take the money and then toss Sarah back into the world without a penny to live on.'

Kenneth put the kettle on and took two mugs out of the cupboard. 'Herb tea? Jane left some of her special brew to try.'

'That's another thing,' said Euphemia. 'When was Jane going to tell me she was going away? She seems to think she can come and go as she pleases, completely ignoring the fact she has already used up her holiday leave. Alistair daren't refuse filling in at reception because he loves her, but that's not his job. He has HR work to do.'

The kettle boiled and switched itself off. Kenneth filled the mugs. The water instantly turned yellow, and the smell of oranges and ginger filled the room.

'It's boring old turmeric, with a hint of cayenne, cumin and orange,' said Euphemia, after taking a sip. 'Hardly a special brew.'

'I like how you can know all that with one sip,' said Kenneth. 'I think it's okay. I quite like curry in a cup.'

'Anyway,' she said, 'I've decided I should go with her and check this place out. Pretend I'm a client and find out what is so amazing about this Retreat.'

Kenneth wrinkled his nose and took another sip of his tea. 'This isn't bad,' he said. 'I'll have yours if you don't want it.' She pushed her mug across the bench.

'Did you hear what I said about me going to Waiheke?'

'Yes. I'm thinking about it.'

'Think all you like,' she blurted. 'I'm going and that's that.'

'Woah,' he said. 'Where did that come from?'

Euphemia was as surprised as he was by her outburst. She shook her head. 'Sorry, I'm worried, I think,' she said. 'How can someone like Nell make sensible women give away their worldly possessions and, in Sarah's case, leave them with nothing? Why do they do that? And I'm worried about Jane. She has nothing apart from her mother's jewellery to fall back on in hard times, and I don't want her to get conned out of it. I'm sure she sold her diamond pendant to pay for Nell's sessions.'

'All credit to you for caring about your friends,' he said. 'But what about us? Sage Consulting? The family? Petal? Who's going to look after your responsibilities here? You know how busy I am. I can't do it.'

Euphemia took the empty mugs and put them in the dishwasher. She wiped the bench again, and she rinsed the cloth under the tap, wrung it dry and put it in the holder under the sink. Kenneth hadn't moved. 'Kezia is over her morning sickness,' she said. 'She can look after Sage with one hand tied behind her back. Nicky can help with Petal and on the days she can't, then Petal can go to doggy day-care. All you have to do is take her there in the mornings and pick her up at the end of the day. The girls have been on at me for ages to get a cleaner. So I will. And a gardener. You can do your own washing, you know how, and you can order take-outs or eat at Ted's. Have I left anything out?'

He rubbed his chin and looked sideways at her. 'No. You seem to have covered everything. I suppose it will be good for you to get away.'

'I'll be observing, not relaxing,' she said more sharply than she intended. 'This is not a holiday.'

He held up his hands and stepped back. 'That's not what I meant,' he said. 'I know why you're going. You're looking after your friends and I admire you for it.'

Euphemia couldn't shake off the feeling he was giving her permission. It was odd, because Kenneth wasn't that sort of husband. He never had been. As long as she'd known him, she had been free to do whatever she wanted to do when she wanted to do it. Unlike other husbands, he didn't put limits on her. He had supported her both in her career and in her running. So why did she feel irritated by their conversation and why was it up to her to organise things to carry on smoothly at work and home while she was away? He walked out the door to go to Sydney without thinking about who was going to mow the lawns or make sure the bills got paid. Now it was her turn. Once she had everything organised to run like clockwork while she was away.

He pulled her into his arms, kissed her on her forehead, then leaned back and studied her. 'Don't look so concerned,' he said. 'I'll be fine. You do what you have to do.' He bent down and this time he kissed her on her lips. Properly. Her irritation seeped away. Euphemia had never been able to resist his properly-kisses. They went upstairs to bed.

CHAPTER 14

It was a warm day despite the clouds cluttering the sky. The soft breeze smelled of the sea. Jane leaned against the balustrade on the ferry and looked across the Hauraki Gulf to Rangitoto Island which they were sailing by on their left. She was wearing a pink, zip-up hoodie over a white t-shirt, pink yoga pants, and white Allbirds. The two-strand diamond tennis bracelet, thin gold chain necklaces and diamond and sapphire earrings plus her huge sunglasses completed the rapper look Euphemia had teased her about when they met at the airport earlier that morning.

'Better than looking like someone's lost shadow,' said Jane referring to the black merino top and jacket, matching leggings, and black trainers which Euphemia always wore when she wasn't working. Euphemia raised her eyebrows and suggested they change the subject. The flight to Auckland took an hour, the Uber ride to the ferry terminal, forty-five minutes. Euphemia just had time to grab a coffee before they boarded the ferry which left precisely at the time stated on the timetable. It was a weekday and after 10 AM so the cabin was full of elderly day trippers taking advantage of the free fares the pensioner Gold Card entitled them too.

'That's your last coffee for a while,' Jane said nodding towards Euphemia's huge takeout cup. 'Enjoy it, but make sure you get rid of the cup before we arrive, or they'll make you stay at a motel to detox before you're allowed to come to the Retreat. Why are you coming, by the way? If you won't obey the rules?'

'I will obey the rules after I get there,' said Euphemia. 'Until then, I'm a free woman.' She saw the look on Jane's face. 'Don't worry, I won't embarrass you. I'll play nice.'

'Are you sure?' Jane adjusted her sunglasses then used a finger to flick away a lock of hair the wind had blown into her mouth. 'After all the snide remarks you've made, I don't understand why you want to come. I'm surprised they agreed to let you.'

'Not as surprised as Nell when I made my appointment. I explained I was grieving Roger's loss too, which I am by the way. I told her how well you looked and how I thought I should deal with my own issues. She was very sympathetic and she went out of her way to fit me in to the same fortnight as you when she saw how much I was going to donate to the Institute. I'm grateful someone was persuaded to rebook for next month.'

Jane studied Euphemia for a moment over the top of her sunglasses then shrugged. 'Your donation is your business. I'm not as materialistic as you. Money has never interested me.'

Euphemia almost choked on her coffee. Jane had been fixated on money and how much everyone had for as long as she had known her. She knew how much each of her friends were worth, how much they had inherited and the prices they had paid for their houses, cars, jewellery and furniture. Her mother had been worse, judging people by their possessions and not their inner qualities. She ingrained this mindset into her daughter who then chose to marry Justin, a man with a bank vault where his heart should have been. He had proceeded to spend Jane's inheritance and she had let him, all for the sake of keeping up appearances. If it hadn't been for the fire destroying almost everything she had left, Jane would still be the snooty socialite who blanked Euphemia at school reunions. Thank goodness for the fire. Jane proved to be much nicer when she was poor. Poor-Jane was brave, righteous, funny, smart and courageous, qualities which endeared her to Euphemia. Qualities which almost compensated for the fact she was a terrible snorer. Euphemia had packed several sets of industrial strength earplugs just in case they were put in adjacent rooms.

'The size of your donation is not why you were given a place so quickly,' continued Jane. 'Nell would have felt your deep and urgent need to be healed.'

'That sounds very spooky.'

'Didn't you read any of the information they gave you? This is a retreat for the soul,' said Jane. 'Instead of a room, we are each assigned our own haven. I find it very comforting to know that at the end of each day I will be somewhere safe where I can concentrate on using all my new techniques to self-heal.'

Euphemia took an extra, large gulp of her coffee and thought again about what she was getting herself into. The Acceptance Institute sounded awfully self-focused. How much navel gazing could she do before she got thoroughly bored and needed to break out? She had questioned Nell about physical activities and only when she was sure she would be able to go running did she make the final payment and commit to the course. If she wasn't able to exercise she would need a proper asylum run by doctors in white coats with pills and medicines.

The engines changed from a high-pitched hum to a low grumble as the ferry slowed on its approach to the island. Bush-clad hills rose from the sea, houses dotted amongst the trees and along the ridgelines under the sky. The wind dropped completely once they were in the land's shelter. Out to sea there were gaps in the clouds through which the sun shone, spotlighting the grey water with circles of blue light. Euphemia took off her wind jacket. Her black short sleeved t-shirt over her black leggings clung to her slim body making her legs look even longer above her chunky trainers. The ferry slowed again, riding up the concrete causeway which sloped into the water between rocks on the shore. Crew lowered the ramp at the front and below on the vehicle deck, engines started. A line of cars drove slowly off the boat, then sped up, quickly disappearing around a bend at the end of the road.

The women were to wait outside the terminal where they were to be met by a driver. Euphemia looked wistfully at the barista, plying his trade from a coffee cart in front of the building, wishing she could have one last hit of caffeine to delay going full cold-turkey. She estimated it would take ten hours for her to lose the caffeine in the extra-large, triple-shot, flat white she had drunk on the ferry. After that she planned to eke out the stash of caffeine pills in her backpack to avoid the worst of any withdrawal symptoms. On one level it was going to be interesting because her super powers were a result of up-regulating her metabolism. Caffeine helped maintain her system in a state of readiness. No one had told her this; she had figured it out for herself. As long as she could maintain a low level of the drug she should be fine and she saw no need to inform the retreat about her supply.

A stocky middle-aged woman came over and stood beside them. Her shoulders were as broad as her hips, and her tummy bulged over the waistband of her skirt but she had remarkably good legs. 'I'm Margaret,' she said. 'You look like you're going to the same place I am.'

'I'm Jane and this is Effie,' said Jane, smiling.

'Nice to meet you and my name is actually Euphemia. Not Effie,' said Euphemia, smiling too.

'Hi, Jane. Euphemia,' said Margaret. 'I know what it's like. I hate it when people call me Maggie instead of Margaret. I'm from Hamilton.'

'We flew up from Wellington this morning,' said Jane.

'I drove. I left my car at the ferry terminal. Do you think it will be all right there? I'm a bit nervous,' replied Maggie. 'You're lucky to have each other. I wanted my friend to come but June said it was all a giant con and she wouldn't be seen dead at a retreat.'

Euphemia could bear the smell of the coffee wafting over no longer. She put down her backpack and was about to order a triple espresso which she could down in one gulp when a van drew up beside them. A young woman got out. She was in her twenties, and wearing a white t-shirt, long white shorts and white Allbirds. Her dark hair was cut short, forming a soft halo of curls around her head.

'Ladies,' she said. 'I'm Claire, one of the healers. Welcome to the Acceptance Retreat. It's good you're getting to know each other. Jump in and buckle up. I'll throw your luggage in the back and we'll be off.' Once they were seated inside the van, she slid the heavy door shut with a thump and ran around, climbed into the driver's seat and took off so fast the women jolted back in their seats.

'Sorry,' she yelled. 'It's this new van. It's electric and the acceleration takes a bit of getting used to.'

This was Euphemia's first trip to Waiheke Island and she hadn't realised how big it was and in places how suburban. She had looked at a map before leaving and seen that the island was the same shape as the toe of Italy's foot. A main road snaked along the central ridgeline running the length of the spine of the island. Minor roads leading down from it to various bays and small villages branched off it at regular intervals. Divided in two the south-eastern half of the island consisted mainly of farmland and vineyards. This side had few inhabitants in contrast to the north-western side where most of the housing and urban development had taken place.

Euphemia noted various landmarks and road signs as the van passed them by on what was a long drive to the Retreat. She estimated they had travelled twenty kilometres before the tarmac gave way to rutted gravel. For half an hour, they bumped along, the windows closed against the dust billowing along beside and behind them. Now and then they would meet another vehicle on a bend, and Claire would have to slow down but the further they got, the fewer vehicles they saw. Eventually they turned off the main road, to stop in front of a pair of high gates set into a six-foot stone wall.

Claire wound down her window and pressed numbers into the keypad with her thumb. The gates swung open. She drove through, the gates closing automatically behind the van. They carried on up a sealed driveway surrounded on both sides by dense bush.

'I love the smell of the horopito tree,' said Margaret leaning out a window. 'You get it nowhere else in the world.'

Jane inhaled deeply, closed her eyes then exhaled slowly. 'Is that what it is?' she said. 'I never knew. Thank you for sharing, Margaret.'

Ten minutes later Claire swung the van past a fountain in front of a large single-storey building and stopped. She got out and ran around to open their door. Euphemia stepped out first, blinking in the noonday sunshine. Jane and Margaret stood beside her, Margaret stretching her arms. They looked around unsure what to do, then a slim woman in her fifties emerged from the building and walked down the shallow steps to greet them. She had long straight dark hair, kohl-lined almond-shaped brown eyes and a clear light complexion surrounding full even lips. She raised her hands in a namaste gesture and bowed.

'Welcome to the Acceptance Retreat. My name is Selina,' she said.

CHAPTER 15

'HAVEN' WAS A TOUGH WORD FOR EUPHEMIA TO GET HER head around. What was wrong with the word room? Because that is all it was. White walls, narrow, oblong windows under the eaves set above head height, with views of the tree-tops outside, a double bed covered with a linen navy-blue duvet and matching pillows, and a single cupboard. A tiny bathroom, with a tiny shower, hand basin and toilet, tucked behind a partition on one side, the only concession to luxury. Alarmingly, the single light switch was outside the door, beside the small board with her name on it. It read Euphemia and not Euphemia Sage. To Euphemia, the word haven conjured up an image of comfort and safety. It didn't apply to what was essentially a pristine cell all alone at the end of a long corridor with many corners.

Her vertebrae concertinaed on top of each other when she sat down on the bed. She checked under the duvet to find there was no mattress, just a thin layer of padding over a hard, flat surface. Euphemia groaned. She hadn't expected a five star hotel, but she also hadn't expected having to sleep on what was a padded wooden board under a measly thin duvet. Now suspicious, she went into the bathroom and turned on the shower. And waited. Five minutes of impotent dribble and the water was still cold. Great. She was just about to march back to reception and tell them she had changed her mind and would like a ride back to the ferry when there was a knock at the door.

Selina didn't wait for her to reply. She walked in. 'I've brought your backpack,' she said and put it on the bed. 'We recommend that all our clients rest for the afternoon after they get here. We will serve the evening meal in the Domed Hall, which you passed through on your way to your haven. Come down when you hear the bell.'

'I'd prefer not to rest,' said Euphemia. 'If possible, I'd really like to go for a run.' Euphemia was both taller and broader than Selina, her size emphasised by the close confines of the tiny room. It was unnerving, and she felt like a clumsy great giant in the presence of a graceful and delicate sylph. She stepped back.

'We recommend our clients don't get ahead of the programme we have specifically developed for them. Rest today. Tomorrow I will see you for your first one-on-one session, where we will discuss your goals for the next two weeks.'

Before Euphemia could object, Selina left the room, and the door closed automatically behind her. A soft click followed. Euphemia leapt forwards and turned the handle. Locked!

'No run then,' she said. 'It's lucky I'm not claustrophobic, or that the place isn't on fire.'

She plumped down on the bed, the jarring in her spine a reminder too late that plumping was not a good idea. Dumbfounded at finding herself locked in a 'haven' in a retreat in the back of beyond in her fifties, she lay back and stared at the ceiling. Paying to be a prisoner was not her idea of a good time. Okay, the Acceptance Retreat literature didn't exactly promise a good time, but it hadn't mentioned incarceration. Certainly not on the first day.

She considered her options. She could bust through the walls and run for help. Possible and very tempting. Her second option was when they unlocked the door for dinner, to demand to be taken back to the ferry and she would return to Wellington alone. The last option saw her busting open the door with one well-aimed kick, shout the place down until Sarah came out of her 'haven' and convince her to return to Wellington and her children. All three options were great in theory, but all three were unlikely to achieve the objective; getting Sarah to see sense would take patience and time. Leaving would achieve nothing; the last thing she wanted to see was Sophie's disappointment when she returned to Wellington without her mother.

It was cold. She unzipped her backpack, took out her merino vest and put it on. It had been a warm outside, but inside it was at least five degrees cooler. She found her light jacket and put that on over her other clothes. These people were too cheap to pay for either proper mattresses or heating. She decided not to think about what dinner might be. Or her rumbling stomach. In the side pocket of her backpack, she had hidden a supply of chocolate muesli bars, which she had vowed to use only for emergencies. If being locked in a cold, bare room against her will did not constitute an emergency, then nothing did. She dug around expecting to feel the wrappings with her fingers, but all she felt were her merino socks. She tried not to panic. That didn't work, so she tipped the entire contents of her backpack onto the duvet, shaking it up and down to make sure it was completely empty.

Underwear (black), t-shirts (black), two pairs of leggings and two pairs of shorts (black), pyjamas (blue), a beanie (black), three pairs of socks (2 x black and 1 x white), one pair of jandals, one hairbrush (pink), one toilet bag (bright red) and that was it. She sorted everything into neat piles to make sure she had missed nothing.

Where were the caffeine tablets in the silver foil she had slid into the pocket of her leggings? Where were the chocolate muesli bars she had tucked inside her socks? More importantly, where was her phone? How was it possible in this day and age to be locked in a room and ordered to sleep? To have her belongings searched, her privacy violated, and her property confiscated? Who did these people think they were taking her phone away? They were treating her like she was a teenager with a TikTok addiction! If there was an emergency at home, what then? What if her family needed to contact her? What if she wanted to finish the book she was reading? She was just getting to a good part in Death Actually. (Ben had invited Maggie to a romantic dinner. Was she going to say yes?) And what if she needed to play Patience to soothe her nerves? She had rights, dammit. These people were running a retreat, not a prison.

It took less than three minutes of concentrated searching to find the hidden cameras tucked into the top architrave above the windows on each wall. If she hadn't used her enhanced eyesight, she would never have seen them since they were so small. She had kept the search casual, looking away as soon as she found them. Whoever was at the other end must not suspect she knew they were there. Based on their positions, they covered the entire room. So much for this being a haven! Nothing could be further from the truth. Next, she checked every surface of the bathroom casually as she put her toiletries away. It was a relief to know she could shower and use the toilet without the staff at the Acceptance Retreat spying on her private moments. She still double checked the toilet bowl to make sure.

When she had tidied away her clothes on the simple shelf provided, she took off her shoes, lay down on the bed and stared up at the ceiling as she considered what to do next. Never in her life had she been anywhere so confronting or so odd. If she had her phone, she would have called Kenneth and told him to send a helicopter to winch her to freedom.

She had meant to call Barbara in Sydney and tell her where she was going before she left, but time had got away on her. They had been talking every day for months about the Switch and the troubles at the Foundation in Mauritius. Several of the better research geneticists had left to take up teaching posts at universities in Britain and it was difficult finding staff of the same calibre to replace them. The research had reached a critical stage, and it was a pity to have it interrupted. Now Barbara would wonder why she wasn't answering her calls. Hopefully, Kenneth would tell her where Euphemia was at one of their Zoom conferences. Since Roger's death, Barbara had been taking a larger role in 'Desserts are Us' and her advice had been just what Kenneth needed.

In her eighties, Barbara was no longer the super woman she had been in her fifties, but her brain was as sharp as ever. She joked she needed all her healing powers to fight the effects of age on her brain and had none left over for physical combat. After the incident on the Bridge Euphemia had suggested she take a holiday to recover.

'Go to your house in Tahiti for a month,' she said. 'Scottie can run the Foundation, and Kenneth has things under control at 'Desserts are Us' thanks to you.'

'Scottie is my tech guy – that's all. While he is one of the best techs in the world and devoted to me, he is not one of us, Euphemia. Alison's father is up to his old tricks and I'm worried the manager in Mauritius is not up to defending our work. I think I may have to go and I'd like you to come with me.'

'Of course I'll go with you,' said Euphemia. 'When were you thinking of?'

'At the beginning of next month.'

This conversation had preceded Sarah's flight to the Retreat and Euphemia had naturally agreed to accompany her to Mauritius in three weeks. It was lucky she was only going to be here for a fortnight so wouldn't be letting Barbara down. She was looking forward to the trip as she was curious about the research and what had been discovered. She also hoped to explore the contents of the archives the Foundation had accumulated in the centuries since Rachel emerged from the pond.

Euphemia only realised when she lay down, that there was no noise. No birds, no traffic, not even the sound of the trees moving behind the glass above her. No people, no footsteps, no doors shutting, no machinery humming, nothing. Just a dense silence. Her room, sorry haven, was sound-proofed. She heard nothing, not even after she dialled up her hearing. This meant no one could hear her. She was alone, locked in a room, her movements relayed by cameras to who knows who, her super powers on hold until she figured out what to do. Some retreat!

CHAPTER 16

THE LOCK INSIDE THE DOOR, CLICKED. EUPHEMIA OPENED her eyes and looked at her watch. It was 5.30 PM. She had been asleep for three hours but it felt like more. She sat up, swung her legs over the edge of the bed, and stayed there getting her bearings. Her room looked the same. Everything was where she had put it. But it wasn't the same. Someone had been here while she was asleep. Lingering in the farthest corner was a smell. Only just detectable; it faded to nothing when she registered its presence. But she kept its olfactory print to match later. Shivers skittered down her spine at the thought of being observed asleep and helpless by a stranger. It puzzled her she hadn't woken up, because her super powers usually ensured she was sensitive to changes in her environment even when she was asleep. At home, she woke and checked the room at the slightest disturbance waking a very annoyed Kenneth at the same time. It was an ongoing source of friction between them, his lack of sleep since she had come into her powers.

Her tummy growled. There had been no lunch offered when they arrived, and she was starving. She stood up and stretched, noticing that despite her concerns, she felt energised. Kenneth's restlessness since Roger's death, combined with her hot flushes and general alertness, had made for a busy bed. She hadn't realised how much she missed waking up and feeling refreshed until now. If this was what a few hours' sleep could do, how would she feel after sleeping a whole night? Her tummy rumbled and gurgled, reminding her again she hadn't eaten or drunk anything except coffee since breakfast. She was thirsty and famished, and now her door was unlocked. She was keen to explore the rest of the complex and find food, any food.

She pulled on her shoes, did up the laces, and looked fondly at her bed before opening the door and venturing down the corridor. Strip windows at ceiling level on one wall revealed tree branches moving silently in the evening light. Strip lighting at foot level activated by movement switched on as she approached and then turned off after she passed by. Right angle corners followed one after the other, disorientating her before finally she reached a set of double doors, which automatically swung open silently in front of her. They closed just as silently behind her, the snick of the internal bolt lock barely audible. She turned another right angle and walked down yet another corridor, not as long, but with the same high windows and strip lighting. This time, the double doors opened onto a large hexagonal room with a glass-domed roof.

In the middle of the room, a huge, round sisal rug lay on polished blonde wooden floorboards. Someone had set six places at equal intervals around it. At each place was a placemat, a name written on thick card above it, a folded linen napkin beside it and a covered bowl sitting exactly in the middle. A jug, just like the one Jane had brought to dinner, sat next to the name cards and a glass beside that. There were no chairs, just flat cushions the same colour as the sisal. The walls of the room were white and bare. Seven doors opened into the space. People smells, incense, the aroma of food swirled in the air currents heated by the sun, under the glass dome.

The first to arrive, Euphemia tried to get an idea of the rest of the complex, but it was impossible to see behind the doors or above the solid walls. One door must open onto the short hall, then the front door they had come through earlier. Looking up through the glass dome, she saw the sky turning slowly to night. She walked around the circle, examining the place cards. They had set her name next to Jane's. Margaret was on Jane's other side. Then Selina, Nell, and Claire's places completed the circle. Where was Sarah going to sit? It had been nearly two weeks since she left Wellington to come here.

Two doors swished opened at the same time. Jane and Margaret walked through. Bed hair and wrinkled clothes, Jane rubbed her bleary eyes and focused on Euphemia.

'That was the best nap I have ever had,' she said, yawning.

'Me too,' said Margaret, as she pulled her sweatshirt down to cover her belly. They gave each other a clumsy high-five and looked around the room. Margaret found her place and groaned. 'I thought they might do this,' she said. 'Eat on the floor. I can get down but getting up again? That's a whole other story. I don't know what happened. One day, I could get down and up without having to think about it. The next day, I have to roll around on the floor to get into the right position so I can haul myself up using furniture for support. I used to think old people having to call someone to help them get up was a pathetic cry for attention. Now I know it's the real deal.' She looked Euphemia and Jane up and down. 'The two of you are slim and fit for your age. You won't have any bother. All I ask,' she said, 'is that you don't watch me. Just focus on something in the other direction and let me get up the only way I know how. Slowly.'

The remaining doors opened, and Claire, Nell, and Selina walked into the room. Their performance, for that is what it was, reminded Euphemia of synchronised swimming without the nose-pegs. Their toes pointed, their heads held straight, their backs straighter, their legs stiff, they marched to their places, crossed their legs, and sat down in a fluid motion with their hands resting on their knees, their thumbs and index fingers joined to make a circle, palms upright.

Selina inhaled slowly, then exhaled just as slowly looking at each one in turn, her eyes suggesting they too take their seats. Margaret was right about the struggle. She got to her knees then swung her thighs to one side falling backwards onto her bottom. She brought her legs up in front of her, one knee higher than the other.

'My hip hurts if I put my leg down,' she offered to the group by way of explanation for the awkward posture.

Jane had no belly to impede her, and her descent was more like Selina's than Margaret.

Euphemia, who could have easily dropped from a standing position with no fuss into the crossed leg position, made a show of hip and knee stiffness. When they were all settled, Selina suggested they think silently about the gift of food, then to eat when they were ready. Euphemia was so hungry she forgot to ask about Sarah.

She lifted the lid from her bowl, having thought briefly about the gift of the food her donation had funded. Cos lettuce leaves, finely chopped chives, yellow and orange nasturtium flowers, chopped spring onions and a sprinkling of pistachio nuts. The leaves were washed. There was no dressing. The salad was in a small earthenware bowl and there was nothing to eat it with. Margaret gasped and clutched her throat. Selina smiled beneficently and removed the lid from her bowl. They watched as she delicately used a cos leaf to scoop nuts, flowers, and spring onions into her mouth. Between each mouthful, she put the bowl down while she chewed slowly and stared up at the sky. Euphemia watched, mesmerised by Selina's Adam's apple bobbing up and down when she swallowed after exactly forty chews.

The salad was fresh, crisp and delicious. It was also gone in less than a minute. Euphemia poured a glass of water from her jug, drank it, and sat back wondering what the next course would be. No one spoke. When everyone had finished their food, Nell clapped her hands and a woman in a pale pink hoodie, track pants and bare feet entered the room holding a tray in front of her and collected the dishes. Selina led the way, recapping her bowl and handing it to the woman. Nell and Claire followed her cue. When the woman stopped behind her, Euphemia reared back in surprise.

'Sarah?'

Sarah Baillie nodded then took her bowl before moving away to collect dishes from Margaret and Jane. She didn't say a word before leaving through the same door she had just come through.

'Why didn't Sarah eat with us?' Euphemia asked. 'We're old friends.'

'Sarah has her role here, as do you,' said Selina. 'This is her life now. She is pleased to do her part to keep the Acceptance Retreat running as it always has.'

Euphemia decided it was better to say nothing. Not yet anyway. This was truly the strangest place she had ever been to, let alone paid actual money to attend. She needed to know more about how it worked before rocking any boats. In the meantime, she hoped that Sarah or anyone would bring the next course soon. The salad was excellent, but she was hungrier than she had ever been, and her enforced caffeine withdrawal wasn't helping. A big fat juicy steak, or mac and cheese with added bacon, was what she felt like now. Unadulterated protein with lashings of fat. Something she could get her teeth into, something which would warm her stomach.

She looked expectantly from Selina to Nell, then to Claire. They had folded their napkins and looked to be getting ready to leave. Selina got up, followed by Nell, both in the same fluid motion from the floor to standing in one move. Selina wished them each a good night's sleep then she and Nell disappeared through their respective doors. Claire stayed and smiled at them in that irritatingly peaceful way she had.

'You are welcome to take your water back to your havens. The jugs are refilled according to your needs. Selina encourages us all to hydrate as often as possible. Tomorrow you will wake at 5.30 AM for a yoga class here in the Domed Hall at 6.00 AM. After yoga, we will have beginner's meditation followed by breakfast at 8.30 AM. At 9.00 AM I will hand out your individualised programmes after which we get down to Retreat business.' Her smile morphed into a tinkling laugh, which grated like fingernails on a blackboard.

Margaret's bottom lip quivered.

'Is that it?' Jane asked. 'There's no more food?'

Claire raised her eyebrows. 'That was the welcome banquet which Selina described in the course literature, yes,' she said calmly. 'The plants were of the finest quality, organically grown here on the island and picked within an hour of being presented to you. Our dietician has carefully worked out nutritional requirements for each of you. The minerals, vitamins, and plant proteins will sustain you until morning.'

'But I'm still hungry,' said Margaret. She had rolled her legs around to one side and was attempting to get up. With nothing to hold on to, she was making heavy weather of it, and growing increasingly red in the face. Euphemia, tempted to offer a helping hand, remembered what Margaret had said and turned away so as not to be caught watching.

'Oh, for goodness' sake, Maggie. Let me,' said Jane springing to her feet and holding out her hand. Margaret took it and Jane pulled her upright.

'It's Margaret,' said Margaret, smoothing down her trousers. 'Not Maggie.'

'Sorry,' replied Jane, rolling her eyes.

'Selina has designed the water to ease hunger pains,' said Claire.

Margaret picked up her jug and glass and looked at both suspiciously.

'The layout can confuse at first, so I will see you to your doors. Jane,' said Claire, indicating one door with an outstretched hand. 'Margaret, yours,' she said, stepping backwards, 'and Euphemia, yours.' She waited for the women to leave, then locked their doors behind them. It was 6.30 PM.

CHAPTER 17

IT WAS STILL LIGHT WHEN EUPHEMIA WENT TO SLEEP. IT WAS dark when once more the quiet snick of the lock drawn back inside the door, woke her. The room may be spartan but thankfully the shower had improved and was now hot and powerful. She was enjoying the sharp needles of water drilling into her hair follicles when without warning it stopped – pleasure was clearly on a timer. The towel provided was small and rough, but it was sufficient, and she dried off. There was no hair dryer, so she used her fingers to clear the tangles from her damp hair then dressed in her usual black merino leggings and t-shirt. Five minutes after opening her eyes she walked barefoot down the corridor and arrived in the Domed Hall to find seven yoga mats laid out in two rows of three with one at the front.

Nell arrived next, quickly followed by Selina, Jane, Margaret, and lastly, Sarah. Euphemia smiled, but only Jane and Margaret returned her greeting. The others solemnly moved to stand at the back of their mats. Claire claimed the one at the front. Margaret and Jane yawned as they joined Euphemia in the back row.

'This morning,' said Claire, 'we will do a simple workout so I can assess strengths and weaknesses with the objective of building on your strengths and eliminating your weaknesses during your time with us.'

'Good luck with that,' muttered Margaret.

Claire's voice was so gentle and accepting, Euphemia had immediately felt the muscles in her spine relax. Jane caught her eye and nodded as if to say, I told you. Her new pink leotard, with matching leggings, showed off her neat figure. Margaret, in contrast, wore a fluorescent green zip-up jacket and track pants which emphasised rather than flattered her stocky outline.

Music started – an instrumental track of soothing sounds set to a gentle rhythm. Euphemia heard waves breaking softly on a beach and wished herself to a tropical island where palm trees swayed overhead and the sun shone, where the sea was warm and where no was around to ruin the peace, tell her what to do or lock her in her room.

'We will start with the child's pose,' said Claire. In one fluid motion, she lay down, her bottom resting on the backs of her legs, her feet splayed beside her hips and her arms stretched out in front of her head. Sarah, Selina, and Nell followed suit, as did Euphemia and Jane who huffed slightly as she moved into position. Margaret kneeled then fell forward onto her hands and knees before pushing back to land heavily on the backs of her legs. 'Ow!' she yelled before rolling onto her side and rubbing her left hip. Claire stayed in position, head down, her arms in front of her, inhaling into her stomach and exhaling through pursed lips. Just as Margaret achieved the closest semblance to the pose she could manage, Claire suggested they move into the table pose, hold it... and then down into the plank position.

'Now lift your legs as high as you can, arching your back, and... hold. Remember to focus on your breathing, slowly in and slowly out.'

Jane was the first to break wind, followed quickly and more impressively by Margaret.

'I've had three kids. That's my excuse, and it's a good one,' whispered Margaret out of the side of her mouth. 'The last two were enormous babies.' Claire, pretending she hadn't heard, moved into the next pose. Margaret rolled onto her side and, trying not to laugh, raised her left leg in the air in front of her.

Jane did the same, but unfortunately, as she moved into a downward dog, a small, high-pitched squeak escaped. She ignored it and carried on. Euphemia was concentrating on inhaling and exhaling so she could feel her tummy muscles soften as instructed. She didn't notice first Margaret, then Jane, roll into balls of stifled giggles on their mats. It wasn't until Claire stopped her softly spoken instructions that she saw them.

'I blame the lettuce,' said Jane, tears rolling down her face.

'The pine nuts,' howled Margaret. She moved to sit with her legs out in front of her, holding her stomach as she rocked backwards and forwards.

Claire got to her feet, her hands on her hips and looked down at them. Selina, Nell, and Sarah stayed face down on their mats, their arms stretched in front of them, supplicants who didn't move. Gradually, the giggles and snorts faded.

'Morning yoga helps our bodies to eliminate our toxins,' said Claire. 'Breaking wind is expected. The exercise helps your systems to achieve homeostasis. Most of our guests have this condition when they first arrive, but as your gut microbiota acclimatises to the diet and your core body functions become healthier, this will happen less and less. Enjoy your laughter,' she said, her face serious. 'It serves to speed the elimination process and enhances mood.'

By now Jane and Margaret were sitting upright, solemn once more, the ridiculousness of their earlier situation thoroughly ruined by the lecture. Chastened, they glanced up. Jane muttered a quick sorry, followed by Margaret, who found something interesting she needed to remove from under a nail.

'We will end with lower body strengthening poses,' said Claire, sitting down again this time with her feet resting, sole up, on her thighs. She maintained this pose as she lifted her hips in the air. The six women in the room followed as best they could but only the three at the back eliminated their toxins. This time no one laughed.

Claire then asked them to lie flat on their mats with their eyes closed and suggested they relax. 'Concentrate on your breathing. Feel the air as it sweeps in and out through your nostrils, your mouth, down your windpipe and to your lungs, then back again. Imagine the swirling particles of life.'

Maybe it was the good night's sleep, or maybe it was the low level stretching of her core and body. Whatever it was, Euphemia lay on the hard floor, concentrating on the ebb and flow of the swirling particles of life in her airways. It was a surprise when Claire spoke next. She asked them to sit upright on their mats with their legs crossed in front of them, their hands resting in their laps and to close their eyes.

Euphemia waited for instructions about how they were to spend the last half hour. She was hoping they could skip the scheduled meditation and move straight to the breakfast part of the day. Her stomach rumbled in agreement. It was not to be. Her stomach growled in protest this time. If they were stay like this and think of nothing, she would need guidance.

Euphemia opened her eyes after a few minutes. Selina, Nell, and their yoga mats had disappeared. Claire, facing them, stared straight ahead at a point over their heads, her eyes unmoving, her pupils dilated. The only movement Euphemia could see was the subtle rise and fall of her chest under her loose-fitting white cotton t-shirt.

Jane glanced from Margaret to Euphemia and cleared her throat before tipping her head towards Claire and raising her eyebrows. Euphemia shook her head. It was best to copy the woman. Any discussion could delay the arrival of the food. It was all she could think about. Last night, they were told the meditation session would be for thirty minutes. It wasn't long to wait. She had plenty of things to think about. Anything to stop her focusing on the pangs of starvation nagging at her brain telling her to find food, lots of it and to scoff it down before anyone else could. She found a point where the wall met the glass dome and fixed her gaze. Questions about Sarah, thoughts of home and Sage Consulting, Petal's battles with the cat next door, Nicky's ongoing struggle about her feelings for Dave, jostled for her attention between yearnings for coffee and toast, bacon and eggs, croissants filled with chocolate, apple Danish and more coffee. Hot caffeine-laden coffee. Black, white, it didn't matter, a cup, a mug, a jug to herself. She licked her top lip, sniffing the air.

Another stomach gurgled. Jane bent over cradling herself then she shrugged and smiled, apologetically.

'Mine's been doing that since we finished the yoga,' whispered Margaret. 'I'm starving. My body temple does not run on lettuce. If breakfast isn't more substantial than that pathetic excuse for a dinner we had last night, I'm leaving.'

Euphemia banished her steaming hot cup of freshly made coffee to the fond memory section of her brain. She was surprised to see Claire had gone now too. Last night's eating mat and napkin were sitting in front of her as was her jug with a glass beside it. The fingernail mark she had imprinted in the plastic handle identified it as the same jug which she had left next to her bed. It was disconcerting and downright annoying to know someone had been in her room again.

Almost as disconcerting as not knowing what they were putting in her water. The cure for her thirst was an arm's length away, and yet she hesitated. Last night she had no choice but to drink it because she had been so thirsty and could not have slept otherwise. She had taken a series of small sips, trying to work out what was in it, but knowing they observed and likely recorded her every action meant she couldn't do it as properly as she would have liked. If she took the jug into the bathroom, it would tip off whoever was watching her that she knew about the cameras. Unable to take the long slow deep sniffs and mouthfuls she needed, she had to make do with a series of quick inhales following by rolling a tiny bit of liquid around the inside of her mouth. With her tastebuds ramped to high, she managed to work out some flavours. These included an acid-sour with an unidentifiable origin, an acid-sweet with pine, and a bitter velvety feeling which clung to the insides of her cheeks and the back of her tongue. That was all, so she memorised it as a baseline to see if today's blend would be any different. If it had been formulated to her specific needs, that meant Margaret's and Jane's water would be different. The simplest way to find out would be to taste them.

She held out her glass. Automatically, Jane filled it from her jug. Before she could drink it, Sarah lent over and knocked it from her hand, spilling the contents into her lap. Without a word, she picked up Euphemia's napkin and mopped away the liquid. Euphemia grabbed her hand, stilling it, as she tried to look in her eyes, but Sarah ducked her head.

'Are you okay?' whispered Euphemia.

Sarah turned away and, taking advantage of Euphemia's confusion, extracted her hand, then stood up and disappeared through the door she had come from earlier. Seconds later, she was back with a tray loaded with the covered bowls from last night. The women licked their lips as she placed a bowl in front of each of them. This done, she disappeared back through the door.

'She was always so talkative, before,' said Jane. 'The girls at the club used to grumble about her never shutting up.'

'Sarah is fine,' said Selina, her voice startling the three women. 'She has taken a vow of silence for two weeks. You can't talk to her because she won't answer you.'

'Isn't it strange that her two weeks of silence coincides with the only two weeks her old friends are here,' said Euphemia.

'Is it?' Selina walked over to stand in front of Euphemia. 'I find it strange you consider your own needs should take precedence over Sarah's.'

'That's you told,' muttered Jane. Margaret rolled her eyes. Euphemia detected a whiff of rebellion in the room. Selina quelled the nascent uprising with an icy stare, then took her place at the fourth corner of this morning's eating square and sat down.

'We eat in silence,' said Selina. 'It is only by concentrating on our food that we can truly appreciate the goodness it brings to our body.' She took the lid off her bowl and made the namaste gesture.

Margaret eagerly lifted her lid, slumping in despair when she saw a single hard-boiled egg. Jane lifted her lid. She had two eggs, as did Euphemia. Margaret's eyes widened in disbelief and outrage.

'There's been a mistake,' she bellowed.

'It is not a mistake,' said Selina. She held up her hand as if that were the end of the matter.

'You can have one of mine,' whispered Jane. Euphemia felt instantly guilty she had not offered to share first.

Margaret almost accepted Jane's offer. Then she shook her head and sighed a deep sigh of resignation. 'No, you have it. Who knows? I might get two tomorrow.'

CHAPTER 18

EUPHEMIA'S FIRST ONE-ON-ONE SESSION WITH SELINA WAS
to take place in a clearing in the bush overlooking the bay below. Rather
than let her find her own way, Claire insisted on guiding her down the
metre wide gravel path through the trees. Weathered railway sleepers
bolted into place with huge steel nails supported the wide steps cut into
the clay slope. Handrails made from recycled plastic, coloured green and
moulded to look like branches stood on both sides. Not all the visitors
to the Retreat would be fit enough to manage the steep path without
support. The clearing was circular. In the centre was a recently mown
area of carefully tended weed-free lawn, the smell of freshly cut grass
lingering in the air. The dark olive greens of New Zealand's native trees
formed the backdrop to a wooden bench enclosing the perimeter of the
lawn, except for a large gap on the lower slope, cut to expose the view to
the rocky bay below. A solitary yacht lay at anchor on the far side of
the bay.

Claire led her to a seat on the bench beside Selina, pausing for an
acknowledgment from the older woman. A look passed between them
and with a sulky toss of dark curls, Claire walked off, the sound of her
footsteps stopping when she reached the cover of the bush. A twig

snapped, a branch got pushed out of the way, the rustling sound of her t-shirt when she folded her arms across her chest marking her within earshot.

Euphemia and Selina sat side by side in silence staring straight ahead. The sky was summer blue and cloudless. There was no wind and it was getting hot. Grateful for the shade of the trees, Euphemia followed a fantail or piwakawaka as it darted after insects, its bright chirrups and tarty bum movements making her smile.

'Pretty birds, aren't they,' said Selina.

'Yes,' said Euphemia.

Five minutes passed before Selina spoke again. 'You have come to the Retreat because you are concerned about Sarah,' she said. 'I assure you she came of her own free will. She came because we can help her.'

'She does look well. Quieter than usual, but well. Better than she did after Roger died.' Euphemia wondered how to say this next bit without being offensive.

Selina took over. 'You're worried about her money?'

'I am. As are Sophie and John, her children. Sarah made some rash financial decisions before she left, evidently at Nell's instigation. We're worried she will end up penniless.'

Behind them Claire stood up, her shoe scuffed the path and dislodged a pebble which rolled into a pile of leaves. Euphemia had heard the sharp intake of breath when she mentioned Sarah becoming penniless.

'Thank you for your frankness,' said Selina. 'And so early in your stay. You know almost nothing about us, yet you arrive with your mind made up. You consider us to be shysters, con artists and you want to rescue your friend and return her to the bosom of her family, preferably with her wealth intact or only minimally diminished. I'm right, aren't I?'

'You are,' said Euphemia. She hadn't expected this from Selina, she had expected more of the 'woo-woo'.

'My question is for you, Euphemia Sage. Why are you the one who has come after her? I expected her children to come to her rescue, not a friend of her husband's. Surely her love for her children would be a better reason for her to give up her sanctuary than anything the wife of her late husband's business partner might say?'

Euphemia tucked her hands under her thighs, idly examining the yacht for signs of life as she considered what to say next. The quick and easy answer would have been to tell Selina she was right. She had known Sarah for a long time, but it was true not as a person in her own right. Only as Roger's wife, just as Sarah had only known her as Kenneth's wife. Their children had played together, grown up together. They were close, whereas she was merely acquainted with Sarah. Their relationship was superficial and not a friendship.

Why had she come? Why had she put her life on hold, her business, her trip to Mauritius, to come to this strange place? Clients often made stupid decisions with their assets and she did not suddenly down tools and follow them to far flung islands to talk them out of their plans.

'I guess,' she said finally. 'Part of me feels responsible.'

'For what?' asked Selina.

'For Roger's death.' It was the first time she had said this out loud since the plane crash. 'For not being able to save him.'

'Could you have saved him?' asked Selina.

Euphemia studied every inch of the yacht while she considered her answer. It was a pretty boat. Even she, a non-sailor, could appreciate the sleek lines of what looked like a yacht large enough to round both horns without having to stop for supplies. It sat low and wide in the water, its wheel set on the right side of the cockpit. The decks were dark-stained teak, the white hull offset by a blue canopy over the cockpit and a blue cover on the mainsail. A radio antenna and satellite dish sat proudly on a crossbeam near the top of the single mast, which was as tall as the boat was long and anchored by stays at the bow and stern. The name, not one of the usual corny names which people called their boats, was *Ad Capere*. Euphemia racked her school Latin for the translation. Ad, she remembered, means to, but Capere had a number of meanings including occupy, or seize, or she remembered in some contexts, take or grasp. No doubt the boat's very wealthy owner would have his or her own interpretation.

She turned her attention back to the woman, an oasis of calm, sitting beside her.

'I couldn't. Save him,' Euphemia said eventually. 'It doesn't stop me wondering, though. All of us there helping felt the same when we later found out the passengers in business class had drowned. I hate to think of Roger trapped in his seat...' She stopped, screwing her eyes up tightly, her fists clenched in her lap.

'Leave it,' said Selina gently. She took Euphemia's hand and stroked it, soothing the tension from her muscles. 'You feel guilty about Roger's death. I can see that translates into feeling a duty to save Sarah. From us.'

'That sounds awful,' said Euphemia, turning to look into Selina's dark eyes. 'I'm sure you mean well.'

'Tell me,' said Selina. She let go of Euphemia's hand and tidied her long dark hair over one shoulder, twisting it into a thick rope which unfurled when she let it go. 'If Sarah wasn't a rich woman, would you still have come?'

Euphemia wanted to say that of course the money made no difference, but she stopped. Of course it made a difference. It would be disingenuous of her to deny it. It was a huge amount to hand over to people she had only known for a few weeks. If Euphemia could stop her from squandering the money which was her children's as much as it was hers, then part of her was discharging her responsibility to Roger.

'I put it out there as something to think about,' said Selina. 'Let's talk about the other reason you came.'

Euphemia had had enough truth for one day. She stood up. 'Let's not,' she said facing Selina. 'I came to make sure Sarah is here of her own free will. What she does with her money is her business. Unfortunately, what she considers to be her money and what is actually her children's inheritance from their father has become confused. I was genuine when I said you mean well. You don't seem to be an evil person. But Sarah is vulnerable and right now an unscrupulous person could take advantage of her.'

'Plainly put,' replied Selina. She got up. Their eyes met and held until she spoke again. 'I respect your honesty. In my experience honesty, much like truth, is a many-sided jewel. All sides need to be seen and appreciated before one can know the true value.' She walked away, her back to Euphemia. 'Claire?'

The younger women emerged and stood awaiting instructions.

'Euphemia is ready for her massage now,' said Selina.

'Of course,' Claire replied. 'This way.'

The one-on-one session was over. Euphemia had no choice but to follow.

CHAPTER 19

NELL WAS NOT A LARGE WOMAN, BUT HER HANDS AND ARMS had the power and strength of a pro-wrestler. Euphemia wondered if she specialised in thumb-only push-ups. By the time the massage was over thirty minutes after it started, the tip of every bony prominence in her back was pulsating with a tenderness all its own. The strap muscles on either side of her spine from her buttocks to the base of her head were now swollen and bruised. Euphemia had attempted small talk as soon as she lay down on the table, but a series of grunts had rebuffed her chat. Silently, she lay with her head in the hole and stared at the floor as Nell climbed onto a stool, bent over her, and went to work.

After Nell had finished her assault, a shell-shocked and battered Euphemia registered the door closing as plaintive whale sounds grew louder and the lighting dimmed to a rose-tinted hue. The small room warmed up and clouds of scented steam puffed over her from the grill above, filling the room with the sharp smell of lavender overlaid with the sweetness of jasmine. Enveloped in her towel, she lay still, letting the novel sensations wash over her as she healed her battered muscles from the inside. It was hard to keep track of time and the myriad of stimuli affecting her, so she didn't. Her mind emptied, and she enjoyed the unfamiliar luxury of lying peacefully in the present. There was nowhere to go, nowhere to be, no one to have to talk to. It felt like freedom.

The steam clouds stopped, the warmth receded, and the light brightened. Only the music and the soothing whale sounds remained. The inflammation in Euphemia's muscles was gone, the pain too. They felt renewed, rather than beaten. The door opened and a cool draft wafted across her bare shoulders when Sarah walked in. Euphemia sat up, holding the thick, fluffy towel around her. She wiped the lavender-jasmine drips from her forehead and pushed the hair back from her eyes.

'Sophie and John send their love,' she said. 'They're worried about you.'

Sarah didn't look at her. She was wearing white surgical scrubs and white Crocs. Her hair was held back with combs behind her ears and she wore no make-up, no jewellery, not even a watch. She kept her eyes averted as she wiped down the shelf next to the massage table, mopping up the moisture, which had pooled into puddles. She dropped one sodden towel into the bucket on her trolley, which she pulled behind her. When that was done, she stood in front of Euphemia, pointedly looking not at her but at the sheet on the massage table. Euphemia climbed down, holding the towel up under her arms, and went to the changing room. In the cubicle, she poured herself a glass of water from her jug. Thirstily, she finished it in one gulp and poured herself another, then quickly got dressed hoping Sarah would still be there when she emerged.

She was. Sarah had stuffed the balled sheet into the bucket with the towel and was spraying the table surface with a cleaning solution which smelled like the one Euphemia used at home, energetically pumping the handle on the bottle, not sparing a single centimetre from her efforts. She used a new cloth to wipe it down.

'I know you can't talk,' said Euphemia. 'But...,'

A look of pure fear crossed Sarah's face but, head down, she kept wiping. Euphemia noticed she was taking a very long time to clean the tiny room. It was as if she wanted contact. Euphemia looked up and kicked herself for not seeing the cameras before. If the place was being monitored, there would be microphones as well.

Euphemia put down her jug. 'Darn it,' she said. 'I left my towel in the cubicle. Will you look after my water?' Sarah nodded, and for the first time looked directly at Euphemia. She was shaking.

In the cubicle, Euphemia was unsure what to do next. She had to communicate with Sarah without being observed or overheard. Unless. There were no cameras in the toilet, a microphone maybe, but she pitied whoever was supposed to monitor that. A diet of eggs, water and green vegetables did not make for quiet ablutions. The toilet had one other thing. Paper. She sat on the loo and finger nailed her message into a sheet, folded it into a tight square, and crossing her fingers that the impressions would survive the folding. She returned to Sarah, who was standing quietly by the door holding her jug.

'Thanks,' said Euphemia, taking it from her. But she hadn't gripped the handle properly, and the jug slid out of her hands and fell with a crash onto the floor. The lid stayed on, but water spilled out from the spout.

Euphemia looked up, shamefaced. 'Sorry, I've always been clumsy. Can I borrow your mop?'

Sarah shook her head and picked up the mop herself. She edged past Euphemia to get to the scene of the spillage. As she brushed past, Euphemia dropped the folded message into the pocket of Sarah's scrubs.

CHAPTER 20

LUNCH WAS THE SAME COLOUR AS THE PREVIOUS NIGHT'S dinner – green. Green pears and green kiwifruit, cut into slices, served without adornment. Even Jane looked crestfallen when she took the lid off her bowl. The three women silently ate their fruit, the atmosphere grim. Euphemia, taking Selina's lead, chewed each mouthful thirty times to make the experience of eating last longer thus fooling her stomach into thinking she had eaten a substantial meal. It worked – sort of. She stopped worrying about what was in the water and instead drank as much as she could to help get rid of the awful gnawing emptiness inside her. Caffeine withdrawal was nothing in comparison to calorie deprivation. Her companions had already lost weight. Water might account for some of that, but loss of sub-cutaneous fat accounted for more. The dark rings under Margaret's eyes were particularly stark.

Sarah delivered and collected their bowls keeping her head down, and her eyes averted. She gave no clue whether she had found Euphemia's message. Etched into the paper had been one blink: Yes. Two blinks: No. A simple enough instruction if the right opportunity presented. Neither the cameras nor the microphones would detect her response, if, and it was a big if, Sarah wanted to communicate. For all Euphemia knew, she might be perfectly happy with the arrangements at the Retreat. She might enjoy being a servant with no voice, forced to attend to the most mundane tasks, and to serve her old friends. Sarah could have found the meaning of life in other people's dirty dishes, old towels, and unmade beds.

'This afternoon is our first group session,' announced Selina after Sarah left.

As she didn't move, Euphemia assumed the session would take place here in the Domed Hall. She exchanged covert glances with Margaret and Jane to see if they agreed. No one had told them not speak to each other, but this was the pattern they had fallen into. She felt like a new kid on her first day at a new school. You had to check out the big kids and the friendly teachers before saying anything which would get you into trouble.

Jane shuffled to get comfortable and tried not to giggle. Margaret did giggle. Claire stared at her and Margaret squirmed until she found something interesting to look at on the other side of the room. Claire, younger than Selina and Nell, had seemed approachable when they first met. But her openness had morphed into semi-rudeness. Curt, it was as if her mind was several steps ahead of everyone. She became irritated if they didn't obey her instructions immediately. Incredibly fit and quick in her movements, Euphemia noticed an intolerance with those who weren't as agile, like Margaret and less so Jane. She didn't hide her irritation, it was obvious in the way she held her mouth and, on one occasion, even rolled her eyes. It surprised Euphemia that Selina and Nell, both consummate hosts, tolerated this behaviour towards paying clients.

Selina signalled the session was about to begin when she raised her hands to the prayer position in front of her and closed her eyes. Nell followed, as did Claire. Jane shifted to sit on her haunches and stared at the floor. Margaret sighed and unfolded her legs, extending them in front of her and leaning back on her hands she gazed at the ceiling. The lotus position was easy for Euphemia. She relaxed, closed her eyes and focused on the only noise in the room, the sound of breathing.

Five minutes passed. Jane choked and started coughing. Margaret leaned across and landed a helpful whack on her back. Spluttering followed, then a grab for the jug. Jane refilled her glass and drained it.

'Margaret,' said Selina breaking the silence. 'Share with the group. Tell us why you came.'

Margaret flushed a deep red. 'Do I have to go first? Jane is better than me at this sort of thing.'

'It's not a contest,' said Nell. 'No one will judge you. Why did you come?'

Margaret cleared her throat and smoothed the fabric of her trousers with sticky palms. 'I ran out of oomph,' she said. 'After my kids left home and my husband fulfilled his manly cliché by running off with his secretary, I needed something to fill the void. So, I worked like a dog for ten years and built an online business. I was good at it. The products were constantly being improved. I had customers around the globe.' She stopped and almost whispered the next part. 'Then stupidly, I sold it to an Australian competitor. A part of me died. I don't know why I did it. They wanted me to stay on as CFO, but I didn't see the point. I could tell they didn't want me around. I had given birth to it, brought it up, and now it was ready to take its place in the world without me. Just like my kids, I let it go. I did well, but the money wasn't important.'

Claire wrinkled her brow, a tight smile on her lips.

'I keep telling myself that I know what I achieved,' said Margaret. 'But I don't know what to do. Every time I think of something, then the futility of building something from nothing only to lose it again takes over, so I don't do anything. I'm stuck.'

Euphemia hadn't seen that coming. The stocky optimist who joked about her appearance was in reality a tired tycoon looking for help.

It was as if Selina had read her thoughts. 'The lesson is in the listening,' she said. 'It is why we have group sessions. To properly hear what others tell us instead of thinking we know them based on first impressions.'

Jane caught Euphemia's eye and nodded pointedly.

'Rich coming from you,' Euphemia muttered back. Jane tossed her head and made a heart sign to Margaret.

'Jane,' said Selina. 'Why are you here?'

'To understand my life,' she said.

'Good answer,' said Nell. Jane beamed. The teacher had praised her.

'Is that a touch ambitious?' asked Selina.

'I don't see why. I'm here for two weeks with nothing to do but eat, sleep, exercise and think about myself. Before I leave, I should have everything figured out. Otherwise, what's the point of coming?'

'Not a lot of eating,' Margaret hissed out of the corner of her mouth.

'We shall do everything to help you achieve your goal,' said Selina. 'But how will you feel if, at the end of two weeks, your life is still a mystery to you?'

'I hadn't thought of that,' said Jane. She rubbed her chin and squeezed her lips between her fingers before saying, 'I don't know.'

Claire shook her head and sighed. She turned to Euphemia. 'Why are you here?' Her emphasis on the word 'you' intentionally unpleasant.

'To support Jane of course,' replied Euphemia hoping to divert her attention from her morning's session with Selina.

The answer surprised Claire, who recovered quickly. 'Why do that here?' she asked. 'Don't you support her at home?'

'She does,' said Jane. 'Euphemia saved my life and my jewellery from Justin. He was my husband, but he died in the fire which he lit. He burned down our house. Without Effie, I would be a penniless, home-less widow. She's my best friend. She comes across as judgemental and a bit cold, but she means well despite the resting bitch face. It's annoying but she is usually right about everything, especially about men.'

Maybe it was the lack of food or the lack of privacy, or maybe it was having her motives for coming to this strange place interrogated by people she didn't trust. Maybe it was not being able to talk freely to Sarah. Possibly it was a combination of all of the above, or maybe it was the first time she had ever been called someone's best friend by someone other than Kenneth. Tears pricked Euphemia's eyes. One broke free and rolled down her cheek, landing with a loud plop, staining a dark circle on her placemat.

No one spoke, no one moved. Selina held up her hand. Everyone except Claire looked at her with care and compassion. Claire studied her. Euphemia, her eyes stinging, felt a soft hand on her back. She turned around and squinted up at Sarah, seeing kindness in the offer of a small cloth. This was supposed to be the other way around. I'm supposed to help her. Euphemia straightened her t-shirt, took the cloth, wiped her eyes, cheeks and blew her nose. Sarah held out her hand for the cloth to take it away.

'Sorry, everyone,' said Euphemia. 'I don't know what happened. I never cry. Not in public. I guess it's been building up. I don't like feeling trapped.' Sarah's expression didn't change, but her eyelids moved. She blinked once, slowly and purposefully.

CHAPTER 21

A DAM HAD BROKEN.

'And,' said Margaret. 'I also don't like being trapped and I don't like feeling hungry.'

'Where is my jewellery?,' asked Jane.

'Give me my phone back,' demanded Margaret.

Day Two and Euphemia's tears had unleashed rebellion. Nell and Selina exchanged worried glances. Claire smiled but tried to hide it behind a frown.

'This is a good time to end our first session,' said Selina, rising to stand. 'Return to your havens, rest and contemplate the reasons you gave for coming here. Dinner will be served at 6.30.' Claire and Nell stood and the three women filed out the same door through which Sarah had left.

'That must be the way to the kitchen,' said Margaret, nodding after them. 'Let's check it out.'

Jane shook her head. 'It will be for staff only. We can't.'

'Why not?' asked Margaret. She rolled to her side and onto her hands and knees, then walked her hands up her body to stand with her feet apart, her arms crossed in front of her. 'I came here to learn acceptance, not to be starved to death. Come on.'

Euphemia thought about Sarah. The long blink had to have been deliberate, which meant she was trapped, too. They all were. Raiding the kitchen to search for food would be a distraction at most. It would do nothing to get them to freedom. Rather than storming the kitchen, she needed time to work out a plan. 'They know how we feel,' she said to Margaret. 'Let's wait and see what we get for dinner. It won't hurt to wait a couple of hours.'

'Speak for yourself,' said Margaret. As if to emphasise her situation, her tummy emitted a long, slow, deep, gurgling growl. 'I. Am. Famished.' She went to the door and pushed. It didn't move. She leaned against it and pushed harder, wedging her feet against the floor for extra heft. 'They locked it. Just like they have every other door in this joint. When I get home, my lawyers will slap this place with whatever people slap places with to ruin reputations and get refunds. False advertising for a start. The public need to know what a con this is. Acceptance Retreat my behind! June was right. It should be called the 'Resistance is Futile Institution for those with too much money and not enough sense'. How much did you girls donate to come here?'

Jane shifted uneasily. 'That's private,' she said. 'Talking about money isn't polite.'

Margaret shook her head. 'Either you have too much to care or so little you're embarrassed. I'm smack bang in the middle and I can tell you I forked out over ten big ones to eat lettuce, drink water and get locked up. There isn't even a glass of world-beating Waiheke chardonnay to help with digestion.'

'Of course, there's no alcohol,' said Jane. 'It's poison.'

'Drunk from the well of Acceptance Institute Kool-Aid, Jane?'

'At least it's non-fattening,' retorted Jane.

'Ooooh,' said Margaret. 'I was wondering when we would see mean-girl and here you are.'

'Stop it,' said Euphemia.

'Aaaaaand,' said Margaret twirling around and pointing at her with her arm outstretched. 'Head Prefect comes to the rescue.'

'Yes, she does,' said Euphemia. 'We should stick together. Starting fights won't help. I get that you're hungry. We all are. I get that this is not the experience you thought it would be. But until we work out what we're going to do, our only choice is to get along.'

Margaret toed a ridge on the mat. Jane huffed. 'I'm sorry for implying you're, you know, weight challenged.'

'Yeah, I'm sorry for calling you names.'

'Right then,' said Euphemia. 'I'm going to my "haven". See you at dinner.'

'Okay,' said Margaret. 'But if it's more lettuce, so help me, I will break down that door and eat anything and everything I find. Then I'm off to get a burger, fries and a large gin and tonic in Oneroa.' She picked up her jug and glass, counted the doors and finding the one which led to her room, left.

'Am I really a mean girl?' asked Jane.

'You were,' said Euphemia. 'At school, you were horrible. You weren't great when you were married to Justin either, but you're not a mean girl now. You're my friend.'

'And you're my friend,' said Jane. 'We look after each other, don't we?'

'We do.'

'See you at dinner.' Jane walked over to her door and stopped. 'Margaret was spot-on though. You do act like a Head Prefect.' She roared with laughter and disappeared.

CHAPTER 22

IT TOOK ENORMOUS WILLPOWER FOR EUPHEMIA TO LIE ON her bed and stare at the white ceiling. Two days without exercise was a long time. Normally her muscles would twitch with pent-up energy, letting her know it was time to go for a run, or lift weights, or do stretches, then repeat all three until she was spent. Rachel's Switch worked by stimulating her cells to produce more essential amino acids and proteins which in turn enhanced her senses and powered up her muscles. Would her super powers decline if her cells were stopped from responding to the messages from her genes? Would her senses and muscles stay primed for action or would they degrade?

Being locked in a tiny room, starved of protein, with her every activity monitored was akin to being put in chains. The only powers she could use without being observed were her senses. Taste, touch, hearing, vision, and smell she worried if these be enough to get her to Sarah?

What would Barbara do if she were in Euphemia's place? The answer was simple. Barbara wouldn't be in this position. Older, wiser, confident in the world and in her powers, Barbara Scarsdale, her distant cousin, had been born with Rachel's Switch in her genes. She was more suspicious than Euphemia, anticipating threats and acting accordingly. Euphemia was an innocent in comparison. Her naivety condemning her to lying on the bed in a room she couldn't get out of without exposing her powers, and counting the paint bubbles on the ceiling to keep from going mad.

Based in Sydney, Barbara had arranged to meet Euphemia as soon as she learned of her existence. Cunningly using Kenneth's new company as cover until she could be sure Euphemia was the real deal. Freddie had told no one she had a daughter for reasons Euphemia still didn't understand. Her mother left her on her sister's doorstep when she was three and then died when Euphemia was in her teens without ever returning to explain her actions. Barbara finding her proved to be a relief. Now she knew she was not the only one in the world with these strange powers and she had someone to ask about them.

Barbara had been reasonably forthcoming about matters of family history, but she was more reticent when discussing the work of the Foundation in Mauritius. Euphemia had gleaned what she knew from snippets dropped in their conversations. Set up to study the genes which coded Rachel's Switch, the Foundation was well-funded and extremely secure. Barbara not only emphasised the need for secrecy about the powers and the research, she repeatedly emphasised that Euphemia was only ever to use the powers when she was certain there was no risk of detection. If it got out there were humans with genuine super powers, Rachel's descendants would be hunted down and become nothing more than lab rats to be studied by scientists employed by whoever could pay the most money. This would have a catastrophic effect on them, their families and the world as the potential for abuse was enormous. Already Alison Sinclair's father had gone rogue, attempting to replicate the powers in midlife women using a cocktail of Euphemia's blood and age-defying drugs. His lack of success thankfully a result of underfunding, his stupidity and being in too much of a hurry to test his concoctions. The Switch sisterhood lived in fear of well-funded geniuses who wanted to rule the world and live forever.

'I do understand the need for secrecy,' Euphemia said. 'But if it means we can't use the powers for good when situations demand it, despite the risk of being seen, what's the point? We can't stand idly by doing nothing to prevent injustice, death, and suffering when it is right in front of us. At least I can't. Truthfully, what would be so wrong if humanity had the code to the Switch? Think how many of the world's problems could be solved.'

'Or made worse,' said Barbara.

'There has to be a way around this,' Euphemia replied, only to have Barbara shut her down again.

'Okay, you be the first,' she said 'You show the world what you can do then come back and tell me what happens. If they let you.'

Euphemia knew then she was too Pollyanna-ish. In reality her normal life with Kenneth and the girls would be gone. Their lives would be over unless you call being studied in a laboratory, living. Sage Consulting would go. Fifty employees would have no jobs. Coming out of the super-power closet would prematurely ruin thirty normal years of Kezia's life. The twins wouldn't have a mother and they could be locked up in separate labs, living their childhoods under a microscope. Nicky's career in the police would also be gone. Undercover operations would be impossible with the world's paparazzi are camped outside your door. Kenneth, Ben and Dave would lose the women they loved to science and their days would spend hiding from ghastly nosy parkers, aka journalists.

Euphemia knew all of this, and yet still she struggled. Inheriting super powers only to use them on the rare occasions when no one would notice was an utter waste. Roger might have lived if she had used her powers to lift the plane out of the sea before he drowned. Then Sarah wouldn't be in this terrible place and neither would she.

It was one thing to grow up knowing in your bones that you are destined to do something meaningful, something important with her life. It was another thing to realise as she had with the onset of the powers that this wasn't just an adolescent pipe-dream. With the onset of her powers she had the means to make her destiny real. To be told the powers were to be kept secret at all costs meant her destiny ran headfirst into a brick wall.

Her promise, made under pressure, to Barbara to be discreet, all but neutered her. Not that her life with Kenneth and the girls meant nothing. They were the most important people on the planet, and she loved them with all her heart. But they didn't need her. Not any more and not as much. The time she had left to fulfil her life's destiny was running through her fingers like water, and there was nothing she could do to stop it. Super powers don't change your life expectancy. It was even possible, Barbara said, that the stress from the Switch on your body can shorten it. Not by much, but enough for Euphemia to know she couldn't sit idly for much longer.

So far she hadn't found any limits to her powers. Okay, she couldn't fly. That was a limit. And she had nearly died when she had been stupid enough to take on a stampeding herd of steers for no reason other than the sheer thrill it brought her. That escapade had taught her a valuable lesson. Over-confidence and hubris were character flaws she needed to keep suppressed. She had to work for her gift. Train hard, then harder again – if she was to succeed and do her best when called upon and if she was to satisfy the craving inside her to be all she could be. Barbara was partly right about being discrete but that did not have to mean impotence. There had to be a way she could be all she could be without destroying herself or her family.

Distracted by a vibration in her bones Euphemia opened her eyes. Above her a branch swung against the window; the vibration as it impacted the glass transmitting through her body like an electric current. Strips of loose bark hung from the single branch exposing smooth bare wood beneath. Shadows morphed into letters carved in the wood which spelt, *Help, S.*

CHAPTER 23

When the women entered the Domed Hall, Selina, Nell, and Claire were sitting in their usual cross-legged position, waiting for them. There were not one but two lidded bowls at each place setting. Margaret squeaked when she spotted them, shivering with excitement as she put her jug and glass down in front of her placemat. She sat down easily, exchanging excited glances with Jane and Euphemia.

Selina cleared her throat. 'Congratulations,' she said when they were seated.

'For what?' asked Margaret. Her fingers inched closer to the bowls.

'For getting to this stage in the course before any group has before. You are three highly evolved women.' Nell and Claire nodded in unison. Selina continued. 'You have achieved what we call, 'the group cohesiveness stage' in less than 48 hours. So fast, you have already progressed to the next stage, the rebellion stage.'

The women shifted positions on the floor as they absorbed this information.

'Damn right,' said Margaret. 'We're no pushovers.'

A beat later, Jane spoke too, her courage growing with each syllable. 'Damn right, we're staunch,' she added.

Euphemia was more concerned she hadn't seen Sarah yet.

'If there isn't decent food in these bowls,' said Margaret, 'you're going to see the rebellion stage beaten by the full roar stage.'

'Yeah,' said Jane. 'Way to go, Maggie.' She leaned over to high-five Margaret then stopped. 'Sorry. Way to go, Margaret.'

Selina suppressed her smile. 'Go ahead. See if tonight's offering is enough to stop you constructing the barricades.'

'Yesss,' said Margaret, pulling her fist down over her elbow when she uncovered the first bowl. The aroma of boiled tofu in a sesame sauce with peanuts drifted around the room. She took the lid of her second bowl and saw a large avocado, sliced and sprinkled with olive oil and balsamic vinegar. 'I can work with this,' she said. 'Thank you.'

Jane was equally enthusiastic about her feta, tomato, and olive salad, and her own sliced avocado. They looked at Euphemia expectantly. She took off the lid off the bowl closest to her. It contained the same salad as the night before but with more nuts. She left the lid on the second bowl. 'I'm happy with this.'

'If you don't want the other one, I'll have it,' said Jane.

Margaret screwed up her face, annoyed she hadn't been quick enough.

'Like the water, the food has been individually designed to satisfy your needs,' said Selina. 'Sharing is not permitted. Let's take a moment for gratitude. After we have eaten, I'll explain tomorrow's updated schedule.'

Euphemia swallowed her last mouthful, taking the standard thirty chews as she had with the preceding mouthfuls, long after the others had finished. Margaret, leaning back on her arms, her legs stretched in front of her, smiled benevolently at everyone while Jane patted her tummy contentedly and yawned.

'Please put your bowls on the trolley before you leave,' said Selina. 'Sarah is resting. You won't see her for a few days.'

'She's all right, isn't she?' asked Euphemia.

'Of course. Like you, she has reached another stage in her journey to acceptance and, like you, she is ahead of her schedule. Wellington women are such go-getters.'

'Auckland women are go-getters too,' said Margaret.

'What stage has Sarah reached?' Euphemia asked.

'Sarah is taking the solitary path to acceptance,' said Nell. 'We can't say more than that without breaching her privacy.'

Selina clapped her hands. 'Tomorrow you will wake before dawn for outdoor exercise. After breakfast, yoga, then you will meditate until lunch. Claire?'

'We're going swimming in the morning, so wear togs if you have them.'

Nell got up, followed by Selina, then Claire, and they walked out in single file.

Margaret got quickly to her feet, deposited her bowls on the trolley and said, 'I'll sleep well tonight.' She bent over picked up her jug and glass and left.

Jane hugging her jug under her arm, said goodnight before she too left. If only every rebellion could be subdued with an avocado, thought Euphemia as she added her bowls to the trolley, it would give new meaning to the term green revolution.

CHAPTER 24

THE LOCK CLICKED. EUPHEMIA OPENED HER EYES. WEAK PRE-
dawn light suffused the room and she swung her legs over the edge of
the bed and stood up. Head down, rubbing one eye with the knuckle of
a hand, she shuffled to the bathroom, her body moving like an old
lady's. Hot flushes bursting across her body, bathing her in sweat, had
ruined her sleep and she was exhausted. They were always worse when
there was a problem she couldn't solve. She stopped in front of the
mirror and pulled at the loose skin under her chin, horrified to see a
turkey neck reflected back at her. Where had that come from? It was so
unfair. When she slept well she felt like thirty on the inside, thirty-five
on a bad day. Outside, she looked her age, fifty-four.

In her youth she had taken pride in not being as vain as her peers.
She had taken her thick dark blonde hair, her unmarked skin, clear eyes,
and straight back for granted. Now she despaired when she looked in
the mirror. Age had taken a toll on her good looks, but worse than that
her enhanced vision meant she could see every line and wrinkle as soon
as they appeared in the minutest detail. Worst of all, she could see the
parts of her skin which were going to become wrinkles as well as the
beginnings of every coarse hair which sprouted overnight. She kept a
pair of tweezers handy to pluck these out by the roots before anyone else

could see them. As of this morning, her round-necked t-shirts would have to go. They made her turkey neck look even worse that it was. A bulk purchase of merino turtlenecks - how cruelly named they were - would be made as soon as she got home. If Diane Keaton could wear them winter and summer, so could she.

If she had been at home after a sleepless night and a soul-destroying morning look in the mirror, Euphemia would have gone downstairs and made a cup of strong coffee. Petal would circle her ankles, making whimpering noises to be fed and the sun would shine through the leaves of the big old oak tree in her garden. After her coffee she would have gone for a run up through the bush-clad hills behind Thorndon and the city in the Te Ahumairiangi Reserve, where the wilding pines were gradually being replaced by native trees. The run would boost her adrenalin levels and her wrinkly neck would fade into insignificance. Exhilarated by exercise, she would be ready for the new day.

At this over-priced Retreat, the most she had to look forward to was a drink of water with goodness knows what in it.

She rinsed her face in cold water, dried it, brushed her hair and put on a headband, to hold it off her face. She had meant to get a haircut before she left, but time was not on her side. By the looks of her neck this morning, time had deserted her completely. Instead of getting her hair cut, she prepared two weeks of healthy meals and put them in the freezer so Kenneth would have something to eat while she was away. He needed a home cooked meal to heat in the microwave or he would default to junk food or worse, three course dinners at Teds. He had worked so hard to lose weight, she didn't want to feel her going away was responsible for him regaining it.

Then the new cleaner had to be shown where everything was and what needed to be done. She organised the dog walker for Petal, then someone to come and mow the lawns, trim the hedges and take the cuttings to the dump. At the last minute, she remembered, one of their cars needed servicing or it would lose its WOF. Nicky promised she would take it in because they both knew Kenneth would forget. Luckily, Nicky was working from the nearby police headquarters for three months and so was available to help. Kezia and Ben were too busy looking for a place to live after the babies arrived and Kezia was keeping the wheels turning at Sage Consulting, so she couldn't ask her to help at home. Kezia had settled into the CEO position at Sage, so well that Euphemia had had to remind her it was only temporary and that she would be back in two weeks. A message which may or may not have got through. Why did she feel like she was being pushed out? Kezia had driven her and Jane to the airport an hour before they needed to be there. She all but shoved them out of the car before taking off back to the office, not bothering to hide the huge grin on her face.

Euphemia's tummy rumbled and gurgled. Salad for dinner was not enough to sustain her, but she had played along partly because it was both strange and interesting to starve. She had never had to diet to lose weight so she didn't understand what other women moaned about when they were dieting. The baby weight after the girls were born went away with breastfeeding and running had kept her weight steady ever since.

Another gurgle, another rumble, and the emptiness in her stomach became an ache. She stripped off her pyjamas and pulled on shorts and a t-shirt, to go under her black merino running gear, ready for the promised swim.

In the end, she need not have bothered. The exercise consisted of no more than a slow walk down to the sandy beach below the Retreat. Claire led the way while Nell brought up the rear. The path through the bush was tricky in places. Jane struggled to keep her footing on the steeper bits, but Euphemia managed it easily.

'I used to go hiking before I started the company,' said Margaret. 'I should get back into it.' They had taken off their shoes and were sunning themselves on a rock, their feet dangling in the sea. They had been told to wait for the others. It was 6.30 AM and behind them the bush was alive with birdsong. Tuis sang the purest melodies to any bird venturing into their territory, warning them to stay away. Piwakawaka, or fantails, chirped away regardless, darting in under branches to catch the insects stirred up from the leaf litter by their footsteps. They heard Jane grunting still half way up the hill and Nell's encouraging prompts as she negotiated the steep slope to the beach. Claire had wandered off to sit by herself further up the beach.

'Done much swimming?' asked Euphemia.

Margaret looked at her. 'How do you think I got these shoulders?' she asked. 'I got as far as the Nationals and would have gone to the Games if I hadn't caught glandular fever. It ruined my last year at school, and I didn't go back to it. I can't remember the last time I went for a swim.'

'Race you to that yacht,' said Euphemia pointing to the boat.

'You're on,' said Margaret, getting up. She stripped off before Claire noticed what they were doing. Euphemia was a fraction behind her when Margaret entered the water. Cool rather than cold, it was clear, and refreshing. Euphemia settled into an easy crawl, keeping a few strokes behind Margaret on purpose. When she guessed they were out of earshot, she swam up and tapped Margaret's leg to get her attention.

'Swim behind the yacht,' she said.

Margaret nodded and sprinted ahead leaving Euphemia to follow in her wake. Too competitive to let Margaret achieve an outright win, Euphemia paced herself to arrive behind the boat a stroke after her rival, with a clean conscience – she had not used her super powers.

With nothing to hold on to and aware they couldn't spend too long out of sight, they trod water in the hull's shadow. 'I want to go,' said Margaret. 'I didn't sign up to this.'

'Me neither,' she said. 'But we're miles from anywhere, even if we could get out of our rooms.'

'Don't you mean havens?' Margaret snorted. 'Good to know we're together on this. I can't think of anything right now, but we're smart women, we can work it out.'

'We'd better get back before they get suspicious,' said Euphemia.

'The whole thing is ridiculous. Have you figured out what they're doing to your friend?'

'No,' said Euphemia. 'I need to find her. Do you know where she is?'

'No idea, but I'll keep an eye out. Race you.'

Margaret used the hull to kick off and, head in the water, she pulled away, her strong shoulders bobbing at the waterline showing off the skill which had almost allowed her to compete internationally. Euphemia watched her go, took one last detailed look around the bay, then set off at a more leisurely pace.

Nell's face was red, her hands folded in front of her chest when they emerged from the water. 'You're not supposed to go off by yourselves.'

'Why not?' asked Margaret, blowing water from each nostril onto the sand.

'Health and safety,' huffed Claire.

'But you said we were going swimming,' said Euphemia. 'I don't understand why you are so upset.'

'It was supposed to be a dip. You won't get extra rations,' said Nell. 'You've ruined the nutritional balance we have spent two days working to achieve. You'll have to start all over again.'

'It was worth it,' said Margaret. 'I'd forgotten how much I enjoyed it. Thanks, Euphemia.' She raised her arm in a high-five and they slapped palms.

'Justine, my daughter, is the swimmer in our family,' said Jane, dusting an imaginary speck of dirt from the sleeve of her pink sweat-shirt. 'She's an ocean swimmer. I can tell you're more used to pool swimming. Ocean swimming is a tough sport. She swam from Oriental Bay out to Matiu Island when she was seventeen.'

'Didn't they have to send the police boat out to bring her home?' asked Euphemia.

'That's not the point,' said Jane. 'She was training for her first Ironman and she missed the tide. It could happen to anyone.'

'Anyone who is a very slow swimmer, you mean?'

Jane's lip curled as she turned away.

'She must be an impressive young woman,' Margaret said tugging her clothes over wet skin. 'Before I started my company, I did the Maui Ironman twice. Tell her to call me if she needs any tips.'

Jane sniffed and stood up. 'She has an excellent coach in New York. An ex-Olympian,' she said. 'But thank you. I will let her know.'

Margaret shrugged and looked at Euphemia. 'Don't suppose you fancy a race up the hill? I've got my wind up now.'

Euphemia wiped her brow and sighed. 'Sorry, that swim did me in,' she replied. Jane cocked her head. Euphemia never got tired, and she had never backed down from a challenge in all the time she had known her.

Nell glared at Claire. 'You were supposed to be supervising them. Now we have to go. We can't stand here chatting all morning.'

'It's better than meditating,' muttered Margaret.

'What did you say?' asked Claire.

'Ignore her,' said Nell. 'Come on, we're late. Selina will be furious.'

'Is fury allowed on an Acceptance Retreat?' asked Euphemia.

Margaret tittered.

CHAPTER 25

LUNCH. KIWIFRUIT (SKIN ON), CELERY STICKS, AND ROCK-
hard chunks of avocado with a sprinkling of dried cranberries and pine
nuts. After their hard-boiled eggs at breakfast, this meal was a massive
disappointment. The women wasted no time complaining, ate every
morsel and looked around for more. Margaret wiped her empty bowl
with her finger, which she licked. Jane watched Selina, following each
piece of fruit going into the poor woman's mouth with the intensity of
a hyena waiting for a lion to finish eating a carcass. If a pine nut had
dropped between bowl and mouth Jane, poised to pounce, would have
dived across and snapped it up before Selina knew what had happened.
Finally, the agony was over. A sulky Claire, muttering that it was about
time Nell pulled her weight, cleared away the bowls. Selina announced
they would now sit together in quiet meditation.

Three hours later, Euphemia's left foot had lost all feeling. She
dreaded the coming agony of pins and needles when she tried to move it.
Jane had nearly fallen asleep twice, her eyes flipping open when her head
dropped onto her chest. Selina, Claire, and Nell remained perfectly
composed, sitting upright in the lotus position, their eyes closed, their
hands resting on their knees, their chests rising and falling in unison.
Much to Euphemia's amazement, Margaret had got herself into the

same position. Whether she could get out of it again remained to be seen. It seemed the swim seemed had released something inside her; or had she been like this yesterday?

Euphemia stopped thinking about Margaret and concentrated on her breathing trying to empty her head of thoughts. She focused on the muscles in her face and upper body, one by one bringing them under control, settling twitches and minute movements. Images of her turkey neck magically disappearing occupied her mind. Surely world peace or saving the planet from global warming deserved her attention more than the craggy, sad, saggy state of her neck. But what can one woman's thoughts do against the problems of the world? To think that in the early 1990s Putin had been driving taxis. If only a super woman had taken him in hand then, before the war in the Ukraine, not to mention the wars in Syria, Chechnya and his own country. Was she wasting her powers despairing over her turkey neck sitting cross legged on a mat on an island in the Hauraki Gulf of a tiny country at the bottom of the world? Of course she was. Should she be looking for the next Putin and his taxi rather than worrying about her neck? She should!

When she got home, she would call Barbara and insist she tell her more about the Foundation. Then she would go there and see for herself what was being done in the name of Rachel's Switch. It was a pity Mauritius was one of the most difficult places to get to from New Zealand but as much as she hated long haul plane journeys, she needed to go.

She opened her eyes when she heard the thump. Jane had succumbed to boredom and fallen asleep, landing face first on the floor, her body folded at the waist like a rag doll, her legs still tucked underneath her. Euphemia scooted over on her bottom and shook her.

'Jane, wake up.'

'No. I won't,' said Jane. 'There's nothing to wake up for. We're stuck here eating vegetables, doing nothing but sit around or stretch stuff. We're doomed.'

'You're being silly, wake up.'

'Why should I? You interrupted the nicest dream. Brad Pitt and me were on top of the Beehive watching a tidal wave roll up Lambton Quay. He was so brave. He's so good in bed. Do you know he...'

'And' said Euphemia, squeezing Jane's arm. 'That's enough.' Jane was apt to retell her sexual exploits in vivid detail if given half a chance.

'Leave me alone,' said Jane, pushing her hand away. 'I'm tired. I haven't slept since I got here.'

Selina and Claire looked surprised. 'Of course you have,' said Nell.

'I haven't,' said Jane. 'I didn't want to bother anyone. I've always been more concerned about other people than about myself. Haven't I, Effie?' Euphemia propped her upright. Jane's eyelids drooped, her breathing calmed, and she started snoring quietly.

Nell came over and shook her.

Jane took a moment to focus. 'Please give me back my HRT,' she whimpered. 'The stuff in the jug doesn't work. I need actual hormones. Real ones. The ones made in a factory by proper doctors in white coats. Not the black cohosh, dried yam junk you're feeding me.' She got up and, standing with her hands on her hips, she glared first at Nell, then at Selina, and then Claire. 'I will not, repeat NOT, spend another night being kept awake by hot flushes. Give me back my patches, or I will not be responsible for my actions.' With her chin thrust forward and her nostrils flared, she bared her teeth and poked her finger at Nell. 'I want my patches back. Now.'

Euphemia had to give it to the staff. They were cool customers. There was no flinching, no blinking or huffy shoulders. They didn't take their eyes off her for a minute, but formed into a huddle. Selina put her hand up to Jane, telling her to wait. Fists clenched at her side and rocking her taut body from one foot to the other, Jane nodded.

Euphemia couldn't believe her luck. An honest conversation she could listen in to.

'You were supposed to check the tapes,' muttered Selina.

'I can't do everything,' Claire hissed. 'Nell hasn't lifted a finger since you put Sarah in solitary.'

'I do so do stuff. I cut up the kiwifruit.'

'You left the skins on.'

'They're the best part, natural roughage.'

'I don't give a fig about roughage. You were supposed to do the dishes. You didn't.'

'Stop it. Both of you,' said Selina. 'We have a situation here. Do we give her the patches or do we wait for the black cohosh to work?'

'We'd better give her one patch,' whispered Nell. 'Remember what Denise was like when we made her wait?'

'I can't deal with another Denise situation,' said Selina. 'Not when we're so close. We're agreed then?' The others nodded. She turned to Jane and smiled. 'You may have your patch. Claire will bring it right away.'

'Why do I have to go? It's Nell's turn.'

'Don't worry,' said Nell. 'I'll go. Anything to stop one of Claire's sulks.' She flounced off to the kitchen, slamming the door behind her just hard enough to send a puff of wind across the big room.

Jane instantly relaxed. Her shoulders dropped, and she hugged her arms around her chest as she thanked Selina profusely. Euphemia thought she was being pathetic.

Margaret tsked. 'Everyone knows implants are better than patches,' she said, then paused and looked at Euphemia. 'What do you use?'

'Nothing,' she replied. 'I'm doing it the natural way.'

'I thought so,' said Margaret. 'I can always tell. The face fuzz gives it away.'

Euphemia's hand flew to her cheek. 'I don't have face fuzz. Jane would have told me.'

Jane screwed up her lips and shook her head. 'I inform you about your various bodily issues on a need-to-know basis only. It's less stressful for both of us. Most of the time you ignore me anyway. Like when your face gets too red, or when you get snippy at the office.' She turned to Margaret. 'When her bloat gets bad, I slip one of my water pills into her coffee. That helps, and she's none the wiser.'

'I am now,' said Euphemia. 'Don't you ever put drugs in my coffee again.' She brushed her fingers over the skin below her ears. 'I can feel it. You should have told me, Jane.'

'Have you ladies quite finished?' asked Selina. 'You didn't come to the Retreat at great expense just to compare menopause symptoms.'

'You wait,' said Jane. 'It won't be long until you get them, too. And you, Nell – you're only a few years away from it. Comparing notes with other women is the best way to find out what doctors don't tell you.

They say to lose weight but there's more to it. Intuitive healing, which you do here, that only works for the easy problems. Trust me when I tell you that menopause is not easy. Margaret knows.'

Margaret nodded. 'I do, and I've got the perfect thing in my haven to take your fuzz away.'

'It's that bad?' asked Euphemia.

'Not if you want to look like an old lady,' said Jane. 'Maybe you do?'

'I don't. I'll take whatever you've got.'

Margaret checked with Selina to see if it was all right to go to her room and collect the cure.

'I want to see what it is before you give it to her, though,' said Selina.

Back in two minutes, and still panting, Margaret handed Selina a box of wax strips. 'All she needs to do is stick it to her face, wait, pull it off, and the fuzz is gone. It's completely natural. No chemicals.'

Selina opened the box, checked inside it, pulled out the contents, checked them and put them all back before she handed it to Euphemia. 'I wouldn't bother if I were you. There's nothing wrong with looking your age.'

'Speak for yourself,' said Jane. Under her breath she added, 'Rich coming from someone who dyes her hair.'

'What did you say?'

Jane scratched one ear. 'I said you have beautiful hair.'

Selina's almond eyes narrowed.

'If you haven't used these before, I'll show you what to do,' said Margaret. 'It'll only take a few minutes. Selina, you don't need to wait.'

Selina looked from one to the other. They smiled at her. She hesitated, then said, 'Okay. Afterwards, practice your meditation. I will see you at 6.30 for dinner. Jane?'

'I'll help Margaret.'

'That's unnecessary and your mediation could do with some work.'

'How do you know?'

'I'm paid to know. I'm right, aren't I?'

'I guess. What about my patch?'

'Here it is.' Nell held out the little square packet.

Jane grabbed it, ripped it open, and stuck the patch on her tummy.

'I feel better already,' she said. Euphemia heard her happily practising her 'oms' as she wended her way down her corridor back to her haven.

'Pay attention,' murmured Margaret taking a strip out of the box. She held it in front of her mouth and spoke quietly so Euphemia had to lean in to hear her. 'Put the strip across the lock in your door before it shuts. It will stop the bolt from sheeting home.'

Euphemia's eyes widened. 'Got it.'

'Good,' said Margaret, speaking normally again. 'I did mine last night, so I know it works. You're not the only one with this problem.' She ran her hands over smooth cheeks and turned so Euphemia could inspect her skin.

'How long does it take for the fuzz to come back?'

'Not long. I kept some strips for me to use in case.'

'Good thinking,' said Euphemia. 'See you at dinner.'

CHAPTER 26

EUPHEMIA DIDN'T MEAN TO FALL ASLEEP. SHE HAD GONE back to her haven after dinner and with her back to the cameras slipped the wax strip over the lock on her door. She and Margaret had agreed to start their exploration at 01:00 AM, when everyone else would be asleep. It was important that if anyone was actually watching the camera feed from her room, they would see that she was asleep too so she lay on the bed and closed her eyes. A rustle of clothing woke her. Margaret was standing beside her, shaking her head.

'I thought I could trust you,' she said. 'Hurry. We haven't got much time.' She was gone before Euphemia got off the bed.

She checked the wax strip was still in place, when she slid the door shut behind her. Full respect to Margaret for her ingenuity. Euphemia ran down the corridor, through the Domed Hall and following her outside into the crisp night air. A sliver of moon in the cloudless sky provided enough light to see Margaret's shadow disappearing around the back of the building. Margaret had stopped and was waiting for her on steps leading to a porch when she caught up.

'This has to be the kitchen,' she whispered and opened the door.

Euphemia held her breath after Margaret disappeared inside waiting for lights to come on, an alarm to sound, but nothing happened. Why were the doors unlocked? She checked for cameras but couldn't find any. Suspecting a trap she cautiously followed Margaret inside. At the end of a short corridor she was confronted by an open door and a blast cold air. Margaret was standing next to a shelf in a cool room stuffing hard boiled eggs in her mouth, ignoring the yellow crumbs falling around her.

'Look,' said Euphemia, pointing at the mess on the floor. Margaret smiled a cheesy mashed- up egg smile and more bits tumbled from her mouth. She pushed the bowl towards Euphemia, who resisted for all of two seconds before she took one, bit into it and then took another.

There had been a dozen eggs in the bowl. In less than five minutes it was empty, the floor under their feet smeared with yellow.

'I need to find Sarah,' said Euphemia. Margaret her face buried inside one half of an avocado shook her head.

'I'm going to look for her. You stay here and clean up.'

'Don't take too long,' came the mumbled reply.

Behind the door, further down the hall next to the kitchen was an office containing a desk. A row of blank TV screens had been mounted on the wall above it. The desk was bare apart from a black keyboard. Euphemia pressed enter and two of the screens flicked into life. Jane's face took up all of one screen, her body as she lay fast asleep on her bed, the other. The resolution was incredible. Euphemia could see her lips fluttering as she breathed out and when her eyes flickered behind her eyelids, a corner of her mouth twitched. She was dreaming and every minute facial expression was being recorded. Euphemia pressed <return>. The screens showed her own bedroom and her empty bed. She pressed <return> again. Another empty bed. Margaret's room. Another <return> and this time Nell's face loomed large, a tear escaping from her right eye and sliding down her cheek, the expression on her sleeping face exposing some deep sadness. Fast asleep on her back, her mouth open, her chin dropped so low it pulled her skin tightly over her cheeks into deep hollows – she looked dead. She checked for breathing movements as she thought there really was such a thing as being too skinny. The next <return>. Selina's long dark hair spread over the pillow like a mass of seaweed on the surface of the sea. She was lying on her side, wide awake, one eye staring at the camera. Euphemia jumped back.

Selina couldn't know Euphemia was looking at her, but it felt like it. Where was Sarah?

The next face was Claire's. Asleep she looked innocent, child-like even as she lay curled into a tight ball on her side. Euphemia couldn't resist focusing in, her suspicion that Claire was sucking her thumb, proving to be right.

She found Sarah lying on her bed, both eyes wide open, staring at the camera. She looked gaunt, her usually bright eyes dull. 'What have they done to you?' she whispered.

'Found her?' Margaret asked from the doorway. Her t-shirt streaked with egg, fruit and what smelled like carrot juice reminded Euphemia of when the girls were young and, like them at the same age, Margaret looked content.

'She looks terrible. I've got to get her out of here,' said Euphemia.

'Tomorrow night,' said Margaret. 'We'll do it then.'

'We don't have time. They'll discover the missing food and they'll keep us locked up.'

'How will they know it was us?'

Euphemia could think of several answers but only said the one which wouldn't offend. 'Easy, they'll watch the tapes and see we weren't in our beds.'

'Okay then we'll make a break for it tonight. Find the phones,' she said. 'We'll call the police to meet us on the road.'

Euphemia found them in the second drawer down. She picked up hers and touched the screen. Nothing happened. 'Dead,' she said. She looked around then checked the other drawers. 'Can you see a charger?'

Margaret shook her head. They checked the rest of the phones one by one. They were all flat.

'I'll see if I can find the van,' said Euphemia. 'You finish tidying up.'

Clouds now covered the sky, and a light wind had come up. The air felt damp and cool. Rain was on the way. She ran as fast as she could to a large outbuilding, pulled opened the door, climbed into the driver's seat of the van relieved to see the key in its cubby-hole on the dash. She pressed the ignition switch. A light came on, glowing in the dark for a few seconds as she watched the bars in the battery icon tick down from twelve to one. The van was as flat as the phones. She got out and searched the shed for a charging cable, but found nothing.

Back inside, Margaret's attempts to clean up had done little to conceal the carnage wrecked on the contents of the cool store. Euphemia checked her watch. Even if they both scrubbed and cleaned for an hour, it would be daybreak by the time they finished. Rearranging the boxes in the cool store, might delay anyone finding out about the raid, but only for a few hours.

'I'm going to run to Oneroa and get help. You keep them occupied until I bring the police back,' said Euphemia.

'That's one possibility but it will take hours,' said Margaret. 'What if the police don't believe you? Grown women don't get held captive against their will. Not women our age. They'll think you're just a dissatisfied customer who doesn't like what she signed up for. I know. What about the yacht? I can sail, we could use that.'

Euphemia thought for a few seconds. The idea had merit and she wouldn't have to leave Jane and Sarah behind. 'Okay, but we have to get the others and they're locked in.'

'We get them out.'

'How?'

'There will be a control panel somewhere. Look.'

'You check the office, I'll check the hall,' said Euphemia.

'Found anything?' asked Margaret after they had been searching for five minutes.

'No, keep looking,' whispered Euphemia. Nothing stood out. She ran her hands along the walls, looked under photographs of beautiful places, but found nothing. 'Stand completely still. Don't make a sound,' she said. The sound of drawers opening and closing stopped. Euphemia stood in the middle of the hall and dialled up her hearing excluding the sounds she didn't want. The hum of the cool store fell away. A possum scratched across the tin roof, then disappeared as she focused her hearing on a hum coming from behind a wall in the office. The hum became a buzzing, which grew louder as she moved towards it then softer as she moved away from it. She followed it until it led her to the architrave surrounding the door to the Domed Hall, the sound of electrons fizzing where circuits joined leaping into her ears. She could feel their tingling presence in her palm as she ran it over the surface of the wood. The current surged to its conclusion. She pushed. A long thin door clicked open and behind it were three switches, each with its own automatic timer, one on top of the other. Helpfully someone had labelled them: Heating, Lights and Doors.

'Found it,' she whispered.

Margaret clapped her on the back. 'You beauty.'

Euphemia was about to flick the switch marked doors when she stopped. 'Houston, we have a problem.'

'We do?'

'This switch unlocks all the doors, not just Jane and Sarah's. What do we do with Claire, Selina, and Nell?'

'Allow me to save you the trouble of answering that question.'

Slowly Euphemia and Margaret turned around. Claire was standing behind them. She had the cutest little crossbow Euphemia had ever seen tucked into the corner of her elbow and it was loaded with a tiny steel bolt. Claire's finger was on the trigger.

CHAPTER 27

'ARE YOU ALONE?' ASKED EUPHEMIA.

'No, the others are hiding behind me,' snarled Claire. 'Of course, I'm alone.'

'How did you know we were here?'

'I'll give you a clue. Margaret has been going on about how hungry she is since she got here. It was only a matter of time before she found a way to the kitchen. Why do you think I left the outside doors unlocked?'

'You've starved us,' said Margaret.

'It was for your own good,' replied Claire. 'Ketogenic diets are natural. Complex carbohydrates are not.'

'Complex carbohydrates taste great. Ketogenic food does not,' said Margaret.

'Your hypothalamus has Stockholm Syndrome, courtesy of the industrial conglomerates who have loaded your food with so many pleasure triggers you are addicted. Our programme is a staged withdrawal of the substances which are ruining your health. If you stick to our diet after you leave, you will add years to your life.'

'Yeah! Miserable years,' said Margaret.

'Okay, that's enough,' said Euphemia. 'Why the crossbow?'

'It stops discussion and speeds up the inevitable.' She lifted the bow, aimed the bolt at a spot over Euphemia's head, and pulled the trigger. Six inches of steel parted her hair before embedding in the wooden door behind. Claire tilted the weapon end to her lips and blew. Then she reloaded.

'Holy crap,' said Margaret. 'You nearly shot her.'

'The key word in that sentence is 'nearly'. You,' she said, pointing the crossbow at Euphemia. 'Get in the office.' Euphemia didn't move.

'What about me?' asked Margaret.

'I'm hardly going to lock you up together,' replied Claire. 'You're going back to your room. We'll see what Selina and Claire have to say about your escapade in the morning.'

'Lock me in the office and put Euphemia in her room.'

'What difference does it make?'

'It would be better.'

'No, it wouldn't,' said Claire. 'Hurry up. I don't want to shoot you but I will. Through the arm. It's not fatal, but it makes a point.'

'We're on your side, Claire,' said Euphemia. She lowered the tone of her voice and slowed her words. 'You look exhausted.'

'That's because I am, Nell does nothing. She's a lazy cow and I have to do everything. Now move.'

'Put me in the office. Not her,' said Margaret again.

Euphemia turned and shushed her. 'I've got this.'

'Doesn't look like it,' said Margaret.

'Leave it,' said Euphemia. Margaret's eyes glazed over, and she stopped talking.

'We are with you, not against you. Claire, I accept your experience. It's been a long night,' said Euphemia. 'You can't hold your eyes open. You want to sleep.' She lowered her voice further to a pitch which she knew would resonate inside the other woman's mind.

'I do,' said Claire. Her eyelids drooped, and she stifled a yawn.

'You can sleep,' said Euphemia. 'All you need to do is go back to your room. Shut the door and crawl under your duvet, pull it over your head and close your eyes.' She spoke in a slow, rhythmic, even comforting tone. 'You will be so cosy and so warm. Your muscles will relax, and the weight will leave your bones as you lie still, at total ease.

You will feel clean air wash through your lungs, your heart will beat lazily in your chest, as you fall into a deep sleep and dream about lying on warm sand in the sunshine, away from this place. Alone, warm, safe. No one to tell you what to do. No Nell, or Selina. You will be at peace. All you have to do is walk through the door and go to your haven.'

Claire's shoulders sagged. The cross bow sank lower. She closed her eyes and her head rolled onto her chest.

'Return to your haven,' said Euphemia softly. 'Forget you saw us. I am no threat to you. I am on your side. All will be well. Tomorrow you will wake from the deepest sleep you have ever experienced. You will feel refreshed, alive and you will know all this has been a dream.'

Zombie-like, Claire shuffled towards her. Euphemia put her arm around Margaret, whose head was also lolling sleepily on her chest, and pulled her aside to give Claire room to pass.

Claire reached the door and pushed. But she didn't go through. Her head snapped up, her eyes flicked open, and she laughed. 'Thought you had me, didn't you? Don't know who taught you hypnosis,' she said. 'But they missed an important lesson. Meditation and hypnosis don't work well together. Meditation allows me to step outside myself to observe the world and my actions in it. Hypnosis works by letting another person into your deepest self and following their instructions. See how they clash? Nice try though. Now go into the office and stop playing silly games.'

She pushed Euphemia into the room. 'While you're there, dream about lying on warm sand,' she said and locked the door. With a key.

Euphemia listened to their footsteps, to the door into the Domed Hall swinging open, more footsteps and then silence.

CHAPTER 28

HER PLAN HAD WORKED. EUPHEMIA WAS FREE TO FIND OUT exactly what was going on at this so-called Retreat. She dragged the chair across to the desk, sat down and pulled the keyboard towards her. She had to work fast because she didn't know how long the reassurance that she was no threat, which she had implanted in Claire's brain, would last.

She checked the screens one by one. Jane was still asleep, as were Selina and Nell. Claire closed Margaret's door and Euphemia saw the satisfaction on her face as she ripped the wax strip away and locked it. Margaret, on the inside, was furious. She hammered on the door, kicking it, yelling at Claire that she had made a huge mistake and to let her out this instant or she would have her fired and the Retreat shut down. Claire hurried back to her room, tucked up under her duvet before Margaret gave up her protest and lay down. Teeth clenched, she glared at the camera, boring it with her eyes before she turned away and curled up on her side.

Sarah was awake. Her hands lay intertwined across her stomach, her hair tangled, her face bloated from crying, her eyes flat as she stared at the ceiling. On the floor beside her bed were documents and a pen. Euphemia focused to read what was on the papers. 'Deed of Gift between Sarah Anne Baillie and the Acceptance Institute'. Sarah had signed it and, on behalf of the Acceptance Institute, so had Selina. Yesterday's date was below the signatures.

'Sarah,' she whispered. 'They did it.'

She checked the documents again. There was only one copy on the floor, Sarah's copy. Which meant the other copies must already be on their way to the lawyers. That's why they were sent down to the beach for a swim, so they wouldn't hear the courier van when it came to collect them. Today was Friday. The courts would be shut tomorrow and Sunday. She had two days to extract Sarah and save the Baillie inheritance.

She checked the time. 4.30 AM. Yesterday, while down at the bay, she noted the high tide mark on the rocks, and then had watched to see if the tide was coming in or going out. Using the Rule of Twelfths, she calculated out when it would be low tide. High tide would have been between 5 and 6 PM last night. If she could get everyone to the yacht by 6.00 AM, the outgoing tide would help speed them on their way to safety. She needed all the help she could get because she had never sailed a yacht before. Margaret said she had but was she telling the truth?

In the meantime, she had half an hour to find out as much as she could about the murky dealings of the Retreat. Staff who use crossbows to threaten clients had to be protecting more than the vegetarian contents of a cool store. Sarah was half starved, locked up and intimidated into signing away her money. Logic and the all-pervasive presence of social media meant there can't have been any other 'Sarahs' over the seven years the Retreat had been operating. Word would have got out if duping women out of their money was a frequent practice. If not from those who had gifted their money in the belief it brought them acceptance, then from their families left to pick up the pieces. Eventually, the word fraud would have surfaced regardless of the embarrassment, and the authorities would have been involved.

So what had just happened to Sarah had to be a rarity, a one-off. Which meant there were other reasons Claire confronted them with a weapon. She wasn't a killer. There had been genuine fear in her eyes when she saw how close the bolt had come to the top of Euphemia's head. That had been an act of recklessness she would not dare repeat.

But who could say what she might do under real stress? What was she really guarding? And for who?

The answer had to be here in the office. Euphemia swivelled around in the chair, taking in the bare walls, the desk, the keyboard, and the screens. People's faces awake and asleep, bodies in different positions on beds. It was the middle of the night, so there wasn't much to see. During the day, when they were stuck in their rooms, the images would have been more interesting. Selena said Claire was supposed to have checked the tapes. That meant there was a system for storing the images and playing them back. Either there was a server close by or the data went to the cloud, which in turn meant there was an internet connection she could use.

She stood up, leaned over, gripped the nearest screen and tore it from its bracket on the wall. A trail of cords led back to a hole which the cords from the other screens still traversed. She pulled the desk away from the wall and put her eye to the hole, her skin registering warmth in the gap. The cool store was on the other side of the wall. The warmth could be from its refrigeration unit, but she had seen this on the wall outside. It took little effort to yank the door free from the lock, and she went into the corridor to estimate the width of the adjoining wall. Her question answered, she returned to the office to study the screens that were still working. She typed instructions then waited for confirmation the data upload had gone through. All she had to do now was escape before Selina or Nell woke up and tried to stop her.

It would have horrified Barbara if she knew what Euphemia planned to do next. So, she thought, it was just as well Barbara was on the other side of the Tasman Sea and would not witness Euphemia's first public display of her powers. She hoped to get the others out and to safety without being too overt, but she was also prepared to do whatever was necessary. The stakes were so much higher than she had first thought, because now she knew what was being done in the name of Acceptance.

CHAPTER 29

SARAH LEAPT OUT OF BED, CLUTCHING HER DUVET TO HER chest when Euphemia kicked through the wall of her room. From the outside.

'It's me,' said Euphemia. 'Quick, put on your shoes, something warm and wait for me. I'll be back.' She waited the second it took for Sarah to nod that she understood and disappeared back through the hole, into the dawn light. When she returned several minutes later, she had Jane in tow.

'Wait here,' she said. 'I going to get Margaret.'

Jane beckoned to Sarah to climb out and jump the three feet to the ground. Together they stood with their arms around the other, shivering, as they watched Euphemia run up to the side of the building, and at the last-minute leap up and kick a woman-sized hole in the wall. The plaster gave way on impact, the cracks spreading out from the centre like when a stone hits a windscreen, then the wall fell inwards in a cloud of dust. They shuffled across and peered at Margaret, who was sitting up in bed, staring back at them, her eyes wide, her mouth open.

'Hurry,' said Euphemia. 'Shoes and warm clothes. There's no time to waste.'

Margaret, already dressed, flung off her duvet. She didn't need to be told twice and clambered out to join them.

'You lead the way,' Euphemia said to Margaret. 'I'll follow.'

Margaret ran off down the track without waiting for the others. They were still thinking about what they had witnessed, then as if someone had slapped them into understanding, they set off after her. Euphemia surveyed the wreckage from her hiding place in the bush. Because of the sound-proofing, she had decided there would be less noise if she kicked through the walls from the outside. It was entirely possible Selina, Nell and Claire had slept through her assault because as yet there was no sound from their rooms. She scanned the overhanging branches for the message on the one outside her room. Fifteen feet off the ground, whoever carved it was either very strong or incredibly athletic to climb that high. Sarah was neither.

The sound of footsteps in the corridor outside Jane's room stopped further conjecture and she hurried towards the path to the beach. Behind her, a door opened followed by a moment's silence. Then Claire yelled to the others to come and see what had happened. Any minute now they would be on her trail. She sped up, galloping down the steps between the trees only to find the others were barely a third of the way to the beach. Jane was struggling with the steep drop, Sarah with the loose gravel. They would have been faster if they sat on the backsides and slid down the hill. This wasn't an option but neither was continuing at the same pace because now yells echoed from the hillsides like bloodhounds baying for scent.

'Margaret, go to the back,' ordered Euphemia. 'Jane, relax.'

'Why?' asked Jane. Too late because Euphemia slung her over one shoulder like a sack of potatoes and took off down the path, leaping over steps, dodging low-hanging branches, and weaving along narrow ledges until she reached the shore, unbundling her onto the sand.

'Swim to the yacht and no matter what you hear, do not turn around and do not come back. Got that? Good.' She didn't wait for a reply, just disappeared back up the track.

Sarah, having been at the Retreat the longest, had lost a lot of weight, and would have been a pleasure to carry after the hefty Jane, if it wasn't for her sharp hip bones digging in to Euphemia's shoulder.

Spurred on by her experiences, when Euphemia put her down on the sand, Sarah waded straight into the water and started swimming. Her hand like a visor above her eyes, Euphemia searched the bay. Jane's neat but efficient breaststroke had her halfway to the yacht. She was thinking her plan may work after all, when a steel bolt ripped through the air beside her head and pinged off a boulder.

Margaret was almost at the beach when Euphemia reached her.

'You're not carrying me,' she said.

'I could,' said Euphemia grabbing her hand. 'But I won't only if you match me step for step. Run and don't stop running until you reach the water.'

Euphemia pulled Margaret behind her and together they left the cover of the bush and zig-zagged to the waterline. She pushed Margaret ahead of her, and just as she was about to dive in, she heard a yell.

'You won't get away with this.' Selina called, her voice loud and clear across the surface of the water.

Euphemia waded in and swam, not caring that she powered past Margaret. Halfway to the yacht, she stopped and looked back. There were two heads in the water. One was Margaret's. The other, Claire's.

CHAPTER 30

By the time Euphemia reached the yacht, Jane had pulled down the stainless steel ladder at the stern and was attempting to push an exhausted Sarah up and onto the boat. Euphemia reached over and, with a firm application of force to her bottom, Sarah slithered into the cockpit and lay on the floor gasping for air, spent.

'No need to be so rough,' said Jane, climbing up after her. 'I would have done it.'

Euphemia didn't have time to debate the etiquette of boarding a boat. She stepped over Sarah and leaned over the wheel to inspect the panels and levers set into what looked like a dashboard. Thank goodness they were all labelled. Not that it helped much. She didn't know what an 'Inverter' did. The 'Nav Instruments' label was self-explanatory, but again as she hadn't done any navigation training, it was a switch she didn't intend to use. 'Power', she understood, but what on earth was a 'Windlass'? Sarah hauled herself up to sit on the bench behind her, shivering, her teeth chattering noisily with cold. Euphemia was too busy trying to work out how to get the boat to go to take much notice. Jane, pushed past her reached under the canopy and pulled out a set of keys attached to a tiny float, which she waved triumphantly under Euphemia's nose.

'We'll need these,' said Jane.

'How did you know where they were?' asked Euphemia.

Jane was about to answer when Margaret pulled herself up the ladder and into the cockpit, followed quickly by Claire.

'I can explain,' said Claire. She held her hands up beside her head. 'I won't cause trouble. Please, please, please take me with you.'

Jane clutched Euphemia's arm and pulled her away. 'She's one of them,' she hissed. 'Throw her overboard. She swam here, she can swim back.

'No, don't,' said Sarah. 'Claire was the only one who was kind after they locked me up. She smuggled food to me when the others weren't looking.'

Claire looked hopefully from one to the other like a puppy searching for a kind owner. Margaret jerked her head towards the water. So did Jane. Sarah's eyes pleaded for her to be allowed to stay.

'Do you know anything about boats?' asked Euphemia.

'My dad had one when I was a kid,' replied Claire. 'I know a bit.'

'You can stay,' said Euphemia.

'But she—' said Jane.

'We don't have time for this. I'm the captain. I say we take her. Hurry, we need to get this thing moving. Jane, you, Margaret and Sarah, go below, and get out of those wet clothes. Use this.' She tossed the bunch of keys to Jane, who sorted through the one she guessed would unlock the doors to the cabin. Two attempts and she was in. She handed the keys back to Euphemia, who repeated the exercise with the ignition.

'Okay Claire, what do I do next?'

'Get the anchor up,' said Margaret lagging behind the others.

'Both of you go up front and pull it up,' said Euphemia.

Margaret sighed, reached across and turned the key. After some coughing, the engine started and the deck they were standing on reverberated with a dull throb. Water bubbled from the exhaust pipe where it met the sea and the sweet smell of diesel greeted their nostrils, riding up on puffs of black smoke.

'It hasn't been used for a while,' said Claire. 'Let it idle to charge the batteries. See those knobs on the ends of the two levers? One drives the boat forwards. The other puts it in reverse. Got that?'

'Got it. Thanks.' Euphemia gave one a wiggle, and it slipped forward. The engine changed from idling to a deeper sound, and the boat started to move.

'Not yet,' yelled Margaret yanking the lever back. 'You'll rip the front off the boat if we don't get the anchor up first.'

'How do we do that?' asked Euphemia.

'That switch,' she said, pointing at the one marked windlass. 'It's an engine which winds up the anchor.'

'Got it. Go below and get dried off and changed. I'm going to need you. How long will it take to get to Oneroa from here?'

'Why Oneroa? Why not Auckland?' asked Margaret.

'Because Oneroa is closer and because Auckland is a busy port, and I don't fancy our chances in a tiny boat mixing it up with the container ships in the shipping lanes.'

'Okay, you're the boss,' said Margaret. 'Claire?'

With them gone, Euphemia had a good look around the cockpit. She lifted the lids on the benched seats and found lifejackets, ropes, two buoys and a half empty bottle of scotch. She pulled herself up and edged along the side of the cabin, keeping her hand on the safety rail as she inspected the big sail rolled up under a cover made of the same blue canvas as the canopy. Three wires held the mast in place: two to each corner at the back of the boat and one to the pointy bit at the front of the boat. There was a metal thing on the front which you could stand on. She didn't know what this was for or why anyone apart from Kate Winslet and Leonardo Di Caprio would want to stand on it. Another sail coiled around the wire at the front and had ropes attached to it. The ends of the ropes wound around stainless steel cleats screwed onto the deck. Perfect toe-stubbers, she thought, making a mental note of their existence. It all looked very ship-shape and mysterious. That the motor worked was a huge relief because she didn't have time to learn the intricacies of sailing.

'Cup of tea?' called Jane. Her head popped up from behind the canopy as she searched the deck. 'There you are,' she said. 'I was worried you had fallen off the back and been eaten by sharks, with none of us noticing.' She climbed awkwardly onto the bench seat and then onto the deck, shuffling sideways along it as she held two cups of steaming liquid in front of her, slopping some as the boat rocked at anchor.

Euphemia had forgotten the magical, simple wonder of a hot cup of tea first thing in the morning. She took the proffered cup gratefully, cradling it between her hands, enjoying the warmth and smell of strong tea wafting up to her.

'It's even got milk in it.'

'UHT, the long life stuff. This is a very well stocked boat. No bacon or eggs, but there's plenty of baked beans. They'll be ready soon.'

Euphemia sipped her tea and sighed. 'You found dry clothes,' said Euphemia.

Jane looked down at the moth-eaten man's jumper and paint-splattered shorts. 'Sarah got first pick,' she said. 'I thought it was only fair after what she told us they did to her after she changed her mind about giving them her money.' She sipped her tea and stared across the water at the beach. 'Do you think they're doing a runner? Selina and Nell?'

'Probably. Which is why we have to get moving,' said Euphemia. 'Sarah signed everything over to them yesterday. We need to get to the police before their lawyers sell off her assets and hide the money.'

'I'm curious,' said Jane. She showed no intention of moving. 'Why have you let Claire come? Aren't you worried she will spy on us for the others?'

'Not really. And if she did, what could she do with the information? We're going straight to the police. My guess is she will make herself scarce as soon as we get there. She's here because she knows more about boats than either of us. We need her.' Euphemia drank the rest of her tea, shook the empty cup over the side to get rid of the last drips, and went back to the cockpit.

'I can tell there's something you're not telling me. You do this every time, Effie, and every time, it's annoying.' Jane followed her back to the cockpit.

Margaret was sitting quietly beside the wheel and looked up when they jumped down. 'What does our capitaine do that's so annoying?'

'Nothing,' replied Jane. 'Give me your cups.' She hooked the handles over a finger, squeezed past Euphemia and went below.

'The batteries will be charged by now,' said Margaret. 'I'll go for'ard and check the anchor when it comes up. Wait for my call before you turn the motor off.'

Euphemia listened to the slow grind as the anchor chain clunked over the metal chute at the front of the boat. There was a solid thunk as Margaret laid it on the deck. The boat had swung free as soon as the anchor was free of the seabed. She pushed the lever with the red knob down a little way, pointed the boat to open sea and it steadily picked up speed, the wake churning noisily in three white ribbons behind them.

'Which way?' she asked when Margaret joined her at the wheel.

'Right,' said Margaret. 'Turn right, but make sure you give that headland a wide berth. From memory, the rocks go out a long way and the tide is on the way out. We don't want to be shipwrecked this early in the journey.'

The sea was flat calm; the sun was up, and there wasn't a cloud in the sky. A seagull glided into the boat's slipstream, hanging over the water watching them beadily, its head low between its wings as it coasted in their draft.

Margaret, sat down and stretched her arms along the top of the seat, turned her face up to the sky, and sniffed the air. 'What a morning. To think I paid to go to a place where they locked us away from this. My first and last spa!'

'Mine too,' said Euphemia. Water slapped against the hull as the boat bucked against the waves when they left the bay and entered open water. 'You said right, didn't you?' She turned the wheel, taking the boat in a wide arc around the headland. 'Look,' she said, pointing. 'A seal. There was a seal on those rocks. It dived in when it saw us.'

'This yacht and the sea are doing for my peace of mind than sitting for hours on a mat meditating ever did,' said Margaret. 'It's perfect.'

'Baked beans,' said Jane, holding a plate up from the cabin. 'Take it quick before they slide off!' she yelled.

Margaret leaned over, grabbed the plate and fork and returned to her seat. 'Proper food. Come to Mumma. O how I have missed you,' she said. 'Hot, tasty and you can't eat it with your fingers. Living the dream Euphemia. Living the dream,' She shovelled several forkfuls into her mouth then stopped and looked guiltily at Euphemia. 'Sorry, you should have had this. You must be starving. I'll finish and take over the helm so you can go below and have a break. It's only three hours to get to Oneroa from here but the boat has a hot shower, a loo and there's plenty to eat. Enjoy.'

Euphemia looked at the speedometer on the dash. They were cruising at 3 knots. She didn't know what that was in real terms, and she didn't know how far away Oneroa was. All she knew was that she was hungry, and the rich tomato smell of baked beans was making her mouth water and her stomach rumble. She took Margaret's empty plate, handed over the wheel and went below.

CHAPTER 31

A LONG CABIN SPANNING THE WIDTH OF THE BOAT
narrowed towards the front where a wooden divider wall separated the
sleeping area from the living area. A loo with a shower head over it and a
hand basin beside it occupied a small cubicle on one side of the bunks.
Sunshine beamed through an open hatch onto the narrow corridor, at
the end of which was a large double bunk constructed sideways and
which took up the very end of the boat. Rolled up quilts and pillows
were wedged tidily into racks on one side of the bed. Windows at regular
intervals along the length of both sides of the cabin let in more light. A
table surrounded by bench seats in a u-shape was on one side of the
cabin, faced by a longer straight bench seat on the other. On one side at
the back were two built-in bunks, and opposite these was the galley.
Shelves, handrails, bench seats, hooks and light holders were all designed
to fulfil multiple functions in the confined space. The seats had lift-up
lids to serve as storage spaces. The table dropped to the level of the
surrounding seats to become another bed. Rows of shelves built into the
walls and guarded by wooden rails held books and charts and lights and
cans of food. Everything was so well thought-out, the polished dark
wooden joinery adding luxury to functionality. There was a place for

everything and everything had its place and, better still, was actually in it.

Cushions on the seats and bunks covered in a waterproof nautical blue fabric with white piping added to the smart ship-shape atmosphere. White ties held back blue paisley curtains on wires above and below the windows. Gleaming brass lamps in pivot holders set at regular intervals down the cabin provided night lighting. Brass rivets fixed the racks to the walls. Brass facings ringed the round windows which were, she remembered, called portholes, and not windows.

Jane stood beside a gas stove stirring a large pot of baked beans. Sarah was pouring tea. 'Your first decent meal in days,' said Jane, handing her a plate piled high with beans. 'There's salt and pepper on the table and I'll bring you tea. It's easier if you sit down and let me wait on you. You too, Sarah.'

Euphemia did as she was told. Sarah joined her. 'Where's Claire?' she asked. 'I thought she was down here with you.'

'She took her plate up front,' said Jane, joining them at the table. 'Thank goodness, its awkward with her here.'

'We're only giving her a ride. We don't need to talk to her. Mmm, this smells so good,' said Euphemia.

They didn't speak again until their plates were empty. Sarah wiped a smear of tomato sauce from her chin and looked sheepishly at Jane, then Euphemia. 'Roger would be furious with me for what I've done,' she said.

'I think he would see the funny side,' said Euphemia. 'I mean, look at us. Half-starved escapees from a spa, on a yacht which none of us know how to sail, going to a place we've never been to a report a crime which may not have happened yet.'

'I did a sailing course,' said Jane. Three months at Evans Bay. It was between the upholstery course and the first aid course. I learned all sorts of boaty things – coming around, tacking, jibing. I've got a certificate to prove it.'

'I stand corrected,' said Euphemia. 'One of us knows boaty stuff.'

Sarah brightened, giving them a flash of the woman they used to know. 'John and Sophie went on that course, too. They teach you how to sail optimists, not fifty-foot keelers. There's a big difference.'

'Okay then, you tell me what a jibe is,' said Jane huffily.

'I have no idea.'

'Isn't it a type of mocking?' asked Euphemia.

'Ha-ha. A jibe is a turn you do when you are going down wind. You put the tiller in the opposite direction of the sail and away you go. Or is it the other way around? I forget the words but my muscle memory will know it when I do it. Laugh all you want but I have got a certificate in sailing, so there.'

'I'm not laughing. I'm not, even though we have a wheel and not a tiller,' said Euphemia. 'Hopefully we won't need to jibe anywhere because it sounds complicated.'

'Don't you trust me?' asked Jane.

'I do trust you. Really I do, but we have the motor, so your sailing expertise will not be required,' said Euphemia. She looked around the cabin. 'Have you looked inside these cupboards yet? There must be a radio because there's an antenna at the top of the mast. I should have thought of it sooner. We can call for help.'

'We've been too busy organising the food,' said Sarah, getting up and clearing away the plates. 'More tea?'

Euphemia shook her head and squeezed out from behind the table. It didn't take long before she found the radio. When she switched it on nothing happened. She took the handpiece off and tried all the switches in different combinations, but to no avail. 'Did your sailing course include radio training?' she asked Jane, who shook her head.

Euphemia stood on the bottom step to the cockpit. 'Margaret, do you know how to use a radio?'

'Switch it on and start talking.'

'I've tried, but it doesn't work. Can you try? Jane, you take the wheel.'

'The correct term is the helm,' said Jane. 'And I'd be delighted.' She and Margaret did a little dance around each other in the confined space of the cabin as they changed places. Margaret pressed the same switches, jiggled the same bits, and looked as mystified as Euphemia.

'Yachts this size are legally required to have a working radio,' she said. 'We should check the fuse on the main board.'

Euphemia smacked her forehead. 'I should have thought of that. Where's the main board?'

'Somewhere,' said Margaret. 'Look.'

'I'll wash up,' said Sarah, leaving them to get on with it.

They found it set into the wall on the other side of the stairwell which led up to the cockpit. It was padlocked shut, and none of the keys on the key chain fitted the lock.

'It'll be easy enough to jimmy it open,' said Euphemia. 'Sarah, can you pass me a knife?'

She slipped the blade under the loop. 'What's that?' She pointed to the far end of the cabin and while Margaret and Sarah were looking, she bent the handle of the padlock open with her fingers. The fuse board swung back to reveal a tangle of different coloured wires. Margaret picked up a yellow wire and showed it to Euphemia. 'It's been cut. So has this one,' she dropped the yellow one and picked up a green one. 'No wonder the radio doesn't work.'

Euphemia took the ends of the yellow wire, stripped off the plastic and twisted the copper strands around each other, then did the same with the green wire. 'Try it again,' she said. Margaret flipped the radio switch. A blur of white noise followed, then stopped.

'Close,' she said, doing some more twisting. 'Try again.'

For the third time she twisted the strands even more tightly together and the same thing happened, then stopped. She sighed and scratched her nose. 'It won't work,' she said. 'There's too much interference.' She tucked the wires back inside the box and closed the door. 'Why would anyone cut the radio wires?'

'Doesn't matter. Another hour and we'll be in Oneroa,' said Margaret. 'We don't need it. Sarah, any chance of another cup of tea? Or, even better, coffee?'

'You're in luck. I found coffee,' said Sarah. She pushed aside pots in the cupboard under the gas stove and pulled out a Bialetti. 'And I found this!' she said triumphantly.

CHAPTER 32

'Everyone! Come and see!' Jane screamed. 'Dolphins!'

Sarah, Margaret, and Euphemia raced up the stairs into the cockpit. Dolphins surrounded the yacht. Some were riding the waves at the front, the bow wave, Jane informed them. While others surfed in and out of the wake at the back. The previously calm sea was alive with fins and tails and black shadows zooming beneath the surface and under the boat.

'Look,' said Sarah. 'A baby.' She pointed at a mother and calf swimming alongside, the mother guarding her offspring from getting too close.

Their silvery-grey bodies leapt in and out of the water, then circled back around, leaping again. One clearly showing off, leapt high and stood on its tail. Another rolled onto its side next to where they were standing and waved a fin at the same time as casting a laughing black eye over each of them.

'It was smiling at us,' yelled Jane. 'It was. It looked at me and it smiled the biggest smile I have ever seen.' She jumped up and down in delight.

Euphemia leaned through the wires of the guardrail to trail her hand in the water. A dolphin nosed it, then dived deep under the yacht coming up on the other side and squeaked.

'Turn off the engine,' said Sarah. 'I want to get in. Swimming with dolphins has been on my bucket list for ever.'

Jane turned the key, the engine noise died and the boat coasted a short distance in silence before stopping. Sarah ripped off her clothes and wearing her underpants and bra, she dived off the back of the boat. The dolphins scattered, but slowly some of the more curious animals swam back and surrounded her, staying just out of reach.

Jane was next in the water, followed by Margaret. Three heads bobbed in the dark blue sea behind the yacht, floating with their arms outstretched on the surface. Euphemia looked around for Claire.

'Claire?' she called. 'Are you coming swimming with the dolphins, too?'

Claire's voice came back to her from the front of the boat. 'No, I'm good. You go. I'll stay onboard and keep watch.'

She sounded fine. Quite normal, in fact. Euphemia could only see a foot sticking out front in of the cabin. Then an arm came up and waved.

Once they were in the water, the dolphins were as interested in the women as the women were in the dolphins. They swam around them, with none of their initial speed. Curiosity had got the better of them and wanted to inspect these pale ungainly creatures.

Euphemia stripped off and dived in. The water was colder than she had expected, but when her hand brushed against the skin of a dolphin; she forgot all about the temperature. Startled, the animal turned and swam off in the opposite direction leaving her with the sensation of its smooth leathery skin. She dived, her eyes open, and swam the length of the yacht, watching the creatures diving under and around her, curious to see what she was doing. One stopped upright in the water, and cocked its head, making eye contact with her before surfacing and diving again. It had a notch in its back fin, and a scar under one eye, and it stayed close as she reached the front of the boat. She had stopped there lay on her back and looked up to see the anchor swinging on its chain above her head. It was supposed to be on deck. Why was it hanging free? From there it could put a hole in the hull if the wind or a wave caught it the wrong way. Treading water she yelled to Claire to winch it up. Claire didn't respond, so she yelled again.

Without warning, the dolphin dived between her legs, rose up and carried her backwards. The anchor plummeted into the sea, right through the exact spot she had been swimming only seconds before. If the dolphin hadn't intervened, it would have knocked her out, before dragging her down as it sank to a bottom she couldn't see. The dolphin was gone by the time she surfaced and looked back up at the yacht. The chain clinked emptily against the hull; the link holding the anchor hung from it, bent out of shape. Someone had to have sabotaged it while they had been motoring to their destination. Someone who wanted to disable the yacht.

Clicks followed a series of high-pitched squeaks sounding beside her. The dolphin with the notch in its fin had returned.

She reached across and caressed its head, feeling its warmth, thinking her gratitude for saving her life hoping to communicate this to the creature. He or she nodded and clicked again before eyeballing her and diving into the deep blue, out of sight.

Euphemia swam back to the rear of the boat slowly. The dolphins had gone, and she was the last one in the water. The others were standing on deck in their sopping underwear, towels and blankets wrapped around their shoulders, their teeth chattering as they talked loudly about what had just happened. Claire was with them, handing around cups of hot coffee, looking happier and more relaxed than Euphemia had ever seen her. She pulled herself up the ladder and hit a wave of excitement as Jane bounced up to her and told her about one dolphin letting her hold on to her fin and pulling her through the water. 'Just like in the movies.' Sarah interrupted her to say she had done that too. Twice! Jane said she would have done it twice but she felt sorry for the poor dolphins and hadn't because she knew once was enough.

Sarah, shook her head and teeth chattering with the cold, stripped off her wet underwear, not caring who saw her body, to towel herself dry before she pulled on her dry clothes. The others followed suit. They were all women; they knew what middle-aged bodies looked like and it didn't matter.

'That was one of the best things I have ever done in my whole life,' said Margaret when she was dressed again. She scanned the water hope-fully for the dolphins and looked sad not to find any.

'Claire, you missed something mind-blowingly fantastic, but thank you for staying onboard so we could enjoy it,' said Sarah. The smile hadn't left her face. 'Who feels like a drink? I saw a bottle of wine in the cupboard. It's red, but that doesn't matter.'

Jane looked around. 'We shouldn't,' she said. 'It's not ours.'

'We'll buy another one when we get to Oneroa,' said Margaret. 'No big deal. It won't be expensive. You get the bottle. There are plastic wine glasses in the cupboard above the table.'

Jane, hunched inside the old sweatshirt, giggled. 'Oh go on. Let's,' she said. 'A little poison won't hurt. I've been so good for three whole months.'

'So have I,' called Sarah from the cabin. 'All because of some stupid theory which makes no sense when you think about it.' She came back with the bottle, unscrewed the top and splashed wine into the glasses Margaret was holding. Everyone took one except Euphemia, who was standing beside the wheel.

'I'd like to make a toast,' said Sarah, raising her glass to the sky. 'Roger, I wish you had been here today. You would have loved swim-ming with the dolphins. Here's to Roger, who taught me a lesson I had forgotten until today. Life is for living. Enjoy!'

'Enjoy,' they echoed. They drained their glasses and held them out to Sarah for another round.

'You're not drinking, Effie?' asked Jane. 'Come on. A little won't hurt. It will warm you up.'

'I'm good,' said Euphemia. 'Has anyone seen the keys?'

'What keys?' asked Margaret.

'Specifically, the key which starts the engine. It was in the ignition when we got in the water and now it isn't.'

Silence fell as they turned away from the wine and looked at the empty keyhole on the dashboard.

'It will have fallen out,' said Jane. She put her glass down and came over to search the floor under the wheel. 'It has to be here.'

Sarah put her glass down too and joined the search.

'They will have gone down the steps into the cabin,' said Margaret.

She climbed down into the cabin and got on her hands and knees, feeling behind and around the steps.

'Found them,' said Claire. They were over there in the corner. Someone must have knocked them out of the ignition when they were getting changed.

'Thank goodness,' said Jane. 'With no radio we'd be stuck here for days.'

'And no anchor,' said Euphemia.

'What? We had an anchor this morning,' said Sarah.

'It fell off,' said Euphemia. 'It nearly killed me when it did.'

'It can't have fallen off,' said Claire.

'Go and look,' said Euphemia.

'Wait a toast,' said Jane. Her face flushed; she was almost laughing. 'To finding the keys! No radio and no anchor. We're lucky we still have an engine. A toast to Claire.'

'To Claire.' They drank again. The bottle was empty.

Euphemia put the key in the ignition and turned it. Nothing happened. She turned it again. Again, nothing happened. The glasses lowered as they listened to the sounds of ropes rattling against the mast and the sea slopping against the hull.

CHAPTER 33

'DOES ANYONE KNOW HOW TO HOT-WIRE A BOAT?' ASKED
Sarah.

'The sailing course didn't cover that. Don't look at me,' replied Jane.
'Effie?'

'Why me?'

'You know about engines,' said Jane. 'You said the ATV at Oakhill
was sabotaged and you were right.'

'Different case entirely,' she replied. 'Margaret, we'd better check the
fuse box again. I'll have a look at the engine. Can one of you, keep an eye
out for rocks or another boat?'

'I will,' said Jane, handing her glass to Sarah and taking the wheel.

'I've done the dishes already,' said Sarah, handing the glasses to
Claire. 'You haven't done anything yet.'

Claire shrugged and juggling the glasses in her hands, went below.

Beside Jane's feet in the floor of the cockpit was a hatch cover.
Euphemia bent down and lifted it open. Sarah bending down beside
her, peered at the engine. 'Do you know what you're looking at?' she
asked.

'Don't have a clue,' replied Euphemia. 'You?'

'The engine in Dad's boat was smaller and older, but otherwise the same. See those,' she said, pointing to three black rubber-covered cables. 'They should be attached to something.'

'They're not.'

Sarah crouched down and felt under the engine, sweeping her hand along its base. 'They're not here,' she said.

'What aren't?'

'I hoped that the nuts which hold the cables in place might have dropped into the well, but they aren't there.'

'Has someone taken them?' asked Euphemia.

'You can't be serious,' said Jane. 'Not again. You do this every time, Effie. It's too much. Really it is.'

'What do you mean I do this because I don't,' said Euphemia. 'It's as much a mystery to me as it is to you.'

Jane let go of the wheel and crouched down beside Sarah and Euphemia. 'Those cables couldn't fall off by themselves, could they?'

'Well, no,' said Sarah. She sat up. 'Someone must have unscrewed the nuts on purpose.'

'Only one person has been on the yacht by herself.' Jane stood up and, before Euphemia could stop her called out, 'Claire, come here!'

Claire poked her head out of the cabin. 'You yelled?'

'Darned right,' said Jane. 'Where are the nuts which hold the cable thingummies onto the engine thingamabobs?'

'What are you talking about?'

'Sarah says the engine won't start because those cables there,' she said, waving her hand over the engine, 'aren't connected. And they can't be re-connected without the nuts. Which we can't find. Which means someone did this after we got on the boat and the only time anyone could possibly have done it and not be seen, because it is a sneaky, underhand, nasty thing to do, was when we were swimming with the dolphins, and you were on board by yourself.' She finished short of breath and with a flourish.

Margaret poked her head out of the cabin beside Claire. 'What's going on?'

'I'm being accused of breaking the engine,' said Claire. She held up her hands. 'See, lily-white. Now compare these to Sarah's and Euphemia's.' She waited while they held up their grease-stained hands.

'If I had done what you're accusing me of, Jane, wouldn't my hands look like theirs?'

'You could have washed them.'

'Look at their fingernails. It will take weeks to get the black out from around their nails.'

'She's right,' said Margaret. 'My guess is those cables aren't important, which is why they're loose.' She slid past Claire, climbed up past Jane, and turned the key. The engine coughed and turned over, but it didn't start. 'It was the fuse for the ignition motor,' she said. 'I replaced it.' She turned the key again, and the engine turned over and this time it caught. 'All fixed. You owe Claire an apology.'

Jane flushed. 'Sorry,' she said, not looking at her.

'You can do better than that,' said Margaret.

'All right,' said Jane. She looked at Claire this time. 'Sorry for jumping to conclusions and blaming you for something you didn't do.'

'Apology accepted,' said Claire. 'I'll make lunch. Soup or baked beans?'

Euphemia and Sarah, glad that Jane had taken the heat for their assumptions, quickly lifted the engine cover back into place. 'I vote soup,' said Sarah. 'I should apologise as well. It's a long time since I looked at an engine and I made the wrong call. Roger took care of the mechanical stuff so I'm out of practice.'

Euphemia was just pleased they were finally on their way again. Not that she regretted the experience, but the dolphins had taken up an hour of their journey time. It was nearly lunchtime, and they were still miles from Oneroa.

'It's dead calm,' she said. 'Perhaps we could speed up.'

Margaret who was at the helm, pointed to a gauge on the dashboard. 'See that?'

Euphemia peered over her shoulder at a needle resting just above a broad red line.

'That's all the diesel we have left,' said Margaret. 'I hope we can get there, but it will be touch and go.'

CHAPTER 34

JANE SAT WITH HER BACK TO THE MAST, LOOKING OUT TO sea. 'Here,' said Euphemia, offering her a mug of hot soup. Jane took it and put it down on the deck. Euphemia, holding her own mug, got down beside her.

'I'm so embarrassed,' said Jane. 'I shouldn't have accused Claire like that. You warned me about always jumping to conclusions and I didn't listen. I've spent the last two months, several thousand dollars and come up here to try and be a better person and it hasn't worked.'

'You sold Justin's pendant, didn't you?' said Euphemia.

'How did you know?' asked Jane.

'I saw you in the jeweller's shop on Cuba Street.'

'Another mistake,' she replied. 'She gave me two and half thousand for it but I know it's worth more. Nell recommended I go to her. I didn't want to be rude so I took what she offered, and I gave it all to the Institute. I feel a fool.'

'We all make mistakes,' said Euphemia. She took a sip of tomato soup. It was too hot, but after days of cold meals it was a welcome change. 'This is very good, considering it came from a can. Come on, drink it. You need to build yourself up again.'

'That's the other thing,' Jane said. 'We ate terrible food, spent most of the time lying on the uncomfortable beds in our 'havens' and we did yoga, which I could have found on YouTube. How could that possibly cost two and half thousand dollars?

'Your money will be in their bank account along with the five thousand I donated.'

Jane punched Euphemia's arm. 'You gave them how much? Five thousand?'

'Keep it down. I don't want the entire world knowing I got taken.'

'Five thousand. I don't feel so bad now. You really got suckered,' Jane picked up her mug and took a long swig of soup. 'You're right, it is good.'

'That's probably because we haven't had salt for a while and our taste buds are reacting.'

'Five thousand? That's a huge amount of money. Whewee!' Jane shook her head and chuckled.

'You can't tell Kenneth.'

'Okay.'

'Promise?'

'I promise. Five thousand is nothing to you, whereas two and a half thousand is a fortune to me.'

'What? Five thousand dollars is not nothing to me.'

'Come on,' said Jane. 'When are you going to admit that you're rich?'

'I'm not rich.'

'For goodness' sake. You're allowed to be rich. It's not a crime. You've worked hard your whole life and, admit it, for most of that time you've lived like a pauper. You don't waste money on holidays, fancy cars, clothes or any of the lovely stuff I used to buy. Your aunt left you her house, so you never had to buy one, and Kenneth invested in the same businesses that Roger did. Euphemia Sage, you are loaded. Stop feeling guilty about every cent you spend and enjoy your life.'

Euphemia opened her mouth to speak, and closed it again. She tried again and then again; the words stuck in her throat.

'If I had your money, I'd know what I'd do. Call Justin a lot of things, they would all be true, but he did know how to enjoy himself. When I remember the exciting things we did and the places we went, I don't regret any of it. Until the money ran out and he refused to get a job and had an affair with Alison then tried to steal Mummy's jewels and almost killed us. That last part wasn't so great.' She drained the last of the soup from her mug and sighed.

Jane was right. Some people would call Euphemia rich. Others would laugh at this description. She liked to think of herself as well-off, comfortable even, but that was only if she kept working. The idea of not working, of not committing the daily act of earning a living, was anathema to her. Aunt Maree and her mother were brought up by their mother on a war widow's tiny pension. It was barely enough to survive, but the state expected women to either to get on with it or marry again and live off their husbands. Many children of dead servicemen ended up in orphanages when mothers couldn't provide for them, and stepfathers didn't want them.

Freddie, her mother, had rebelled against their parsimonious upbringing, running away from their tiny home in Eastbourne to find glamour, fame, and fortune in no particular order, as soon as she was old enough. Aunt Maree, six years younger than her wildly adventurous sister, had been left behind to console her mother, who didn't understand or condone the strange yearnings of her eldest daughter.

Aunt Maree excelled at school and became an engineer when female engineers were uncommon. Undaunted, she held her own in the male dominated construction business so much so the firm promoted her to manage large projects when such a thing was unheard of. Aunt Maree supported her mother financially in her later years, taking her to live in the home left to her by her father's parents. It was Aunt Maree who opened the front door of this house in Thorndon to a three-year-old Euphemia and who had stopped work immediately and devoted her life to bringing her up. The same aunt taught Euphemia by example to be careful with money while investing wisely in the world's share markets so Euphemia would never have to worry about money again.

Yet she had. Worried about money. Euphemia only had to look to her mother to know what happened when money was squandered on fashion and lifestyle. Freddie died in poverty, dependent on a man she barely knew to put food in her mouth and a roof over her head. That same man had listened when Freddie betrayed the family's secret, and probably caused her premature death. Her mother, too proud to ask Aunt Maree for yet another favour, had died unable to afford the ticket home to see her only daughter. Was it any wonder Euphemia had never allowed herself to feel rich?

Kenneth, like Roger, hadn't cared about money, so long as there was enough and he could play golf when he wanted to. He left the actual bill paying to Euphemia. A hard worker with simple needs, he was wise with his investments just as Euphemia was with hers.

'Thanks,' she said.

'For what?'

'For making me see things. You're right, I am rich in a way. I have enough money to do what I want and not many people can say that. I'm lucky.'

'You are so lucky. You know,' she said, 'I never thought I would be so poor I couldn't do what I want. I wasn't brought up to be poor. Poverty doesn't suit me as much as it suits you. If you need any tips on how to spend your money before you get too old you know who to come to.'

'I do. But you're are wrong about the five thousand dollars. No matter how well off you are, it is still a lot of money, and I am not happy about it going to the Acceptance Institute. I dislike being duped and I hate the thought of how many others they have done this to. That's why we need to get to Oneroa before sunset.'

'Well that's not going to happen.'

'What? Margaret said it would take two hours, three max.'

'Yes. If we had gone the other way.'

'Sorry?'

'I thought you knew. This is the long way around. See those hills, in front of us. That's the Coromandel Peninsula. I wondered why we were going this way.'

'Why didn't you say?'

'Because,' said Jane. 'You and Margaret had it all sorted and you didn't ask me. We're heading in completely the wrong direction. We'll be lucky to get to Oneroa by tomorrow.

CHAPTER 35

Euphemia sprinted down the boat and jumped into the cockpit beside Margaret. Jane followed more sedately along the deck.

'What are those hills straight in front of us?' she asked pointing.

'Thompson's Point,' said Margaret. 'We go around that and we're nearly there.'

'That's not Thompson's Point,' said Jane. 'If it was, it wouldn't be that big. That's the Coromandel Peninsula.'

'Oh my,' said Margaret. She let go of the wheel, climbed onto the bench seat, put her hand up to shade her eyes, and looked around. 'You're right,' she said finally. 'Rangitoto is back there. Silly me, I've taken us in completely the wrong direction.'

'Ya think?' said Jane.

'We should have turned left, not right when we left the bay. My fault entirely. It's the weirdest thing, since I was a kid I've had problems working out right and left. I usually rely on others for direction.'

Euphemia took a long, deep breath in. Then she breathed slowly out again. 'Put it in neutral or whatever you do to stop a boat,' she said calmly. 'It's not your fault. It's my fault for trusting you. It wasn't your responsibility to say which way we should go.'

'It was totally your fault, Margaret,' said Jane. 'You're a know-it-all and a blow-hard, which makes people believe you. People,' she added, poking Euphemia in the back, 'who should know better.'

'I said I was sorry, what more do you want me to say? It's not like I did it on purpose.' She turned her back on them and sniffed loudly.

'Don't pretend you're crying, because I know you're not,' said Jane. 'Effie, what do we do? This way there isn't enough fuel to get to Oneroa.'

'I know,' said Euphemia. 'Sarah, Claire, can you come up, please?'

Claire came up first, followed several minutes later by a drowsy Sarah wiping sleep from her eyes.

'What is it?' Sarah asked when they were sitting down facing each other. 'Why aren't we moving?'

'There's been a mistake,' said Euphemia.

'It's my fault,' said Margaret. 'I feel awful.'

'So you darned well should,' said Jane. 'You took us the wrong way.'

Sarah sat up, alert now, concern on her face. Claire yawned and leaned against the guardrail, her eyes closed, her face up to the sun. 'It's no biggie,' she said. 'We turn around.'

'We haven't got enough fuel,' said Euphemia.

'We sail then,' said Claire. 'It's not like we're out here in a dinghy. This is a fifty-foot yacht.'

'Do you know how to work it?'

'No, not entirely, but we're smart women. We can figure it out. It's hardly rocket science.'

'She's right,' said Jane, nodding. 'I passed the Evan's Bay sailing course with merit. I can do this. From now on, I'll be the captain. Now, someone tell me where the wind is coming from. Ideally we want it coming from the opposite direction to where we want to go.'

'We're doomed,' said Sarah, half meaning it.

Euphemia put her arm around Sarah's shoulders and hugged her. 'We're not doomed. Claire's right. It will be fun. Using the sails will conserve what's left of the diesel for emergencies and to help us get into a mooring later.'

'Let's turn around,' said Jane. 'It's a good idea to start by pointing the boat in the direction we want to go.' She looked up at the mast. 'That's handy. There's a wind thingy, up there.'

'Oh goody, a wind thingee,' said Claire. 'I feel better already with you as captain. I'll take the cover off the main sail thingee shall I? So it will go up the mast thingee when the engine stops.'

'No need to be snarky,' said Jane. 'Euphemia, tell her.'

'You're the captain, you tell her. I'm going below to check supplies.'

CHAPTER 36

'I'M PUTTING THE SAIL UP,' YELLED JANE FIVE MINUTES
later. 'Hold on, everyone.'

Euphemia climbed out of the cabin and joined the others standing
in the crowded cockpit. Jane flicked the switch for the sail winch, and
their heads tilted back as they followed the sail up the mast until it
reached the top where, released from its ties, it flapped listlessly in the
light breeze. Suddenly, a puff of wind caught it. The boom swung
wildly from one side of the boat to the other and stopped with a
juddering thud when it reached the end of the rope. The yacht tipped
over and they all went with it, falling against each other, scrambling for
anything to hold on to, a pile of bodies heading towards the water.
Euphemia grabbed Sarah's sweatshirt as she was about to slide between
the wires of the guardrail into the sea and hauled her back on board.
Jane, clinging to the wheel, was the only one to keep her footing.

'You idiot, Claire, you're supposed to hold onto the ropes or tie
them down. One or the other.'

'You're the captain,' Claire yelled back from underneath Margaret.
'You didn't tell me to do it.'

'I'll do it,' said Margaret, pushing her aside. She stood up, climbing
onto the deck to go forward just as another gust of wind caught the sail

and it swung back the other way straight towards her. Euphemia caught the boom with one hand inches before it thwacked into the side of Margaret's head. Feet apart, she held it firmly against the bucking wind and grabbed the rope before gradually letting it out and securing it to a metal cleat on the side of the boat. The sail slackened again, fluttering against the mast. Jane turned the wheel, another gust filled the sail with an almighty whoomph and the yacht took off, leaning to the opposite side this time. Sarah, Margaret and Claire looked up at Euphemia from the floor of the cockpit.

'How did you do that?' asked Margaret. 'With the boom?'

'Instinct,' said Euphemia. 'Go below. There are life jackets on the side bunk.' She held up one end of the thin u-shaped collar she was wearing to show them what she meant. 'Put them on. Jane, here's yours.'

Euphemia took the wheel, holding it steady while Jane put it over her head and buckled up.

'I found some navigation charts in a locker,' said Euphemia. 'I should have looked for them before. It wasn't fair to rely on Margaret. If we keep the coast on our left and head west, we should get to either Onetangi or Palm Beach before dark. Either will do. We'll anchor in the bay, and I'll swim ashore and get help.'

'Except we can't anchor, can we?'

'We'll figure that out when we get there.'

'If you say so,' said Jane. The others had gone below and she sat down opposite Euphemia, wedging her feet against the seat on the low side of the boat to stay upright. The wind had picked up, and the yacht weaved from side to side as it ploughed through the waves, the boom rising high then dipping again towards the water. Using the wheel for support, her legs braced and her feet wide apart, Euphemia steered a steady course, keeping the wind behind them, the sail ballooned taut above and to one side. Without the noise of the engine, the sounds of the yacht and the sea dominated. The hull creaked, then groaned as it slammed into the waves. The ropes rattled against the mast, and the turbulence of the wake was a continuous wash cycle behind them. A seagull flew down and perched on the back guardrail, studied Jane, then let go, the wind catching it under open wings as it fell back, drifted higher and then dived low over the wake before rolling left and away back up into the sky.

'This is incredible,' said Euphemia.

'Isn't it though?' said Jane. She got up and, without letting go of a handrail screwed into the top of the cabin, staggered over to stand wide-legged beside Euphemia.

'Kenneth would love it.'

'So would Alastair.' Jane paused. 'But only if he could bring his bike. He loves his bikes more than he likes me.'

'No he doesn't.'

'Maybe he does. And so what?' She shrugged. 'I don't care as long as we can be together. He's good for me and I'm good for him. We're different and that's okay. For the first time I've found someone I like who I don't have to be with every second of every day. He doesn't expect me to run after him or tell him how well he is doing every second of the day. I don't have to baby him along so he doesn't get upset. Alastair is just as happy being on his own as he is when he is with me, and I feel the same about him. The Retreat and Selina's sessions did help me, you know. They made me see why I put up with Justin and also made me realise I don't have to do that ever again. I can be me. I don't have to prop up a man any more to be part of a couple. Selina had a special way about her. She got me so I listened to what she said.'

Euphemia felt the same. Selina's questions in their one and only session had got to the core of why she was feeling so unsettled. She still had to work out the answers but for the first time in her life, someone had dared to ask her the questions she was asking herself. Selina hadn't assumed she was competent in every situation or that she didn't need help.

'I don't have to be with Alastair to keep the relationship going. I can be me and that's okay,' said Jane. 'I'm still working out what me is. Which is also the point. Maybe I never will. Maybe I'll die not knowing, but I do know I will know more than I know now, and more than I knew yesterday. If you know what I mean?'

'That's a lot of knows,' said Euphemia laughing. 'But I know what you mean.'

'Everyone has to keep searching for answers, for experiences. You can't get to a certain age or stage and just pack up and say you've done all you're going to do. Age is no excuse for chickening out of life.'

Euphemia stared open-mouthed at this new woman. Jane had been browbeaten for years into middle-class conformity, first by her mother and then by her husband. The new Jane was standing beside her, her eyes lit with the excitement of the moment, new energy surging through her body. She stood on the tips of her toes and leaned over the roof of the cabin eagerly searching the sea ahead, unafraid for might would come, on a yacht she didn't know how to sail.

'Full credit to you Jane French. You have figured out your life just as you said you would,' said Euphemia.

'Yeah,' said Jane smiling. 'Listen to me. I said Yeah instead of Yes. Mummy would roll in her grave if she heard that and do you know what?'

'No, tell me.'

Jane put her head back and screamed at the sky. 'I. Don't. Care. What. Mummy. Thinks. Any. More.'

Jane's abandonment was infectious. Euphemia started laughing. Jane did too and together they laughed until they wept, until Euphemia, squatting down, one leg wrapped around the other to stop herself peeing, handed over the wheel and scuttled into the cabin to the toilet before she wet her pants and disgraced herself completely.

'What was that all about?' asked Sarah when she emerged from the loo.

'Acceptance,' said Euphemia. 'Sheer unadulterated magisterial acceptance.'

CHAPTER 37

THEY HEARD IT COMING BEFORE THEY FELT IT. THE WIND ripped across the waves and slammed into the sail, stalling the yacht in the water. Claire fell off her seat, landing on the floor. Margaret too got knocked over, putting her hand through the partition as she fell. Sarah tossed over the back of the seat, her head just missing the edge of the table, tried to sit up and couldn't. Luckily, the kettle which was coming to the boil stayed behind the guards surrounding the gas hob, but water splashed from the spout, dousing the flame.

'A warning would be helpful.' Margaret called out.

'There wasn't time,' said Jane. 'Come up and take over if you think you can do better.'

'A pet hamster could do better,' muttered Claire as she followed Euphemia and Margaret up the steps.

'Crikey, where did that come from?'

'Over there,' said Jane. They turned and looked out to sea. Earlier, the hazy blue outline of the Barrier Islands had been clearly visible in front of the yacht. Now they were completely obscured by a curtain of dense grey cloud stretching from sky to sea coming straight towards them. In front of it, the sea had turned to a sickly grey green beneath a mess of white-topped waves. Euphemia turned around to look at the flat blue calm below the cloudless blue sky they were leaving behind. Above, the sail tugged restlessly at the mast, not sure which way to billow, opting for pointless flapping as the boom tugged at the rope.

'I'll get the sail down,' said Jane. 'It'll need two of you to tie it onto the boom so it doesn't fall over the cabin.' She flicked the switch to winch the sail down, but nothing happened.

'I'll check the fuse box,' said Euphemia. She jumped down the steps into the cabin, only to return a few minutes later shaking her head. 'Looks okay, try again.' Jane flicked the switch again. Nothing.

'You'll have to bring it down by hand,' she said. 'Margaret, Claire, get up there and start pulling. Hurry! No, stop. Hold on. The next squall is on its way.'

'We don't know how long this is going to last,' Euphemia said. 'Sarah throw the jackets hanging next to the loo up here. Claire, check under the seats for safety harnesses. From now on, everyone outside the cabin must be tied on at all times.'

'I thought she was the captain,' said Margaret, pointing at Jane.

'Yeah,' said Claire.

'The captain is telling you both to grow up and do what Effie says. Now!' yelled Jane.

Sarah tossed the pile of jackets onto the floor and they each took one and put it on.

'Sweet mother of sanity,' said Jane. 'Put them under your life jackets, not over them.'

Dressed in her yellow waterproof jacket, attached to the guardrail by a rope and carabiner, Euphemia led the way forward. Claire followed her while Margaret watched. The front of the boat dropped low into the trough of a wave as they stepped onto the roof of the cabin, except the roof was no longer there. Their feet found only air, and they fell, rolling across the side, down onto the narrow deck to jam against the guardrail, the sea within touching distance, through the wires. Euphemia lifted Claire off her and they tried again. With legs wide apart, knees bent and one eye on the sea ahead, they grabbed the boom for support and walked along it to the mast. Claire unwound the rope from its cleat and together they grabbed a handful of sail and pulled down. The sail dropped a few feet, then jammed. They tried again, but to no avail.

Euphemia focused her vision and, high on the mast, saw a knot in the rope which blocked the little tube the edge of the sail was supposed to run down.

A gust of wind, this time fully laden with salt spray, hit them. The sail swung the boom out of their grasp and across the boat until it slammed against the end of the rope. The yacht skewed around, dropping side on to the rolling swell. Water poured into the cockpit and the open hatch at the front. It swept across the top of the cabin, washing over their feet, taking ropes and anything not tied down with it. The boat rolled, the top of the mast dipped into the sea, the sail filled with water and for a moment it felt like they were going down until, caught by another wave, it thankfully rolled upright again.

'The hatch,' yelled Euphemia, pointing. Sarah and Margaret disappeared into the cabin.

Jane dragged the wheel around and, once again, they were pointing into the waves.

'I'm going up,' yelled Euphemia.

'You can't,' screamed Claire, the wind whipping the words from her mouth. She turned her head away from the salt-spray stinging her eyes and wiped the hair from her face. When she turned back, Euphemia was halfway up the mast.

Hand over hand, foot over foot, she climbed it the same way people climb coconut trees until she reached the top where she hooked a rope onto the crossbar. The mast was still swinging wildly from side to side, dipping down one moment, then sideways the next as the yacht made hard work of the sea. She wiped her eyes, squinting against the wind. Up here, she could see the weather was getting worse, not better. This wasn't a summer squall that would be gone as quickly as it had arrived. It was a full-blown storm. Thick grey clouds blanketed the sky in every direction, blocking out any view of land. Bands of heavy rain swept across the water, wind spinning the tops of waves into air-borne foam, which flew up only to be pelted down. They could have been in the middle of the Pacific Ocean hundreds of miles from anywhere. Equally, she knew they could be heading straight into the side of a cliff. Shipwrecked with no one knowing where they were.

The sooner she got the sail down, the sooner they would be safe.

Not safe exactly, but safer. She might know nothing about sailing, but she knew about physics and gravity. If the boat rolled in full sail, there was no coming up again and they would go straight to the bottom. The knot, soaked, swollen and tight, was difficult to prise open, but she worked away at it until it disappeared. She looked down for Claire to tell her to pull, but the deck was empty. Only Jane was visible, holding the wheel with all her might, peering through the rain as she tried to antici- pate which way the storm would push them next.

Her only option was to jump. Which she did, flying to the bottom holding onto the rope, dragging the sail down with her. Still, the wind caught the fabric, sending it billowing out over the sea, then whipping it back in her face, before she finally managed to bundle it into her arms, wrap it around the boom and secure it. The sail down she pointed the boom to the back of the yacht, which she guessed was as neutral as it could get, and secured it, doubling the ropes back and across before fastening them into the cleats and the holders behind them. A quick survey of the decks to check the hatches were secure and she could see the waves had taken life-rings, buoys, and a stick thing with a hook on the end. She didn't know what they used it for, but right now it didn't matter.

'Jane, are you okay?'

Jane nodded, pushed her hair out of her eyes, and grinned. 'This is great!' she yelled.

'Well, hang on. Because it's going to get a lot worse,' said Euphemia. She pointed to the compass. 'Head north as much as you can,' she said. 'It's open sea. Safer than running into the side of the island.'

Jane's grin faltered for a second. 'Aye, aye, Captain' she said, taking her hand off the wheel to flick a quick salute.

Euphemia returned with both thumbs up then went below, to be greeted by chaos. Seat cushions upended, books and papers tossed out of racks, bottles, cups and cutlery floating in two inches of water which sloshed backwards and forwards across the floor. Claire's bottom was poking out of the door to the loo. Between wind gusts, she heard loud groans followed by vomiting. Margaret was attempting to mop up the grubby water slopping around the cabin, but the bucket kept falling over, spilling everything she had just collected. Sarah was stuffing tins of food back into cupboards, the remains of broken jars piled high in the sink.

Sarah stopped what she was doing and held out an open box of crackers. Euphemia took a handful and crunched into them, only realising how hungry she was when she tasted the tang of rosemary and garlic. She held out her hand for more. Sarah shook some into her palm, then passed the box up to Jane. 'How much longer?' she asked.

'I don't know. But we need to be prepared. It's going to get worse before it gets better. Tie everything down in here. Jane and I will take turns up top.'

'I'll help,' said Margaret. 'You take a break.' She picked up the bucket and carried it up the steps. Bracing herself against the seat, and holding onto the top guardrail, she tried to empty the contents over the side. The wind caught the bucket, wrenching it from her. It was gone, bouncing off the waves behind them until it disappeared into the grey mist. Euphemia watched it go, annoyed that Margaret hadn't tied a rope around the handle before going up on deck. It would be the obvious thing to do in these conditions but it was too late to say anything now, and it was more important to maintain morale for what was coming than to vent for mistakes made now. Like the hatch being left open and the life-rings on top of the cabin not being tied down and the stick with the hook on the end going overboard. There were too many mistakes for it to be just carelessness.

'Sarah,' she said. 'Somewhere in here there will be flares, emergency lights, and, I am hoping, an inflatable life raft. Can you help me look?'

'Is it that bad?' Sarah asked.

'Better to be prepared, that's all. You take that side of the cabin and the back bunk, and I'll search up front.'

She stepped over Claire's ankles, then stopped to see if she was all right. The poor girl had nothing left in her stomach to bring up and was instead dry heaving into the loo. She lifted her head and smiled weakly at Euphemia.

'How are you doing?'

'Been better,' she croaked, then groaned as another wave lifted the boat. Claire clung to the porcelain while Euphemia held onto the door. The yacht almost did a headstand as it surfed down the steep side of the wave in to the trough where it bottomed out, wallowing sickeningly until the nose lifted again. Claire turned back, retching repeatedly into the loo.

Euphemia found the life raft, stowed in its airless state under the double bunk at the front of the boat. She called to Sarah to help and together they heaved it out, replaced the wooden slats and cushions and laid it on top. It was heavy, but then it was also big enough to take six people. It said so on the side.

'Hopefully we won't need it,' said Sarah.

'I'm sure we won't. But it would be better to have it near the opening so we can use it if we need to. You take the front and I'll take the back and we'll carry it down to the bunk opposite the galley.'

Euphemia could easily have managed this by herself, but she realised it was better to keep people occupied. And it helped if they were invested in managing the situation as a team. That way, they would hopefully act in the best interests of the group when things got worse and not as individuals desperate to save only themselves. She prayed to the god she didn't believe in that it wouldn't get that bad. Her super powers could only go so far in these seas.

CHAPTER 38

JANE LOOKED BOTH ELATED AND EXHAUSTED WHEN SHE CAME below. There was fire in her eyes and weariness in her bones and muscles. She changed into dry clothes and wolfed down the cold baked beans on the plate, which Sarah handed to her. At the sound of the can opener, Claire had groaned loudly, gagged twice, and crawled off to the front bunk, pulled a tarpaulin over her head and lay curled up against the hull for support. Margaret was at the helm now, the doors to the cockpit sealed shut against the weather. The three women sat huddled together around the table, sharing what body heat they had left as steam rose from their wet clothes.

'How long has it been?' asked Sarah.

Euphemia checked her watch. 'A couple of hours.'

'We'll be out here in the dark. We need lights in this weather or no one will see us.'

'I'm pretty sure they'll come on automatically. The battery isn't flat,' said Euphemia.

'Thank goodness,' replied Sarah, sinking into the collar of her jacket.

The nose of the boat rose, then fell as it went over the crest of a wave, sliding down the other side, shuddering as the rudder grabbed the water. They gripped the edge of the table, waiting for the moment to pass and some sort of equilibrium to be established. A tiny scream came from under the tarpaulin at the front.

'What do you think they're doing at home?' asked Jane. She didn't wait for them to answer, but carried on through gritted teeth. 'Alastair will finish work about now. If the weather's fine, he'll detour around Oriental Bay on his bike. What day is it?'

'Friday?' said Sarah.

'Saturday,' said Euphemia.

'Then he won't be at work. He had a club ride this morning. Coffee after. I hope he hasn't kept up with the kale smoothies while I've been away.'

'He must really like you, because they were truly disgusting,' said Euphemia.

'Healthy though.'

'Are they? Really? Nothing that tastes that bad can be healthy. It's like drinking lawn clippings.'

'I wish I could call him and tell him he doesn't have to drink them anymore,' said Jane.

'Tomorrow,' said Euphemia. 'We'll get through this, sail to the nearest harbour and we'll be back in Wellington in no time.'

'I hope you're right,' said Sarah. 'Will John and Sophie ever forgive me for what I've put them through?'

'They'll just be pleased to see you again. Nothing else will matter. If you'll have us, Kenneth and I will do everything we can to get your money back.'

'Kenneth.' Sarah put her hand to her mouth and gasped. 'I owe him an apology for the way I spoke to him. I was so rude.'

'He's a big boy. He can take it.'

'He was right, though. I should have listened to him.'

'He's usually right,' said Jane. 'He's a wise man and Sage Consulting would not be where it is today without him.'

'Ahem,' said Euphemia. 'I'm sitting right here.'

'You're good at what you do, Effie. But he's a man and there's a difference,' said Jane.

'What difference?'

'It's just that men are still, well, you know, better.'

'I don't know that at all. How can you sit here and say that to my face? You've seen how hard I work and the clients who come to me and not Kenneth for advice.'

'That's because you're always at the office. You should take time off like he does. Get a hobby. Play golf.'

'I don't want to play golf. I run. That's my hobby.'

'Not what I would call a hobby, more like a....' Jane screwed up her face as she tried to find the right word. 'Thing. Anyone can do it. There's no skill involved. Just one foot in front of the other. Running is like walking except faster.'

'You're not a feminist, are you Jane?' Euphemia, already horrified that any woman would hold such antiquated views about the competency of men and women in business, was shocked that Jane, her friend, her employee, could believe such things. In the twenty-first century.

'I never said I was,' said Jane. 'I believe in women voting and that sort of thing, but I'm not a feminist. I wear a bra and I don't go around telling men off.'

'That's not what feminists do, and Gloria Steinem wore a bra.'

'I don't know who you're talking about.'

'Only a very famous founder of the feminist movement back in the 1970s. That's who she is.'

'I was at school then. After school I did my OE in Europe with Mummy. The women back then in New Zealand weren't very interesting. Or famous.'

'She's an American,' said Euphemia.

'That explains it,' said Jane. She sat back, folded her hands across the front of her yellow parka and nodded to emphasise she had been right all along.

'Sarah, you're a feminist, aren't you?'

'What does that even mean? On the one hand, I support women's rights but I've always had Roger to take care of the important stuff like money and repairs around the house. I'm not like you,' said Sarah. 'I didn't work when the children were young. Now they're grown, I'm stuck at home. Employers don't want someone old who doesn't know her way around a computer.'

'I didn't know about computers,' said Jane. 'That hasn't stopped me from working and being an independent-enough woman.'

Euphemia bit her tongue. Hard. She tasted blood behind her pursed lips as she remembered the agony they had silently endured during Jane's first weeks at Sage Consulting. Patiently and repeatedly taken through the basics of the appointment software, Jane still made mistakes and double booked people or forgot about them all together.

The front of the boat ploughed under a wave, and they stopped talking, holding their breaths while the brave yacht struggled and broke free, but not before it rolled, tipping them out of their seats across the top of the table and onto the wet floor. Euphemia got to her feet first, helped the others back into their seats, and told them to hang on and stay put.

She staggered up and opened the door to the cockpit. Water poured down the steps, running down the cabin to the front then surging back again as the boat tipped to the side. She climbed out to see Margaret clinging to the wheel, her arms wrapped around it, her feet sliding out from under her first one way, then the other.

'I've been yelling and yelling,' she said. 'My hands are frozen, and I can't hold on much longer. It's getting worse.'

'Go below,' said Euphemia. 'I'll take over.'

* * *

FOUR HOURS LATER, the sea had died down to a steady roll as the swell from the north beat its way down the coast. It was dark. There were no stars. An occasional squall brushed the yacht with pelting rain, but otherwise the wind had dropped and along with it the noise which had been battering their ears for the last eight hours. The battery had come through and the white lights on top of the mast and at the stern advertised their presence to other vessels, along with the requisite green and red side lights. Euphemia let go of the wheel and peeked inside the cabin. They were asleep. Sarah and Jane had curled up on the seats around the table. The lump under the tarpaulin on the front bunk hadn't moved and Margaret's feet jutted out from the side bunk where she must be wrapped around the life raft.

The compass pointed to northeast, out towards the open sea. Euphemia didn't know how far they had come in the storm or where they were in relation to the many islands which lay along the East Coast of the top of the North Island. For all she knew, they could be in the same place they had been when she brought the sail down close to their destination. All she had to do now was keep them upright while watching for ships and land. When daylight came she would re-orientate herself. So much for beating Sarah's documents to the Institute's lawyers. It would have been faster for her to have run into town than risk all their lives on a yacht she didn't know how to sail to take them to a place she didn't know how to get to.

She couldn't believe Margaret had taken them the wrong way. The woman had been clear to the point of being adamant that she knew the way to go. Euphemia decided it was best to go along with her, trusting the certainty in her voice. She shook her head at the events of the last day. What sort of super woman gets duped like that? Barbara would never have let it happen to her. But Barbara would never have gone to a place she knew nothing about, only to be starved, locked up and spied upon. Alternatively she would also never have discovered what was going on behind the scenes or figured out the real reason the Retreat existed. Euphemia's gullibility had its advantages. The prime one being it didn't make people suspicious.

She had fitted into the regime at the Retreat so well no one questioned how she had kicked out their walls so they could escape. They were all too glad to be free. She had used her powers in the most public way possible, and there hadn't been a whimper of curiosity, just gratitude. Gratitude and, ironically... acceptance.

CHAPTER 39

'You should rest,' said Margaret, climbing up beside her. 'I'll take over.'

Euphemia nodded, then yawned. It was 3.00 AM, and she had been at the helm for six hours, during which she had piloted the yacht through the worst of the storm. The muscles in her legs and back ached, her hands were numb from gripping the wheel in the cold.

'Thanks,' she said. 'You're right.'

'Go below. There's a hot drink on the bench.' She held her own steaming mug of a chocolaty smelling drink in one hand and took the wheel with the other. 'I'll wake you when it's light.'

Euphemia shuffled down the steps, holding onto the handrail because she didn't trust her legs to bend at the knees after being in the brace position for so long. The hot drink was exactly what she needed. She took a sip, luxuriating as the warmth ran down the inside of her chest to her stomach, her hunger settling with the sugar hit. It was so sweet, Margaret must have put half the packet into her cup.

Jane's head appeared over the top of the seat. She opened an eye beneath tousled hair, saw who it was, smiled groggily and lay down again. And started snoring. Softly at first and then, as was her style, the snorting started and grew louder and louder until she made that choking sound in the back of her throat which Euphemia knew so well. Silence followed. An unnerving silence which lasted for seconds longer than was comfortable to listen to without feeling the need to check for signs of life. Euphemia leaned over to look at her and was greeted by the snorts, starting again in earnest. She picked up a pillow. Soaked through, it was useless for what she had in mind. The wet would wake Jane before the smothering was done. Surprisingly, Sarah, on the opposite bunk, slept on regardless, as did Claire up the front under her tarpaulin.

Euphemia shunted her murderous intent to the back of her mind, cleared a space next to the life raft, and lay down. Her eyes closed. Her head swam before the snoring grew louder, then faded to nothing. As she drifted off to sleep, she made a mental note to take Jane to an ENT surgeon when they got home. It might be a drastic measure. It might even be expensive, but it would be worth it to fix the snoring.

She dreamt that desserts of all shapes and sizes surrounded her. Some were hot, some cold. Hot fruit pies with cold ice-cream. Chocolate-covered strawberries, her favourite. Baked Alaskas, the meringue crushed and broken into crumbs, the ice-cream inside melting and running off the plate. Caramel sauce oozed from nougat speckled eggs, feijoa crumbled under lashings of whipped cream. A tall Pavlova topped with cream and slices of kiwifruit displayed in circles beckoned. They were all at the end of her very long spoon. She reached out and had scooped up a strawberry only to have the spoon dashed from her hand. The strawberry rolled across the floor to a boot, which slammed down, crushing it to a pulpy smear.

The desserts disappeared. The boot lifted, and it nudged her side, rocking her until she opened her eyes. Sunshine shone through the window onto the filthy floor of the cabin.

'Get up, the others are waiting,' said Margaret.

Euphemia eased herself upright, pain splitting her head in two. 'Are we there?'

'As far as you're going. Get up.' She toed Euphemia's thigh again. 'Move.'

Euphemia stopped herself from grabbing the boot, lifting it high and upending the woman on the floor. Instead, she looked up, confused, and rubbed her eyes. 'Why are you kicking me?'

'Get up. The others are in the raft.'

'What raft?'

Margaret sighed. 'Move,' she said, grabbing her by an arm and pulling her to her feet. Euphemia's head protested. Her eyes betrayed her, and she lost her balance, staggering against Margaret, who impatiently pushed her off. The inside of Euphemia's mouth was dry. When she tried to swallow, a bitter taste ricocheted from the insides of her cheeks to the back of her tongue. 'You drugged me,' she said thickly.

'I did,' said Margaret. 'Now hurry up. I haven't got all day.' She pushed Euphemia in front of her, up the steps and into the cockpit. It was a beautiful, sunny morning. The sea looked nothing like the roiling, heaving cauldron of last night. It was dead calm. Not a whiff of breeze disturbed its surface under the clear blue sky. All she could see was ocean and sky stretching in every direction. There was no land in sight. In the life raft tied to the back of the yacht, sat Sarah, Jane, and Claire looking up at her, fear on their faces.

'Effie, are you okay?' asked Jane.

'Get in,' said Margaret, prodding Euphemia in the back.

'Or what?' said Euphemia.

'Or I will start my yacht and when I reach six knots, if the raft is still the right way up, I will cut them free to sink or swim as the gods of the ocean see fit. I don't care.'

'The company you built up from nothing,' said Euphemia. 'You didn't sell it, did you?'

'Clever girl. Now get in.'

'And you own the Acceptance Institute.'

'I do.' Margaret unhooked a rope across the back of the boat and pushed Euphemia down the steps. The choice was to either step into the raft with the others or to turn around and disable Margaret. She decided on the second option. It was simpler. She knew all she needed to know. Plus she was really very tired of being told what to do and when to do it by bossy women.

'Look away,' she said to the women in the boat.

'Why?' asked Jane.

'Just do it,' said Euphemia.

'Get in the raft,' said Margaret, giving her another push.

'Push me once more and I won't be responsible for what I do,' said Euphemia through clenched teeth.

Margaret pushed her again.

Euphemia ducked down, gripped Margaret around both knees, hoisted her straight up in the air, then with her hands beneath her feet Euphemia propelled her over the back of the raft like a missile headfirst into the sea.

'Wow!' said Sarah. 'I mean WOW!'

'How did you do that?' asked Claire. 'That was amazing.'

Jane turned around. 'What did she do? What is WOW? What was amazing? Why has Margaret gone swimming? What did I miss? That's not fair, Effie. I turned around like you said and I missed it.'

CHAPTER 40

'COMFORTABLE?' JANE RAISED HER MUG OF TEA TO Margaret, who was lying tied up like a calf at a rodeo at the bottom of the life raft. It was bobbling around in the wake at the end of a twenty-foot rope as the yacht puttered along under sail.

Margaret glared back at her beneath her wet hair and mouthed two vulgar words. Jane smiled, raised her mug again, and sat down next to Sarah. Euphemia, at the helm, looked up at the sail flapping now and then in the light breeze. They were making steady progress on their journey back to Waiheke. Claire passed a mug of coffee to Euphemia and climbed up to join them.

'Don't you think you should tell us what's been going on?' said Sarah.

They looked at Euphemia, who turned to Claire and said, 'You first. You're the cop.'

'What? No one tells me anything,' said Jane.

'How did you know?' asked Claire.

'I suspected you might be,' said Euphemia. 'Better pull Margaret closer so she can hear what we have to say.'

Jane wound in the rope. 'Euphemia told me to bring you closer,' she said. 'She wants you to hear the next bit. I'll catch you up. Claire is a cop. And BTW you're done for.' She grinned and flounced back to her seat.

Margaret snarled and mouthed several more very rude words.

'We're not listening to filth, are we, girls?' Jane said, turning her back on the raft.

Euphemia was mystified as to why Jane was taking so much taking pleasure in Margaret's fall from grace. She hadn't been this chirpy after her triumphant dumping of Kevin at Oakhill Station last year, or when Alison Sinclair was publicly dumped by Justin. Something about Margaret's situation had exposed a mother lode of schadenfreude, that delight in another's misery which is usually concealed in polite company.

Euphemia keeping her eye on the sea ahead, called back to Claire over her shoulder, 'I knew you weren't in on the scam when you left me in the office and took Margaret back to her room. That plus the way you drove the van.'

'What do you mean?' asked Claire.

'You drove it like a cop, carefully but professionally, especially when we got onto the gravel. You'd had lessons. Empathic healers aren't usually rally drivers, or is that me being prejudiced? Anyway, the thing that clinched it was you were also a terrible yoga teacher. You sped through the poses, and they were too basic. Yoga at the Retreat used to get five star reviews on Trip Advisor from women who had spent their adult lives going to classes. I could have lifted your sessions straight from the internet.'

'I told you it was like a You Tube class. How did you know? You don't do yoga,' said Jane.

'Research. Claire copied the same class I found on the internet before I left. With a few extras thrown in, but not many,' said Euphemia.

'I should have copied the intermediate and not the beginner's level. No one noticed except you and Jane.'

'And me,' yelled Margaret over the sound of the wake. 'Selina made a big mistake hiring you.' She lifted her head from the puddle of water on the bottom of the raft. 'I knew you were a fake...'

'No one cares what you think,' yelled Jane.

Claire raised her eyebrows but carried on. 'That's why she let me come aboard. She wanted to monitor me.'

'Spy,' yelled Margaret.

'And I wanted to keep an eye on her, but the storm came up and I got seasick. I am never going on a boat again in my life. I hate to think what she would have done if Euphemia hadn't been on to her.'

'I would have got away, that's what,' Margaret yelled. 'I'm letting the rope out,' said Jane. 'She keeps interrupting.'

'Don't,' said Euphemia. 'I want her to tell us what she has been doing.'

'It's obvious,' said Jane. 'She's been stealing money from guests like Sarah. She makes them sign over their assets to her and banks the lot.'

'Why do you keep her around, Euphemia? She's not very smart, is she?' yelled Margaret.

'That does it,' said Jane. She got up and untied the rope and let it out. Except in her haste, she let it go completely. The little raft slid up one side of the wake, bounced down on the other side, turned over, then over again. Jane's hand flew to her mouth. In shock, she pointed at the upside-down raft floating away behind and to the side of the boat. No body, in particular, no Margaret, bobbing to the surface beside it.

Without hesitating, Jane kicked off her shoes, climbed over the guardrail and dived in, disappearing before surfacing and striking out to the spot where the raft had overturned. Sarah and Claire yelled at Euphemia to stop, to turn the boat around.

Euphemia turned the wheel, and ran to release the ropes from their cleats. The boom swept across the back of the boat, arriving at the end of its arc with such a thud; the yacht heeled over, side on to the waves and the breeze. The keel rose from the water; the sail landed flat on the ocean and began filling up, pulling the boat further over and down. Claire and Sarah, thrown into the sea, their faces white with the horror of their situation, trod water behind the stricken yacht.

Euphemia, still hanging onto the wheel with both hands, yelled at them. 'Swim to the raft. Help Jane find Margaret.' Claire didn't need to be told twice, and struck out, swimming neatly through the water. Sarah swivelled around after Claire then turned back to Euphemia.

'Go,' yelled Euphemia.

'I can't leave you,' Sarah yelled back. Sensibly, she had inflated her life jacket. 'Tell me what to do.' The contents of the cabin popped up and floated around her, seat cushions, cups, plates, knives, forks and shoes bobbed on the surface.

'Swim around the mast. Try to keep the sail flat on the surface. Don't let it fill with water,' said Euphemia. She had braced herself upright across the upended cockpit. Sarah set off. Sensibly, she started at the top of the mast and slogged her way down the length of the sail, lifting it as she went until it became too heavy, and she had to stop.

Quickly estimating the height of the mast and the weight of the boat in order to calculate the force required to right it Euphemia got the answer. It was a lot. And getting bigger by the minute. Each second wasted was another hundred gallons of heavy water pouring into the cabin. It was an impossible task. Or was it? There was no way she could right the yacht from on board. A bubble of air erupted from inside, nearly knocking her off her feet as it surged past her.

'It's hopeless,' screamed Sarah. 'The sail's filling up. Get out before she goes down.'

'Hold on for as long as you can,' Euphemia called back. 'Just make sure you can swim free if she goes.'

Euphemia waded into the cabin, retrieved a rope, and dived in. She swam to the top of the mast and tied the rope to another. 'You're doing well, won't be long,' she said to Sarah as she swam around the front, then out to sea and out of sight.

Sarah was too busy baling water from the tip of the sail to notice.

CHAPTER 41

JANE LEANED AGAINST THE WALL OF THE ONEROA POLICE station, wrapped in a blanket. Beside her in the same grey woollen standard police-issue blankets sat Sarah and, on a chair opposite, Claire. Their hair was still damp, their bare feet stuck out from the bottom of the blankets, and they were holding mugs of hot tea in their hands. The ambulance with Margaret in it, its siren on full had just left on its way to the helicopter pad. From there she would be airlifted to Auckland Hospital.

'Margaret will be fine,' said Claire. 'The paramedics are taking her to Auckland as a precaution. There's nothing wrong with her that a spell of contemplation in a prison cell won't cure.'

'Are you sure? I don't like what she tried to do, but she doesn't deserve to die,' said Sarah. 'If it hadn't been for you Jane, she would have.'

'Claire helped,' said Jane. She pulled her blanket up over her shoulders and sipped her tea.

'No,' said Claire. 'You're the hero. You got to her before she sank too far. You carried her to the surface and kept her afloat. I helped you get her onto the raft. That's all I did.'

'If you say so,' said Jane. She smiled into her cup, bridling with pleasure. 'I've never been a hero before, but you're right. I am. Life-saving lessons at school really paid off. You know, I have my bronze medallion.'

'You told us,' said Sarah. 'In the police car.'

'And the bar to the bronze medallion,' said Jane. 'That's much harder to get.'

'You told us that, too. Three times. Once on the raft, once in the police car and now, here.'

Jane sniffed. 'I won't mention it again.' She put down her mug and pulled the grey wool blanket tightly around her.

'You're allowed,' said Sarah. 'You're a hero, and you don't need a qualification to prove it. Margaret would have drowned if you hadn't done what you did.'

'After this is over, I'm going to recommend you for a medal,' said Claire. 'For bravery. You deserve it.'

Jane looked up from the depths of her grey blanket, her face flushed. 'I did what anyone would do. Under the circumstances. All I did was to swim the three hundred yards to where I saw her go down, then dive under and look for her in the middle of the ocean. When I got to her, she was sinking fast. I don't know whose idea it was to tie her up, but the poor thing didn't stand a chance.'

'You were the one who said to tie her up,' said Sarah quietly.

'If I remember correctly, it was a joint decision,' said Jane. 'Anyway, it doesn't matter. I pulled her towards me, breathed into her mouth giving her all the air I had in my lungs. Then it was simple enough to swim her to the surface, sixty feet above.'

'Probably twenty feet, not sixty,' said Sarah. 'If you swam up too fast from sixty feet, you would get the bends and you don't have them. Neither does she. So it can't have even been twenty feet because I have heard of people getting the bends at twenty feet.'

Jane rolled her eyes. 'Gosh, aren't you finicky? It was a long way up. Leave it at that.'

'Good idea,' said Sarah. 'What you did was amazing, but you'd better get the details right before you talk to the press.'

'Will they be interested? 'They won't. Will they? I've never talked to the press before. Will they want a photo? They can't take one now. My hair is a mess. I haven't had my roots done for three months. Nell said not to put chemicals on or in my body and especially not on my hair. I will not have my photograph taken until I have been to a hairdresser, a good one.'

'We have to give our statements first,' said Claire. 'We can get tidied up after.'

'I'm going to need more than a tidy up,' said Jane. 'I need the works. Hair, face, Botox, make-up, and clothes, not gym gear. I want to go home and have my people work on me. Not strangers.'

'Who said the magic word?' asked Euphemia as she walked in, her blanket around her shoulders.

'Hero?' asked Jane.

'Not hero, although you are one. Home, that's the magic word,' said Euphemia. 'I like Waiheke. The beaches are beautiful, and the police have been lovely, but going home to Kenneth and Petal is better.' She looked at Sarah. 'They want to talk to you now,' she said. 'Don't worry, it'll be fine. Tell them what you told us in the life raft. They've already got statements from Selina and Nell.'

Sarah stood up and followed a young constable into a room at the end of a short corridor.

'More tea, anyone?' asked another constable emerging from a tiny kitchen. 'I found some Tim Tams hidden at the back of a cupboard.' He waggled the packet at them.

Claire sprang up and grabbed it. 'Double chocolate, my favourite. You have a friend for life.' She ripped open the packet and passed it around. 'And I will have another cup of tea,' she called.

'Me too,' called Euphemia and Jane together.

Jane hesitated when the packet reached her, her hand hovered over the biscuits sandwiching chocolate cream and coated in a double layer of thick milk chocolate. She went in but stopped mid-pick. 'I've been so good for so long and I've lost a lot of weight. I feel renewed and incredibly healthy, but...' She stopped, took two from the packet and bit into one. Her eyes shut and as she slowly chewed the biscuit, a smile spread across her face. 'Bliss,' she said, and took another bite.

Constable Hunter, who looked barely old enough to be out of school, let alone a member of Her Majesty's police force, returned with a tray of steaming mugs and offered these to the women.

'A local reporter has asked to interview you,' he said. 'Before the Auckland lot get here. The ferry arrives in half an hour and there's eight reporters on board. Two news crews will arrive by helicopter in ten minutes. One from TVNZ and the other Al Jazeera.'

'How do you know that?' asked Claire.

'It's a small island,' he said. 'The ferry captain lives in the next bay to my grandmother and the helicopter pilot is my sister. The local reporter is my cousin.'

Claire, impressed with the detailed intel, nodded. 'Ladies, what do you want to do?'

'The story of me rescuing Margaret and saving her life must come out some time, but I am not talking to anyone looking like this. I don't want my grey hair on TV and I don't want to be called old. They make out that anyone over fifty has to be not only decrepit but feeble-minded, too. Have you seen those ads for retirement villages? Patronising rubbish. No,' she said putting her hand up. 'I am not available for interviews. I will fabulous and young again before I say a word.'

'Me too,' said Euphemia.

'Me too,' said Claire.

'You don't need to worry,' said Euphemia. 'You are young!'

'You're also the investigating officer, so you aren't allowed to speak to the press,' added Constable Hunter.

'Which reminds me,' said Jane. 'You haven't told us what was really happening at the Retreat.'

'Ladies,' interrupted Constable Hunter, 'since you don't want to talk to the press, I'll take you to the house where you'll be staying tonight.'

'What about clothes?' asked Euphemia. 'We can't walk around in blankets.'

'Your belongings have been brought up from the Retreat. We also found your phones in the office, and Constable Morton has charged them for you. They're waiting for you at the house.'

The women thanked him so profusely he retreated into the kitchen, blushing to the roots of his short blonde hair.

'I can't believe Selina and Nell turned themselves in,' said Jane. 'Why?'

'Conscience?' suggested Euphemia.

There wasn't time to continue the discussion. Constable Hunter locked the kitchen door and led them out the back door to a car. The house they were going to was only a short distance from the station, and when they pulled into the sandy driveway beside the little wooden batch, Jane whooped with delight. 'It's gorgeous,' she said. 'It's right on the beach.' She leapt out of the car, forgetting that a grey police blanket was the only thing between her, her underwear, the cool evening air and the neighbour who was having a barbecue on his deck. Constable Hunter quickly looked away. Euphemia picked up the blanket and handed it to her.

Jane looked at it and shook her head. 'I don't need it. It's a beautiful evening. I'm going for a swim.' She ran down the beach in her bra and knickers straight into the water and dived over a wave.

'You think she'd be sick of the sea after what we've been through,' said Claire.

'I blame two double chocolate Tim Tams after three months of sugar abstinence,' said Euphemia.

CHAPTER 42

EUPHEMIA FELT LIKE SHE HAD BEEN AWAY FOR MONTHS instead of only a week when she face-timed her family later that night. Tacked onto the end of the evening bulletin had been news of their rescue, but it mentioned only cursory details of a storm and a yacht capsizing out to sea. No names, and it ended with the statement that one person was taken to hospital for a check-up, but that there was no reason for alarm. There was nothing about what happened at the Retreat. As they hadn't expected to hear from her for another week, they hadn't considered she might be involved.

Kenneth was pre-occupied with a marketing issue when she spoke to him. Kezia was still at work and in a hurry to get a set of accounts finished so she could look at a house with Ben. Nicky and Dave were out to dinner at a new restaurant with police colleagues, so they couldn't say much other than they would call her again in the morning. Petal was the only one who smiled when she heard Euphemia's voice and she couldn't be sure that the smile hadn't really been for Jane.

'Barbara's private secretary, Scottie, wants you to call him,' said Kenneth. 'He said it wasn't urgent.'

Deflated by the lack of family interest in their ordeal, Euphemia ended the call. 'They take me for granted,' she said to Jane. 'They assume I will always be there when they need me, and that I will always be okay.'

Jane nodded sympathetically.

'They don't think that sometimes I might need them.'

'Petal was pleased to see you.'

'That's something, I suppose.'

'Justine hasn't returned my call or texted me back either, but she will. She's busy and you know what New York is like. She will be in the middle of some big deal with venture capitalists or investment bankers and won't be able to answer her phone. I left a message about me saving Margaret and maybe being on the news, so I'm sure she will probably call tomorrow.'

'Justine will be so proud of you.'

'Do you think?'

'Undoubtedly.' Euphemia made a mental note to message Justine tomorrow and order her to call her mother immediately. It wasn't her fault she was a spoilt brat and a millennial to boot. Her parents had made her that. At least her father had. Jane had gone along with his lax parenting techniques to keep the peace. Now he was dead and her mother was on her own, the least the girl could do was to stay in touch.

Sarah emerged from the bathroom, her hair washed, and wearing a pair of jeans, a crew-necked cashmere jersey and make-up. After a month of eating the Acceptance Institute diet, her clothes hung off her skinny bones. The jeans would have fallen around her knees if she hadn't gathered them over her hips with a belt. She rubbed her hands together. 'Anyone else as hungry as I am?' she asked.

'What do you have in mind?' asked Jane.

'It's a lovely evening and we have another hour before the sun goes down. How about fish and chips on the beach?'

Euphemia's mouth instantly filled with saliva. 'I vote Yes.'

'And that's a Yes from me,' said Jane. 'Waiheke oysters are famous. We'll get some of those too.'

'Waiheke is also famous for its wine,' said Sarah. 'I've heard that the 'Man O' War' chardonnay had an excellent vintage last year. '

'Better than perfect,' said Euphemia.

CHAPTER 43

A FLOCK OF SEAGULLS GATHERED AROUND THEM AS THEY SAT on the warm sand eating their meal. Now and then one would scuttle closer, make a dive towards the food laid out on the paper, dart in, sneak a chip and fly off before the others could get their share of its booty. Much screaming, arching of necks and stamping of red feet followed. Black beady eyes watched each morsel travel from paper to human mouth, ready to pounce if an opportunity presented. Which it didn't. As soon as they sat down and opened their parcels of hot food, the women ate. And ate. And ate. Not stopping until the last crumb of fish batter was gone. The seagulls looked in horror at the empty packets. This never happened. No one ate everything. There was always something left over to scavenge. Their world order tipped on its axis they departed, taking to the air in disgust as they soared off in search of less ravenous targets.

Sarah bundled up the greasy paper, collected an empty wine bottle, and carried them up the beach and stuffed them in the nearest rubbish bin. On her return, she refilled their glasses from the second bottle and sat down.

'They were right about the chardonnay. It is very good,' said Jane, inspecting the wine in her disposable plastic glass.

'Indeed it is,' said Euphemia. 'Does anyone else feel like this past week has been a dream and they have just woken up?'

'Isn't that strange?' said Sarah. 'I said that same thing to Sophie when I called her. She said to say thanks, by the way.'

'You're welcome,' said Jane. She was lying on the sand, her glass perched on her belly as she stared up at the sky.

'Thanks to Euphemia, not you,' said Sarah.

'Oh,' said Jane. She lifted her head and carefully sipped her wine.

'She said that I sounded like Mum again and not like the eco-health-zombie I was when I left. She's going to come to the airport and drive us home tomorrow.'

'That's nice,' said Jane.

'It is,' said Euphemia.

'Why do you think Selina and Nell confessed?'

'The cynic in me says they did it before they got caught, so the authorities will go easy on them,' said Euphemia. 'They got sick of Margaret's thing and wanted out and that's why they were raking in the cash. It was their escape fund. Imagine working hard for years and losing the lot in the Bitcoin crash and selling to a woman who used them and the Retreat terribly. Then, having to start all over again with nothing when she goes rogue. No wonder they did what they did.'

'I did it,' said Jane. 'I lost my home, my husband, my daughter, my furniture. Everything. I started again, and if I can do it, anyone can.'

'You do have a very expensive jewellery collection and a good friend in Euphemia as back-up,' said Sarah.

'Jewellery I can never sell.'

'Ahh well. That's not quite true, is it Jane?' said Euphemia. 'You paid for the Retreat by selling your diamond pendant.'

'What were you saying, Sarah? About Euphemia being my good friend? She does this every time. I never get away with anything. The ladies at the golf club wouldn't catch me out like that. They're too polite.'

'They don't care about you,' said Sarah. 'Or anyone for that matter.'

Jane sat up and brushed the sand from the backs of her arms. 'Yes, Effie, I sold a pendant. You got me! You're right. As usual.'

'Okay that's not what I meant. Your mother brought you up never to sell. Sooooo,' she said. 'Was it as traumatic as you expected it to be?'

'I haven't thought about it. Besides, I still have the fake. No one will ever know.'

'Justine will.'

'Only after I die.'

'That's the spirit. Finally talking some sense. '

'Since my sessions with Selina, I've made some decisions about my future. I won't sell everything, but I don't see why I should live like a pauper on the wages you pay me when Justine is having a fabulous time in New York. We put her through private schools and university, paid for overseas holidays, skiing, sailing, fencing lessons – the lot. We paid for her teeth to be straightened, her nose re-aligned, her jaw chiselled, her boobs enhanced, and her lips plumped. And when I say we, I really mean me. I sold the antiques Mummy left me and spent every last cent of my inheritance on that girl. She can't even be bothered to take my call or message me back. She will always be my daughter but Justine is her father's creation. It's time she stood on her own size 9 feet.'

'She must find it hard to find shoes,' said Sarah.

'Actually,' said Jane taking another sip of wine. 'It's easier. Mid-range sizes sell out. She waits for the sales and gets the best shoes half price.'

'Typical Justine!' said Euphemia.

'Isn't it? Not that I begrudge my daughter, who I love more than anything. I am very proud of her making it in a tough city like New York. But I have decided I'm going to enjoy what's left of my life. I'm going to do what I want to do for a change. Mummy, Justin, if you're listening, roll over in your graves now. You ain't seen nothing yet.' Jane raised her glass of chardonnay, slopping a little over the side. 'To me,' she said and drank the lot.

Sarah and Euphemia stared in wonder at this new creature sitting on the beach. She was vibrant and happy and totally drunk. 'I'll drink to that,' said Sarah.

'Me too,' said Euphemia.

'We'll need another bottle,' said Sarah, holding up the empty one.

'Yeah, nah,' said Euphemia.

'You're too sensible.'

'Boring, isn't it?' Euphemia was having trouble focusing on the horizon where the sea blurred into the sky. Or was it the other way around? Whatever, earlier the horizon had been a straight line and now it wasn't. Now it was a curvy, floaty thing, and it made her queasy looking at it.

'Yip. Really boring,' said Jane. She lay down again.

'Yip. It is,' said Sarah lying down beside her.

'Kicking in the walls of your room wasn't boring,' said Jane.

'I've been wondering; how did you do that?' asked Sarah.

'I took a run up,' said Euphemia. She didn't like where the conversation was going. 'Flimsy building materials.'

'If you can call concrete flimsy,' said Jane. She hiccupped and rolled over to Sarah giggling. 'She kicked it in because she has super powers.'

'I know, Roger told me.'

A chill ran down Euphemia's spine as suddenly the horizon looked very straight. She pulled her knees up into her chest, wrapped her arms around them, and stared out at the sea.

'Do you really think we're that stupid?' asked Jane. She sat up and poked Euphemia's arm. 'We've been through a lot together. I've got eyes and ears, Effie. Putting a bandage on a femoral artery will not stop someone bleeding to death. You did something from the inside to stop the bleeding. I was your window dressing for the police. I didn't mind.'

Sarah sat up. 'How did you really do it?'

Jane put her finger up to her mouth. 'It's a secret.'

'It won't be much longer the way the two of you are talking.'

'Oh Effie, don't be like that. Didn't you learn anything at the Retreat?'

'Maybe.' Euphemia shuffled away from them

'Effie's in a huuuufff,' sang Jane. 'Effie's in a huuuufff.'

'Stop calling me Effie.'

'Tell us what you learned at the Retreat, then, Euphemia,' said Jane. She hiccupped again, then held her breath, blowing out her cheeks like a child.

'I learned it is important to do what needs to be done when it needs to be done and not to worry who sees. If you must know.'

Sarah and Jane sat quietly, each woman thinking through the consequences of what Euphemia had said.

'You're going public?' said Jane.

'Certainly not. The less people know the better. You are not to tell a soul, either, of you. Promise?'

'Promise.'

'Promise.'

'Next time there's an emergency, if I can do anything to help, I won't worry who sees me.'

'You're talking about Roger and the plane crash?'

'Yes. I should have tried harder to save him. If I had, you wouldn't have come to the Retreat and Sophie and John would have their father.'

'And the people you did save might have died instead.'

'Possibly.'

'There's your answer.' Sarah put her hand in front of her mouth and muttered the next words through clenched teeth. 'We do know you have super powers, but even you can't do two things at once. Women are brilliant at multi-tasking, but no one can do the impossible. The Retreat gave me exactly what it advertised; acceptance. I accept Roger is gone. I don't blame you for his death. You did all you could at the time. For the rest of my life, I will miss him. I accept my sadness and my grief, but they're my feelings to do with as I like. Euphemia Sage, you're off the hook.'

'To be honest, I loved every minute of the Retreat,' said Jane. 'It was better than climbing Mt Taranaki and getting winched off by helicopter. That was over so quickly, I didn't have time to get scared. This time, it sooooo scared me. We were going to drown.'

'Me too,' said Sarah. 'I've never been so afraid but so exhilarated at the same time. They should add sailing to the programme. That was the best bit by far.'

'I agree,' said Jane. 'We'll put it on the feedback form and maybe they will add it in.'

'Feedback form?' asked Euphemia over her shoulder.

'There is usually a feedback form,' said Jane.

'You realise the Retreat is no more. Selina and Nell sold it to Margaret when they lost all their money in the Bitcoin fail in 2018.

They've been managing on a shoestring budget, which is why we there was no cook and all the food was green and cold. They hocked off their gym equipment and they kept us locked in our rooms so we wouldn't see how rundown the grounds were. They had reached the end of their tether, which was why they were so desperate to get their hands on your money. And mine. They weren't booked up at all. We must have seemed like an answer to their prayers when we wanted to come and stay.'

'What do you think will happen to them?' asked Sarah.

'Not much. They confessed, and they'll have to return your money. I guess they'll start again somewhere else. They're too young not to.'

'I've got an idea,' said Sarah. 'I can't tell you what it is yet, but as my Roger used to say, it's a winner.'

CHAPTER 44

Euphemia's phone beeped as they walked into the house. Used to not having it, she forgot to take it down to the beach, something the old Euphemia would never have done. A list of text messages covered her screen. They were all from Scottie in Sydney and they all said the same thing. 'Call me.'

She excused herself and went into the bunk room.

'Where have you been?' asked Scottie as soon as he heard her voice.

'It's complicated, but I'm here now. What's wrong? Is Barbara all right?'

'No, she isn't. She needs to talk to you.'

'Let me speak to her,' said Euphemia.

'I can't,' said Scottie, his voice catching. 'She's had a stroke. She's in hospital. It doesn't look good.'

'Which hospital? No. Don't tell me now. Text me the details. Does anyone else know?'

'She wants to see you first. Before they make the news public.'

'So you haven't told Kenneth? What about James, her solicitor?'

'Only I know and now you. How soon can you get here?'

'Tomorrow. I'll be there tomorrow. Tell her I'm on my way.'

Scottie ended the call leaving Euphemia staring at her phone. It was too soon. Too soon to lose a new friend and the only link she had to Rachel's Switch. There was so much Barbara had yet to tell her about it, about the cousins she hadn't met, and the Foundation. She googled the timetable for the ferry back to Auckland. The last one was leaving in half an hour. If she ran fast, she could catch it, take the early morning flight to Wellington, collect her passport, and fly on to Sydney. It meant she wouldn't be able to give her official statement to the police, but the others were more than capable of telling them what happened. A family emergency took precedence.

Sarah was fast asleep on the sofa when Euphemia returned to the living room. Jane was making tea.

'Would you like a cup?' she asked.

'I don't have time. I have to go to Sydney. I'm catching the last ferry. Will you explain to the others?'

'What's happened?'

'Barbara, Kenneth's business partner, you met her at Kezia's wedding, she isn't well.'

'I'm so sorry. Of course you have to go. I'll explain everything. You can trust me,' she added.

'I do.' She gave a very surprised Jane a quick hug, grabbed her backpack and ran out the door.

CHAPTER 45

ONE DAY A PERSON CAN BE HALE AND HEARTY AND THE NEXT, they are hooked up to bleeping machines and IV lines, unable to move, dependent on others for care. Barbara looked frail and old against the white linen of her hospital bed. Her Margaret Thatcher crown was gone, her hair hanging lankly around her face in grey strands. Her skin sagged, draping over her bones like a wrinkled tablecloth, but it was her eyes which revealed the truth of her situation. Normally bright blue and sparkling with life, they radiated nothing but uncertainty and fear – a last look back from the precipice of the abyss.

Euphemia took her hand, cradling it, in the vain hope of transfusing her vitality to her friend. Once, that might have worked. Now all she felt in Barbara's brief clasp was a papery dryness and the weakness of age and illness.

'Thank you,' said Barbara, the words came out slurred by the droop on the left side of her mouth. Scottie reached across with a tissue and wiped away a dribble. Barbara met his eyes and smiled weakly and lopsidedly.

'I'm sorry I wasn't here sooner,' replied Euphemia. 'I've had an adventure which I'll tell you about when you get home.'

'Don't be silly,' wheezed Barbara sharply, a flicker of her old fire in her voice. 'There's no time for sick bed etiquette.' She closed her eyes, took two deep breaths and opened them again. 'There's a lot I must tell you. For the safety of the Foundation and the others. You're the leader now, so listen.'

Euphemia wanted to protest, to decline the mantle dumped on her without her consent but what would be the point. Barbara had issued a decree from her sick bed. 'One question,' said Euphemia. 'Then I'll be quiet.'

Barbara held up one bony finger, its nail exquisitely manicured and painted lime green.

'Why me?'

'Your father,' said Barbara. 'Because of him, you have the strongest powers of anyone since Rachel's eldest daughter.'

'Who was my father?'

'Who IS your father, you mean?' The line on one machine went crazy. An alarm sounded in one continuous tone. The little colour there was in Barbara's face disappeared and she closed her eyes. A nurse arrived puffing slightly and did something to a machine strapped to a pole. After a few minutes the bleeping stopped, and the line settled back to a steady run of ups and downs against the black. The nurse smiled at Barbara, patted her arm, and left.

Barbara opened her eyes again, flicking them at the water jug. Scottie leapt across, picked up a cup with a lid and straw and held it to her lips. At the same time, he lifted her head forwards off the pillow. She sucked the straw slowly and awkwardly.

When he had wiped away the runoff, she fixed her eye on Euphemia. 'You'll find your father when the time is right, or rather, I suspect he will find you. There is a spy at the Foundation. Your old friend Alison's father is cleverer than I thought. He stole important but not vital documentation and until Scottie flushed him out, he had the codes to the databases.'

'I thought it wasn't safe to have databases and that the archives were all hard copies.'

'A distortion of the truth, which I don't expect you will hold against me. The physical archives are being transferred to a safe house in Coldsham. Scottie is taking care of the digital records.'

'Coldsham? Where Rachel was born, and where my mother died.'

'Yes.' Barbara lay back on the pillows, spent. She didn't open her eyes. 'Go there! Do whatever you have to do.'

'What do I have to do?'

'You will know.'

'But I don't.'

'You do, and you will. Just not yet.'

Barbara's breathing settled into a series of wispy sighs as she drifted off to sleep.

'That's the longest she has stayed awake since it happened,' said Scottie. 'She'll be asleep for hours now. Best if we come back later.'

'And go where?'

'To Barbara's house. I've got a lot to show you.'

CHAPTER 46

THE NEWS OF BARBARA'S DEATH CAME THAT AFTERNOON VIA a phone call to Scottie. In the absence of any known family, she had nominated him as her next of kin. His face fell as he listened to the doctor's explanation that she had died in her sleep and hadn't suffered. After the call ended, he said nothing. He looked at Euphemia, nodded, and left the room. He started sobbing as soon as he shut the door.

Stunned by the news, Euphemia did what she always did when she needed comforting. She called Kenneth. He had brought her passport to the airport early that morning, so he knew Barbara was unwell. Neither of them had expected her to actually die. Barbara Scarsdale was a force of nature, a brilliant woman not only ahead of her time but with an iron will whose determination to get things done overshadowed everyone around her. For her to no longer exist was incomprehensible on so many levels.

'I'm already at the airport,' he told Euphemia. 'I'll be there soon.'

For a few seconds, all they did was listen to each other breathing. There weren't the words to describe their feelings. She heard his boarding announcement, and told him she loved him and she couldn't wait to see him. Then she told him to be careful and to fly safely and to keep his seat belt fastened at all times.

'My plane won't crash if that's what's worrying you,' he said. 'Statistics alone will keep it airborne. Remember that. And that I love you.'

He was right, of course, but being right was not enough to still her vivid imagination. Lately there had been so many disasters, so many people she loved injured or in danger, people dying, and her adrenalin levels had not had time to return to normal. Jittery with the fear of more people she loved being hurt, she tried to tell herself to breathe slowly, in and out through her open mouth while she focused on the here and now.

She walked over to one of the French doors set in regular intervals along the length of the room and looked at the magnificent view of Sydney Harbour with the Bridge in the distance. The Australian flag fluttering at the top, a reminder of her struggle with Rupert after he tried to kill Barbara. Unable to cope with what he had done, he had jumped rather than face justice. In her nightmares, Euphemia still heard his scream as he fell.

In the days and weeks following his death, she had got to know Barbara. They spent hours chatting about what it was truly like to have super powers, and how to live with them. They laughed about exploits gone wrong and shared the tragedy of situations which hadn't worked out despite their best efforts. Barbara told her about the women around the world who shared their secret. Middle-aged women, who more often than not, society ignored so they could exercise their powers without others noticing. Women who quietly and unobtrusively used their powers to do good and right wrongs.

Barbara knew them all, stayed in touch with them and she ran the Foundation, where scientists were researching the genetic basis of Rachel's Switch. She and her team of solicitors in Sydney ran the businesses which provided the finance for the work at the Foundation. Scottie was an integral part of the organisation, despite his youth. He had managed the data, and had access to the files, but not the contents. Only a descendant of Rachel could access the knowledge they held.

Now it was up to Euphemia, someone no one else in their 'family' had met, to tell them Barbara had died. Oh and by the way she was also, Barbara's chosen successor and their leader. It would not be easy, not least because she didn't know the women, how many there were, their backgrounds or where in the world they lived. As to taking over the management of a Foundation, which did research she knew nothing about... what could be easier? As if this wasn't daunting enough, then the news that Alison's father was up to his old tricks added urgency to her tasks. Tasks she hadn't asked for. Tasks she didn't want, on the other side of the world twelve thousand miles from her home, her husband, her work, Petal and her pregnant daughter. It would be impossible.

Underneath the deep sadness at losing Barbara, a creeping itch of resentment was forming. Euphemia was tired of doing what other people told her to do, even more tired of having responsibility foisted upon her. Selina had opened her eyes to the possibility of choice, of choosing to do what she, Euphemia Sage, nee Marchamp, wanted to do. With the rest of her life. She had watched on as acquaintances took long holidays with their husbands in the south of France, played with grand-children, taken up hobbies, travelled to wild and exotic places, explored hidden gems in New Zealand and stayed in luxury lodges. They had reached the time of their lives when work was no longer a priority, when they could enjoy themselves. Why did she now have to give that future up to do what Barbara had all but ordered her to do?

The Retreat had been a revelation. The time on the yacht had confirmed her plans. On her return to Wellington, she meant to tell Kenneth to delegate the management of 'Desserts are Us' to new hires so they could take time off. Together. They were going to travel. Travel, which did not include him sneaking his golf clubs onto the luggage trolley at the airport when it was too late for her to object. Jane was right about their financial situation. They were more than comfortable, they were better than well off. They could afford to indulge themselves in the last years of their lives, because who knew how long they had left?

Euphemia turned away from the view and sat down in the rubble of her plans. What was the saying about life giving you lemons? Could superpowers ever equate with a surfeit of citrus? There was only one answer and she knew what it was. Barbara had quoted Spiderman to make her feel better. She sighed when she remembered her words, 'With great power comes great responsibility.' Damn it. For the first time in her life, Euphemia had an inkling of how her mother must have felt and why she had tried to outrun her destiny. The irony did not escape her.

* * *

EUPHEMIA HADN'T BEEN to Barbara's house before. It was beautiful. Set on the hill above Rose Bay, its spacious grounds beautifully landscaped, it was an elegant home entirely consistent with the woman she was. A carefully tended lawn surrounded by established trees and flower borders ran down to the beach and a small jetty. She guessed the house had been built in the early twentieth century. It was huge, large enough for servants when servants were affordable and lived in. The centre of the house consisting of two living rooms, an entrance hall, a study, kitchen and dining room, fronted a wide portico, one end of which was populated by sun loungers overlooking a pool. An outdoor barbecue, dining and seating areas occupied the other end. Two wings which she supposed contained bedrooms bookended the living area.

This room, comfortably furnished in soft yellows and greens, was where Barbara spent most of her time, according to Scottie. A modern oil painting soared above the fireplace, its chaos of colours and shapes mesmerising in their beauty. A grand piano, sheet music scattered across its surface, stood at one end. Barbara's only granddaughter, Abbey, had been a musician and had just completed a doctorate in music from Sydney Conservatorium of Music when she was run down by a drunk driver. Barbara, heartbroken and bereft, became a recluse until she learned of Euphemia's existence, coming out of her self-imposed exile to become a member of the Sage family. She attended Kezia's wedding, was looking forward to being a step-great-grandmother and now she was dead.

'Man plans, God laughs.' Wasn't that the saying? Euphemia was not religious, but this was a perfect fit for how she was feeling. Choice had been a mirage held out to her at the Retreat, only to disappear when life intervened. If she was being truthful, this was the way it had always been. And she had survived and been happy then and she would again. Her super powers might be amazing, but they could not vanquish a destiny set out for her long before she was born. The only thing she could do was to greet it with open arms and a smile. Was that life's only true choice in the face of events? A smile?

'Mrs Sage?' Scottie poked his head around the door. 'I've made coffee.'

'Anyone who makes coffee without being asked can call me Euphemia,' she replied.

Scottie blushed, pink colour-washing the pale skin under his freckles. In his twenties, he had red hair, green eyes, and a pert nose. A black nose ring hanging from his septum matched the black stud which pierced his bottom lip. A gold chain looped pirate-like from the matching ring in his left ear to the nose ring. A gaping hole had replaced his right earlobe, kept open by another larger black ring. Euphemia could see the wallpaper through this aural porthole. Other than the face jewellery, he wore a black short-sleeved t-shirt over a kilt which covered his knees. Above the top of his black Doc Martin lace-up boots, his muscled legs were covered with a thick thatch of red hair.

'If you don't mind,' he said. 'Mrs S would be easier. It's what I called Barbara, Mrs Scarsdale. I like tradition, plus it fits with your new position in the organisation. Of course, that's only if you want me to stay on.'

'Mrs S sounds fine,' said Euphemia. 'Let's have that coffee, then you can take me through what I need to do.'

'Yes, Mrs S,' he said, smiling. The diamond implanted in his left front incisor sparkled.

CHAPTER 47

THE NEXT THREE DAYS PASSED IN A BLUR. THERE WAS THE funeral to organise and daily meetings with Barbara's solicitors to attend. Kezia and Ben, Nicky and Dave arrived the day before the funeral. They elected to stay in a hotel rather than in the home of a woman they had only just got to know.

'It would feel like we were invading her privacy,' explained Kezia. She and Euphemia were sitting in the outdoor café on the mezzanine floor of the hotel, which overlooked Circular Quay. The Sydney Opera House gleamed white on the other side of the bay, the bridge lurking in iron majesty behind them. It was late morning and quiet. The lunch crowd hadn't arrived yet. Both were wearing light linen dresses, sunglasses and summer sandals, their long legs curved under their chairs.

'I know you, Kezia Sage,' said Euphemia. 'You and your sister are really avoiding the possibility of having to do any housework.'

'I want to relax,' replied her daughter. 'In less than a year, I will have two children and a messy house. If we can find a house.'

'No luck?'

'You wouldn't believe the prices. It's not like it was in your day. Oh I forgot, Aunt Maree left you her house.'

Euphemia raised an eyebrow.

'Sorry, Mum, I'm tired, and not being able to find a place where I can stash two babies is getting to me.'

'I do understand.'

'Do you? Ben and I have got good jobs, and we still can't afford a place we like that's close to the city. The ones we do like and can afford are miles out in the country. We would spend any savings on transport getting to and from work. It's a nightmare and the babies keep growing inside me. I felt them move for the first time on the flight over. It's a weird feeling, like having butterflies inside my tummy. Butterflies who decide to practise kung fu when you least expect it. Do you think they are fighting already?' She didn't wait for Euphemia to answer. 'You are going to come to my scan next week aren't you? I need you there when we find out the sex of number two.'

'You don't want to wait and find out when they're born?'

'No.'

'Okay, I'll be there. Girls are wonderful, you know.'

'I know, but my girls would come with over four hundred years of baggage. I'm not sure I could wrap my head around that and be a good mother.'

'Have you said anything to Ben?'

'There's no point. Why worry him when there's nothing we can do?'

'Nicky?'

'Not yet, but one of us needs to say something. She's my sister and we shouldn't keep her in the dark.'

'I'll do it when we get home and things quieten down. Where's your father?'

'He's gone to see James and the other solicitors.'

'It was thoughtful of Barbara to leave him control of the Foundation's shares in the business. Now he doesn't have to worry about Sarah and Ted having a controlling interest. It means'

'He's going to be busier than ever.'

'Exactly. So how would you feel about taking over Sage Consulting full time?'

'Why? What are you going to do?'

'Barbara left me her house and the bulk of her estate. She was a rich woman with her fingers in a lot of pies. It's going to take me time to understand what needs to be done.'

Kezia bit the inside of her cheek. 'And when the babies arrive?'

'It won't take that long. I'll be back by then because nothing could keep me away.' She reached over and squeezed Kezia's hand. 'Either I will look after them, or I can cover for you at Sage. No matter, you take as much maternity leave as you like. I will make sure we're staffed.'

Kezia took a long drink of water from the glass on the table in front of her. The server swooped across, ice tinkling against the sides of his jug, and refilled it.

'Actually I'd like to stay on as the CEO of Sage,' she said. 'I'm good at it and I've made a lot of progress in taking everything online. Other firms have been asking if they can use the software I've developed. So much so, I'm considering franchising it.'

Euphemia raised her eyebrows. 'I've only been away a few days.'

'It's an idea I've been working on since before the wedding. Barbara was helping me. She said I'd need a business that could run without me there to oversee it every day. Scottie's helped too. I asked him to work for me but he said he needed to stay with Mrs S.'

'That's what he calls me. When were you going to tell me and your father?'

'Dad knows and thinks it's not only a great idea but that it could be a massive,' said Kezia. She shut her eyes and withdrew her head into her neck waiting for the inevitable explosion.

It didn't come.

After a moment of silence, she cocked her head to one side, opened one eye, and peeked at her mother. 'You're not mad at me for not telling you sooner, are you?'

'Of course I'm mad at you. I hate it when anyone goes behind my back. That it was my daughter makes it worse. Frankly, I don't understand why you needed to keep it from me. I've never stopped you from doing anything before.'

Kezia bowed her head and fiddled with the nail on her left thumb. 'True,' she whispered.

'I have always encouraged you.'

'True.'

Euphemia took a deep breath as she looked across Circular Quay to the green and yellow ferries coming and going from the different wharves. 'It's a marvellous idea,' she said finally. 'I'll help in any way I can.'

'I love you, Mum.'

'I love you, too. So you must have thought about what you are going to do when the babies arrive.'

'Ben is going to take a year off. He's looking forward to being a full-time father and house husband and his bosses have agreed. It will give him time to decide if he wants to stay in the police, move into IT, or he could do both. He aced the course at police college.'

'I know, he beat Nicky.'

'Did he now? She said she came top in all her classes. I'm going to have a chat with my sister about telling the whole truth and nothing but the truth.'

'Leave Nicky alone.'

'Or what, Mum, you'll ground me?' Kezia laughed.

Euphemia thought about her options. 'Or I won't come to your scan.'

'That's low, even for you.'

'I can go lower if you push me.'

'No. That's low enough.'

CHAPTER 48

BARBARA HAD STIPULATED IN HER VERY DETAILED WILL THAT she would like a small funeral. She did not want any fuss. There was to be one bouquet of flowers and this was to be placed on her coffin. She definitely did not want either a sermon or a eulogy. Despite these instructions and the lack of publicity about her death, when the day came, St Andrew's Anglican Cathedral Sydney on George Street was full to overflowing with mourners. The building was constructed of local stone and native timbers painted to look like stone in the middle of the nineteenth century. Its Gothic revival style reminded the settlers of their home in England. Buttresses supported the green hammer-beamed roof, tall columns of intricately carved stone, stained glass windows, and patterned-tile floors testified to the skill of the architects and master-craftsmen who had worked on recreating the past for the future.

Seated in the pews were representatives from the business community, state, council, and national politicians from both major parties, and people from the many charities Barbara had supported throughout her life. Most moving was the music. The Sydney Conservatorium had received a large endowment from Barbara in memory of Abbey. They sent their choir, organists, and a small jazz ensemble to play in her honour. The service was brief, over in less than thirty minutes. Afterwards, the Sage family waited by the hearse, while people speculated on who these Kiwi relatives were and why hadn't they heard of them before this. Scottie, wearing his kilt, waited with them, adding to the mystery. James and her legal team facilitated introductions and accepted condolences with the family. Eventually it came time for the hearse to leave and as it was a weekday and businesses didn't run themselves, the mourners dispersed. Euphemia thanked the choirmaster, the organist, and the dean, and they told her how much they would miss Barbara. There was nothing left for them to do but return to the hotel, collect their luggage, and fly home.

Somewhere high over the Tasman Sea, Kenneth looked up from his laptop. 'I've missed you,' he said, taking her hand.

'I've missed you too.'

'Kezia's told you about franchising her software?'

'I don't understand why it was such a big secret.'

'She knew you would want to help, and she didn't want to add to your workload. She was thinking of you. Our daughter wanted to show you how well she can manage on her own. She wanted to surprise you.'

'Well she did. But why didn't you tell me? I don't like secrets and I don't like secrets between us.'

'I know. She insisted I didn't. You don't understand how much she looks up to you and how she wants to make you proud.'

'I have always been proud of her.'

'That's automatic mother proud. It comes with the territory. This time, she wanted to earn your approval.'

Euphemia sighed and leaned her head on the headrest. 'Okay, I get that. Next time, and there better not be a next time, Kenneth Sage, tell me anyway.'

'Deal.' He leaned across and kissed her cheek. 'Speaking of secrets, when were you going to tell me your plans?'

'Oh,' she said. 'Kezia told you.'

'Ah, huh! I'm going to leave that on the table for now. I will not use it against you.'

'I was going to tell you when the time was right. You've got to admit the past six months have been hectic. We've had no time to talk.'

'Okay, you tell me your plans and I'll tell you mine.'

'I'm going to Britain with Scottie next month,' said Euphemia. 'I will be away for three months. Kezia will look after Sage. Nicky will take Petal and you're old enough to look after yourself.'

Kenneth rested his hands on the tray table in front of him. 'I can't manage three months without you. I won't.'

'Then come and visit,' she said.

He nodded slowly. 'I could do that. Why so long?'

'There are Switch matters which need sorting out. Barbara left a complete set of instructions. Scottie will be there to help. He knows the Foundation inside out. Once I've taken care of a few problems, and he is all set up, then he will stay on and run things day to day. I can oversee things from home.'

'Are you going to tell me what these problems are?'

'No.'

'This secret thing is feeling very one way,' he said. 'Just saying.'

'Sorry. I have to do this, and I have to do it this way.'

'It's come at the worst time for 'Desserts are Us', you know that. I need your support, your advice, more than ever.'

'Sell it,' said Euphemia, taking his hand and looking into his eyes. 'Sell it to Ted. He's keen to be a tycoon or he wouldn't have come to you for help. England is so beautiful in spring. The Cotswolds are especially gorgeous. Come with me. We could rent one of those thatched cottages you see on chocolate boxes. We could go to an English pub for lunch every day and explore the history and the gardens. There's the Royal Shakespeare Playhouse in Stratford-upon-Avon. It isn't far from Coldsham. You love Shakespeare.'

'I do not.'

'You could learn to love it.'

'I could not.'

'Okay, then Coldsham has a wonderful golf course. I'd let you take your clubs this one time. Please, Kenneth, it's everything we talked about.'

'Everything we talked about before 'Desserts are Us', you mean.' He slowly disentangled his hand. 'Jane told me what happened at the Retreat. I'm thinking you can't go anywhere without getting into trouble.'

'That's not fair,' she said. 'I wanted to help Sarah. It wasn't my fault Margaret was a baddie and things went sour.'

'I'm not sure about you anymore. I see how excited you get when you use your super powers.'

'Have you had a chance to read your menus?' The flight attendant stood beside their seats, looking down at them. 'Would you like the chicken or the fish?'

'The fish, please,' said Euphemia.

'I'll have the same,' said Kenneth.

'Anything to drink?'

'Water, please,' said Euphemia.

'A large scotch and ice for me,' replied Kenneth.

The attendant moved on to take the orders of the people sitting in front of them.

'You're not being fair,' said Euphemia quietly. 'If anyone looks excited, it's you when you sign up a new distributor for 'Desserts are Us'. I didn't think when I married you I would come second to a chocolate gateau.'

'You don't,' said Kenneth. 'You come second to kiwifruit sorbet.'

'That's not funny.'

'Yes, it is. It's just that it's not very funny, but it is a little funny which counts as funny.'

The attendant arrived with their drinks order. Kenneth inhaled his scotch, then took a healthy sip. 'Johnnie Walker Black,' he said, returning his glass to the tray. 'I needed that.' He turned to her again. 'Face it, we can have everything, Euphemia. We're the lucky ones, we're alive. Roger and Barbara are not. We've spent our lives working together, living together, loving each other more than most couples. But our priorities have changed as we inch closer to the big golf course in the sky. You and I expect different things. And that's okay.'

Euphemia didn't like where this was going. She took his hand, squeezing it as she stared at the back of the seat in front of her. Making eye contact would only cause tears, and she didn't want to embarrass herself.

Kenneth loosed her grip on his hand and lifted it to his lips to kiss it. 'Don't look so scared. I love you and you love me and we can do this.

You go to England.' He kissed her hand between each sentence, soothing her with the gentle tone of his voice. 'I will miss you. You will miss me. We will talk every day. You do your work. I'll do mine. Once a month we will have a wildly romantic reunion somewhere special. We can afford it. Neither of us has to give up anything.'

Euphemia turned and looked at him, her eyes betraying her feelings. She could trust him and she knew he was right. They had grown so strong together that each could survive without the other. For a short time. Then they could reunite and nurture their love, re-kindling the attraction, which had always simmered below the surface of their day-to-day lives.

'Are you sure you don't want a proper drink?' he asked. 'Jane told me you had to drink jug water and eat disgusting food at the Retreat. You can indulge yourself now and again. You don't have to be good all the time.'

'It might work,' she said.

'It will work,' he replied, finishing his scotch. The attendant arrived and prepared their tray tables with placemats, cutlery, and glassware. She placed hot rolls on their side plates.

'Another scotch, please,' said Kenneth. 'And a large gin and tonic for my wife. We will share a bottle of Chablis with the fish.'

The attendant nodded. 'I'm sorry, I forgot to take your dessert orders before. The choice today is either a chocolate gateau or a kiwifruit sorbet.'

'I'll have both,' said Euphemia.

'So will I,' said Kenneth.

CHAPTER 49

BEN SITTING NEXT TO KEZIA, HELD HER HAND AS THEY focused their eyes on the screen at the end of the bed. Euphemia sat in the chair near the door, out of the way. This was their moment, and she didn't want to intrude on their happiness. The same woman who did the first scan shook large dollops of gel onto Kezia's rounded stomach. She took the probe and ran it over her skin, smoothing the gel with it before positioning it lengthways immediately above Kezia's pubic hair. She pushed it in. The twins' heart beats in stepped unison sounded loud enough to touch in the tiny room. Ben, who hadn't heard them before, wiped a tear from his shining eyes, and tightened his grip on Kezia's hand. They laughed, then looked anxiously up at the screen.

Two skinny legs, patchy white against the darkness, kicked out. An arm drifted across the body of its sibling.

'Look, it's sucking its thumb,' said Ben. An alien face, all forehead and dark shadows for eyes, a thumb implanted in its mouth, came into view.

'I'll do the routine checks for each one in turn,' said the sonographer. 'It will take longer because there are two of them, so bear with me.'

Expertly, she swept the probe rapidly over Kezia's belly, stopping now and then to press a button and freeze the picture on the screen. She used a toggle to run some measurements on the babies' skulls, chest, and spine, taking recordings as she moved down their bodies. The thumb sucking continued.

'Can you see the sex?' asked Ben.

'A moment longer,' said the sonographer. After a few more sweeps, she stopped the probe and pressed another button, which enlarged the images on the screen. 'Uncross those legs, little one,' she said. 'Mummy and Daddy want to know what colour to paint the nursery.' The baby kicked out, the probe bucking under the impact. 'You've got a rugby player in there,' she said.

'Yes, but which team?' asked Ben. 'The All Blacks or the Black Ferns?'

'The All Blacks.'

'It's a boy,' said Kezia, unable to disguise her relief. 'And the other one?'

The screen changed again, just as this baby rolled, hunching its back to the probe. The sonographer changed position, digging deeper, as she tried to sneak the probe up on the baby from the side.

'Sorry,' she said. 'This one's not playing ball. I can keep going, but it looks like it's gone to sleep. It won't be turning over for a while. You have one boy. We'll have to wait until the next scan to work out if he has a sister or brother.' She handed Kezia a paper towel to wipe off the gel.

'We'll call him Alexander,' said Ben. 'After my father.'

'Sure,' said Kezia. 'Alexander Kenneth.'

'Done. That was easy. What do you think, Grandma?' asked Ben, his eyes red from happy crying.

'Marvellous,' she replied.

Kezia pulled up her trousers and climbed off the bed. 'Everything looked okay?' she asked. 'My babies are healthy?'

'They look fine,' said Jill. 'But the radiologist will check the scans this afternoon.'

'Good news then. That's a relief,' said Kezia, thanking her.

Ben had to go straight back to work, so it was just Euphemia and Kezia who stopped for coffee at the same café. It had been raining earlier and Euphemia propped her umbrella against the table as she sat in the same chair.

'I'm not worried after that,' said Kezia. 'The sex of baby two doesn't matter. What matters is that they're both healthy.'

The cobblestones rumbled behind Euphemia. She heard the familiar swish of an electric scooter zooming through the lane, the weight of its rider the same as the rider eight weeks before. It was a similar time of day, so odds on, it could be the same man. She turned and glimpsed the same outline coming towards her, getting closer and not slowing down. Euphemia swivelled back to Kezia, accidentally knocking her umbrella into his path. Less than a second later, and because he was going too fast to stop quickly and avoid hitting the obstacle, he flew over his handle-bars, his rat-tail streaming behind him before he hit the cobbles, his arms stretched out in front of him. The only noise was the sound of a scooter wheel circling pointlessly in the air.

'You didn't,' said Kezia, looking at her mother.

'Didn't what, dear?'

'Teach that man a lesson.'

'You're catching on.'

CHAPTER 50

THE PRESS CONFERENCE ENDED. CLAIRE STOOD UP AND joined Euphemia and Sarah at the back of the room. 'That went rather well,' she said, dusting off one sleeve. She was wearing her blue police uniform, her medals lined up across her chest. Her hair neatly cut, her curls blow-dried into conformity, there was almost no resemblance to the wild Retreat-Claire who had met them at the ferry. Even the way she talked had changed from her previous free-wheeling familiarity to clipped official police-speak, which revealed little. Her commander had done most of the talking. Claire had sat alongside him, nodding when he turned to her, her face set and unmoving unless she was required to confirm something he said. Then she said, 'Yes, Sir', 'Correct, Sir', or 'No, Sir.'

The whole thing had lasted fifty minutes. Twenty minutes was such a short time to reveal that they had mounted the undercover operation to stop the pilfering of clients' funds by the operators at the Acceptance Institute. It was only once they had embedded the operative that they realised a more sophisticated form of theft was taking place. The theft of facial expressions. Margaret's company was harvesting the facial expressions of midlife women and selling these to overseas companies who specialised in developing artificial intelligence algorithms. Midlife middle-class women being the demographic group who spend the most money, clues to their emotional states and thought processes were invaluable. These clues were then used to trigger sales decisions algorithms both in stores and online.

'Ohhhhhhhh, I get it,' Jane said loudly when the commander explained why this information was so valuable. She was sitting up the front at the table next to Claire. Quiet laughter followed as the commander couldn't help himself and broke into a broad grin.

'Effie tried to tell us. The cameras!' she explained to the reporters who turned their attention to her and away from the commander. 'She knew. It was Margaret. She had us fooled for a little while, but I knew she was a bad'un when she tried to take my friend away from me. I didn't understand, Effie, but I do now,' she called to the back of the room. She raised both hands and gave her a double thumbs-up. 'You're forgiven.'

'Perhaps you would like to run the rest of this briefing, Mrs French?' suggested the commander.

'No, you do it. You're the man.'

Another round of titters followed, the reporters unsure whether this was praise or a backhanded insult.

'I think they have the gist of it. The details are in your briefing notes, ladies and gentlemen. The police comms team will be only too happy to field questions. Their contact details are also in your notes.'

A reporter raised her hand. 'Ms Selina Kelly and Ms Nell Taylor have been convicted of theft and given community detention. There are some in the wider wellness community who say this is a very light sentence. Would you like to comment?'

'Now, Jessica, you know better than that,' said the commander. 'The police never comment on sentences handed down by the courts. I will say that the women, in mitigation, not only turned themselves in, but they alerted the police to the escape attempt. If it hadn't been for them, we may not have found the stricken yacht *Ad Capere* so quickly and lives might have been lost. In such circumstances, the courts often take a more lenient view. Next question? Tova?' he pointed to a dark-haired young woman sitting at the back.

'Is it true Mrs French has been nominated for a bravery award?'

Jane blushed and looked down.

'I can confirm that is the case,' said the commander. 'She deserves one.'

'And Mrs Sage who, I see, is standing at the back of the room?'

'I am not aware of any actions on Mrs Sage's part which would warrant her receiving such an award, but I would be happy to be provided with further information. Now, if that is all, I have a police force to get back to.' He pushed his chair under the white tablecloth covering the long table. Claire stood to attention as he left the room.

'Mrs French, Mrs French,' called the reporters. 'Could we ask you...'

Jane was in her element, pointing at one reporter after another, basking in their attention as she detailed how she had saved Margaret's life. Euphemia noted the simple pearl necklace and earrings, the plain cashmere jersey and straight skirt. Jane had visited her hairdresser and there was no hint of grey in her new hairstyle. She had regained the weight she had lost at the Retreat and she radiated a new confidence as she fielded the reporters' questions with grace and self-effacing humour.

'Doesn't she look great?' said Sarah who had arrived late and was standing beside her.

'She does,' said Euphemia. 'I'm going to miss her when I go to England. The Retreat helped her to come into her own.'

'It did, didn't it?' Sarah nudged her arm and leaned across. 'I bought it. The Retreat is mine, lock, stock, yoga mats and barrel. Selina and Nell have something special to offer women our age. You made me realize what was going on, so it's ironic I am going to live there after all. I will do the day-to-day organisation and Selina and Nell will provide the counselling as they always have, but with less pressure. Margaret was a real taskmaster.'

'Does that mean better food and no locked doors?'

'Exactly. Better food, better activities, and a happy hour between five and six. Mocktails for the guests and Pol Roger for the owner.'

'No cameras?'

'No cameras. Sophie and John are happy because I got it at a bargain price and, with all the publicity, the place is booked out for the next nine months. I've always wanted a business of my own. I believe I can help women to find happiness and earn a good living at the same time.

Besides, Waiheke is a much better place to spend the winters. I may even get a yacht. Two feedback forms have suggested I add sailing to the programme.'

'Good for you.'

'In the spirit of acceptance, I have even forgiven Kenneth.'

'Roger will be happy.'

'Selina assures me he is delighted.'

Euphemia looked at her sideways to see if she was joking. Sarah looked perfectly serious apart from a tiny twitch in one muscle at the corner of her mouth. 'You'll never know,' she muttered.

'Know what?' asked Jane, joining them now that she was free from the attention of the press.

'Nothing,' said Sarah. 'You did so well up there. Congrats. Now, I must dash. I have a Retreat to run to. We'll have a reunion when you get back from England. Okay?' She kissed them on each cheek, shouldered her Chanel bag and left.

'I'm going home to rest,' said Jane. 'Having your photo taken and answering questions is exhausting. Alastair will look after reception.'

'That's not his job.'

'Yet, he's so good at it.' Jane picked up her handbag and left through the same door as Sarah.

'She can be so...' said Claire.

'Can't she just?' said Euphemia. They walked out the door together, stopping at the top of the streets which led down to the street. 'It was you who carved the message in the branch outside my window wasn't it?

'I confess, it was me. Things were dragging on and I thought it would stir you into action.'

'It did. You're a clever young woman, Claire. What are you going to do next?'

'Since my face got plastered all over the Waiheke Times Community Newspaper, courtesy of Constable Hunter's cousin, I am no longer any use as an undercover operative. I've always fancied working for Interpol. The boss has arranged a secondment for me to see if I like it. I'll be in Europe, so we may run into each other.'

There was something about the way she said this which made Euphemia look twice at her. 'We may,' she replied cautiously.

'If you need anything ever, call me,' she said and handed Euphemia a card. 'Likewise, if I ever need a yacht righted in the middle of the ocean, I may call on you.'

CHAPTER 51

'Petal, baby' said Euphemia. 'I'll miss you too.'

Petal was lying on top of the clothes in Euphemia's packed suitcase, which was sitting open on the bed. Her tawny soft fur contrasting with the neatly folded black merino running gear, her black goldfish eyes following her every move as Euphemia collected her toiletries from the bathroom.

'I won't be away long, I promise.'

Petal buried her head under a bag containing Euphemia's underwear.

'I can still see you,' said Euphemia, sitting down on the bed beside her. 'You have to get out so I can finish packing.'

Petal snuffled deeper. Euphemia picked her up and cuddled her under her chin, rocking her as she caressed the warm folds of skin around Petal's neck. 'Nicky will take good care of you. Kezia and Jane will take you to the office so you can see all your friends. Alice, your lovely dog walker, will come every second day to take you down to the café where you can sit in the sun while she reads her book and drinks her long black.'

Petal jerked her head back and stared at Euphemia, alarm in her eyes.

'I know you corrupted her,' said Euphemia. 'I know you, Petal Sage, and I know you don't like walks. But that's okay. You make me happy and I love you, just the way you are.' Euphemia put Petal down on the floor, and made room for her small toiletry bag on one side of the case. She closed the lid, zipped up the case, inserted the tabs in the lock and spun the dials on the combination lock. Petal watched everything, then gently placed one foot on top of Euphemia's running shoe and looked up at her.

What could she do but pick her up again and cuddle the fat little body into her, holding her tightly as she whispered her apologies? 'I will be home soon, I promise.' She kissed her. 'Would a treat help?'

Petal immediately wriggled loose, launched herself into the air and landed in the doorway, looking back to make sure Euphemia would be true to her word and follow her downstairs to where she kept the treats. Her tail flipped wildly from side to side, her little legs dancing a salsa on the spot. What had once been a sad puppy was now an enthusiastic glutton looking forward to a tasty morsel or five.

Euphemia lifted her suitcase off the bed and carried it downstairs behind the swaggering bottom of her little dog. 'I'm giving a Petal a treat, then I'm leaving,' she called. 'The Uber is here.'

Kenneth met her in the kitchen. 'I wish you'd let me take you to the airport,' he said.

'I'd rather say goodbye here.' She found the bag of chewy treats in the pantry and opened it. 'I hate goodbyes and I hate other people seeing me hate them.'

'We know that, but it's tradition.'

'Not my tradition,' she said. 'I've never gone away without you for this long before.'

He pulled her into his arms and leaned down to kiss her when a little dog squeezed between them and pawed Euphemia's leg. 'Give her the whole bag,' he said impatiently.

Petal looked at him appreciatively and licked her lips as Euphemia let the contents of the packet tumble to the floor around their feet. Petal set to and hoovered them up.

'Where was I?' he said pulling her into his arms again. 'That's right,' he said, stroking a lock of hair behind her ear as he looked into her eyes.

He bent his lips to kiss her, but before he could make contact, there was a loud honk from outside.

'That's the Uber driver,' said Euphemia.

'I don't care who it is. I'm going to kiss you and I'm going to do it properly and I will not be interrupted again.' He bent his head down again and did just that. 'I'll see you in a month?'

'In New York,' she breathed, unwilling now to move out of his arms.

'I can't wait,' he said against her lips.

'Neither can I,' she whispered back.

Kenneth dropped his hands to her hips and eased her away. 'If you don't leave now, and I mean right now, I will take you upstairs and commit marital relations with you and you will miss your plane.'

'I could leave tomorrow,' she said. 'I could say I was unavoidably detained.' Her phone rang in her handbag at the same time as the Uber driver honked the horn again, but this time he didn't stop. The noisy combination of phone and car shattered the mood. She turned, picked up her suitcase, and opened the front door. 'New York, in a month,' she said. 'I love you, Kenneth Sage.' She waved to the Uber driver, who finally took his hand off the horn, then she ran down the path to the car. She didn't look back. It was just as well, because the driver pulled out of their driveway before she had shut her door or done up her seatbelt.

* * *

EUPHEMIA HAD ASKED for a window seat so as not to be disturbed when the rest of the passengers boarded. Still wearing her dark glasses so she didn't have to make eye contact with anyone, Euphemia leaned against the side of the plane and stared idly out the window to the houses on the hills beside the airport. Below on the tarmac, the baggage handlers were loading the last of the cargo into the hold. Next, the fuel hoses were unclipped, and the machinery was driven back to the hangar. She had developed a routine for the three and a half-hour flight to Sydney. As soon as they took off, she would put on her noise cancelling headphones, lower her tray table, take out her laptop and work, only stopping when the meal was served.

For this flight, she had asked her travel agent to make sure there would be no one sitting in the middle seat of three. The thought of having to make polite small talk to a stranger was anathema.

'Excuse me, is this seat taken?'

Euphemia turned to say that yes, it was in her most unfriendly voice. 'What are you doing here?' she asked.

'I couldn't let you travel to the other side of the world on your own,' said Jane. 'You need someone to get you out of tricky situations, or better yet, stop you from getting into these situations in the first place. Who better than me?'

Euphemia took off her sunglasses and watched Jane try to wrestle an enormous piece of hand luggage into the overhead locker. The queue of passengers waiting to get to their seats grew more and more restless as it became clear her bag would not fit. Eventually, the flight attendant arrived and took the bag to the front, but only after telling Jane it would have to be checked in when they got to Sydney.

Jane agreed then plumped down in the aisle seat ignoring the snarls of the other passengers as they walked past her.

'We're going to have such fun, Effie,' she said.

Euphemia laughed, 'We are, aren't we?'

THE END.

ABOUT THE AUTHOR

Rosy Fenwicke lives in Martinborough, in the Wairarapa Wine Region of New Zealand. A multi-genre author, she has written the first four books of THE EUPHEMIA SAGE CHRONICLES - cozy mysteries with a smidgeon of urban fantasy.

COLD WALLET, a psychological thriller set in the world of cryptocurrency, was a quarter finalist in the Booklife Fiction Prize, 2021, and a finalist in the National Indie Excellence Awards, 2022.

DEATH ACTUALLY, is the multi-strand heart-warming story of Maggie, a forty three year old funeral director who lives in small town New Zealand. Themes are, '*Love. Death. And In Between.*'

For more information on Rosy's books and/or to sign up to her newsletter please go to : rosyfenwickeauthor.com. You can also follow her on Facebook, Instagram or TikTok.

DIRE TRAITS. BOOK 5, THE EUPHEMIA SAGE CHRONICLES. AVAILABLE 2023